WHEN THE BOUGH BREAKS

WHEN THE BOUGH BREAKS

David Mark

SEVERN
HOUSE

First world edition published in Great Britain and the USA in 2024
by Severn House, an imprint of Canongate Books Ltd,
14 High Street, Edinburgh EH1 1TE.

severnhouse.com

British Library Cataloguing-in-Publication Data
A CIP catalogue record for this title is available from the British Library.

ISBN-13: 978-1-4483-1199-6 (cased)
ISBN-13: 978-1-4483-1200-9 (e-book)

All Severn House titles are printed on acid-free paper.

Typeset by Palimpsest Book Production Ltd.,
Falkirk, Stirlingshire, Scotland.
Printed and bound in Great Britain by
TJ Books, Padstow, Cornwall.

Praise for David Mark

"A dark, creepy, twisted mystery that will keep readers
awake far into the night"
Booklist Starred Review of *The Burning Time*

"An irresistibly charming detective cracks another
colorful case"
Kirkus Reviews on *The Burning Time*

"An involving, nail-biting police procedural from a
masterful storyteller"
Kirkus Reviews on *Flesh and Blood*

"A hair-raising procedural [that] highlights unselfish love,
sacrifice, and man's inhumanity to man"
Kirkus Reviews on *Blind Justice*

"Deliver[s] the kind of grisly torture and murder scenes that
have rightly linked Mark's work with that of Val
McDermid"
Booklist on *Blind Justice*

"Polished prose, lovable recurring characters, and a stunning
revelation make this a mystery to savor"
Kirkus Reviews Starred Review of *Past Life*

"A fine police procedural . . . Ian Rankin fans
will be pleased"
Publishers Weekly on *Past Life*

"[Mark is] on the level of Scottish and English
contemporaries such as Denise Mina, Val McDermid,
and Peter Robinson"
Library Journal Starred Review of *Cruel Mercy*

About the author

David Mark spent seven years as crime reporter for the *Yorkshire Post* and now writes full-time. A former Richard & Judy pick, and a *Sunday Times* bestseller, he is the author of the DS Aector McAvoy series and a number of standalone thrillers. He lives in Northumberland with his family.

www.davidmarkwriter.co.uk

For Steve, and all at the RLF.

'The soul that has conceived one wickedness can nurse no good thereafter.'

—Sophocles

PROLOGUE

18th November 1995
Pegswood Byre, near Alston, Cumbria

'**U**p, Wulf. *Alarm's gone. Up and at 'em, lad.'*
He feels the words tapping, good-naturedly, inside his skull.
'No shirking now. No rest for the wicked.'
Feels the words pecking, insistent, at the bowl of his cranium. Thinks: sharp beaks and splintered shells.
'You're a fucking monster, Wulf. No sleep for you.'
Feels himself caving in: a mosaic of cracks and splinters held together by wet, matted hair. Thinks of coconuts. Roller coasters.
'You were gonna kill her, Wulf, lad. Do her, and do yersel'.'
He tries to push himself up. Winces, as half a dozen grey-brown hairs are wrenched free at the roots.
'What's gone on, lad?'
A word is pecking at his head. An eggy, gloopy, onomatopoeic sort of a word. Unguent? Incongruous? Angleterre?
He rummages around in his clouded brain. Keeps himself steady. Something's stirring – some dormant terror, stretching its limbs.
'Swallow, lad. Breathe.'
It's not pain, exactly. Not numbness, either. It's more a discomfort: a sensation of having been stuck down, pressed down – a flower crushed between the page of a hardback book. He finds himself recalling the fists of grizzling babies – remembering the tug and tear of those little pink fingers clinging to his beard. Wonders which of the little rascals is playing silly beggars. He can't quite remember their names yet. Can't quite recall if he's a dad, or has one. It'll come to him, he's sure. He just needs to rest. Needs to lie here, with his face stuck to the cold, sticky floor – each

rasping breath sending little wavelets across the rich, reeking puddle of red.

His vision tilts. He realizes he can't hear properly. Perhaps he's folded one ear against his cheek while he slept. *Daft clod. Coagulate!* Aye, that's the word. Coagulating. Congealing. It feels as if something is trickling out of him and gelling at the nape of his neck. His throat hurts, too. He can taste metal.

He becomes aware of wetness at his chin. Christ, he's drooled in his sleep. She'll take the piss; he knows it. She'll tell him he's an animal – tell him that his open mouth reminds her of bovine nostrils, all mucus and crust and ooze.

He tries again to push himself up. Has he slept on his arm? Nothing seems to be responding to his instructions. One of his teeth feels loose. And the light seems wrong. Has she fixed the bulb? Who did she get to do that? Who's she talking to now? Not Barry – no use, that one. Just a fling. A flash in the pan . . .

A hot, damp pain rises from his neck. It snatches his breath. He swallows, baring his teeth, as if gulping back hot, acid bile. Tastes blood. Gulps it down and feels the constriction in his throat. He reaches up. Fingers the wet, slithery fold of neck and hair and throat. His fingertips touch plastic. He picks at its edges. Gasps in a proper breath as he wrenches the noose from around his throat. He angles his head and pulls again at the cord, sucking in a deep, cool breath. The noose slips free, and he pulls it over his head: a hare being freed from a trap.

Through bleary eyes, he stares at the ligature. Green. Green cord, like the gamekeepers use. He pulls at the cord as if reeling in a fish. Finds the end. It's frayed: white threads protruding from the green casing. Half-blind, he stares upwards. Sees the far end of the cord, turning lazy pirouettes as it dangles from the iron hook in the ceiling joist. His vision clears for a moment. Sees the rocking chair on its side. Broken plates. School shirts and football kits dangle from the old white clothes horse at the far end of the spindly floral sofa. There's a posy of dainty wildflowers sticking out of an empty plastic cider bottle by the sink. He recognizes the lipstick shades of hesperantha and nerines. He feels the floor lurch and puts out a hand to steady himself, his eyes landing blindly upon the colourful, childish daubings in their unmatched frames, hanging haphazardly upon the woodchipped walls. He knows the stains they cover. Hung them himself – trying to make it all a bit prettier, a bit cosier – a bit more like home. Wonders whether the damp patches are bigger now: whether the mould in the upstairs bathroom has colonized the entire stone wall around the drafty, single-pane windows. By the far wall, an oil painting of a weeping, sad-eyed little boy. The image was cursed, wasn't it? Had she told him that or had he told her? An American artist. Italian-sounding. Rosebud lips and great twists of fabric about his neck: tears like jellyfish. It had been looking at him as he staggered in. Looking at him as if he already knew. Looking at him as hands became fists and as the world turned red . . .

Memories flood him. He's returning to himself as if pulling on a skinsuit. He forces his appendages into thick legs, chunky arms – repossesses his gut, his barrel chest, his big, hairy head. Feels a tingling in his fingertips, a chilly prickling sensation in his toes. He's dizzy, suddenly. Dizzy and sick. Drunk, too. He raises his head and feels his beard stick to something syrupy. He lets out a breath. Licks sweetness from his lips. Tastes almonds and old coins.

Recollection hits him like a train. For a moment, he feels as if he's hurtling at high speed through a collage of shredded images and blurry snapshots. He sees himself banging on the cracked wood of the back door. Sees his own face looming back at him from the darkened glass. Tastes again the sticky sweetness of the liquor. Hears the echo of his pitiful mewing: his pleas to be admitted, to be heard. Hears himself call her name. It becomes a mantra. *'Trina . . . Trina . . . Let me in! Trina . . . Trina . . . Let me in!'* He's angry. Angry and sad and confused and drunk. He's the man he was before her. Before *them*. He's the man he was before Sal and Jarod. He's the bad man again. He's the bad man he becomes when he drinks.

He dies a little inside as a vision unspools inside his head. He sees himself lose patience. Sees himself put his shoulder to the wood. Sees himself stumble into the little boot room by the back door. Sees himself breathe in the damp and the

earth and the cowshit and the fried food and all the mingled
scents of this place that was once home. There was something
else, too, wasn't there? Something underneath. Something that
makes him think of meat wagons and afterbirth.

He pushes himself upright, a sound like Velcro tearing as
he wrenches himself free of the pool of drying blood beneath
his cheek. Smears a hand across his face, pushes his fingers
into his hair. Takes stock of himself.

He's on his knees on the flagstone floor of the kitchen.
Blood on his face, in his hair, on his hands. There's a low
buzzing sound in his head and a pain running from his crown
to the nape of his neck. He thinks of zippers. Thinks of cracked
pots and hard-boiled eggs. Thinks of the phrenology skull on
top of the three-bar fire.

He turns slowly, blinking as if staring into the sun.
Everything's hazy. Instinctively, he touches his face. His
glasses. Where are his bloody glasses . . .

He pats the floor around him. Screws up his face as the
pain tunnels through his hair, his flesh: grinds into the bone
at the base of his skull.

He lets out a low moan. His eyes are all tears and redness.
He feels as if he's in the grip of a fever. Remembers the
hallucinations he used to suffer in childhood, the nightmares
and apparitions that slithered and crawled around his bedroom
while his mother held him still: sobbing against her chest as
he cried and thrashed and begged for it to stop; for her to
take it away, to make them quiet, just for a moment – one
blessed moment without the static, sibilant hissing at the centre
of his brain.

He touches flesh. Cold, clammy skin. Thinks of slaughtered
swine. Thinks of church candles. Thinks of the tramp he'd
fished out of the harbour at Maryport: his putrid skin sliding
off the bone like slow-cooked lamb.

She's lying half on her side. One big ham-hock arm is
draped across her middle, the other pointed straight out to her
side. She's wearing her nightie – the pink one with the white
flowers. A fluffy burgundy slipper still covers her left foot.
The right is naked: chubby pink toes and chipped red polish.

He begins to shake. Trembles as he moves closer. Feels his

heart punching at his ribs. Reaches out and takes her arm and pulls her on to her back.

There's a gash in her throat – a livid purple hole torn in the folds of her flabby throat. His spectacles stick out of the gory mess in a gruesome mosaic of smashed glass and spattered blood. Her face is a yellowy grey: the colour of the ceiling above a smoker's bed. There's blood in her nostrils. Blood in her hair. Whole constellations of red pin-pricks pattern the dead whiteness of her irises.

He blinks. Takes it in. Lets the full horror of what he has done flood his senses.

He says her name. *Trina.* Moves forward and touches her face with the back of his hand. Looms over her the way he used to when this was his home, and he was her man, and her arms fastened around his broad back like rope, and she made her farmyard noises and bit his neck, and he had all that he wanted in the world. Her kids called him Uncle Wulf. He knows they'd have called him Dad, eventually, if she'd just left them alone.

A dark, malevolent memory stalks, arachnid-like, around the inside of his skull. He remembers rage. Despair. Remembers the cool, clear voice of his addiction. *Drink, Wulf. Drink it down. Then do what you must.*

He had come here to end a life.

He raises his hands to his hair and feels around for the source of the thudding pain. His fingers find a hot, sticky mess just below his crown. He'd fallen, hadn't he? Fallen or slipped. No, she'd hit him; that was it. She'd hit him across the head as he was kneeling at her side, taking her pulse, trying to breathe life back into her. But that wasn't right, was it? How could she have hit him when she was already on her back? He must have slipped in her blood. Slipped, or fainted, or . . .

He slumps into a sitting position, his back against the cupboard door. Looks down the length of himself. Hears the distant wail of sirens.

He readjusts himself. Reaches into the back pocket of his trousers. They've already taken his warrant card, but he still has half a dozen business cards tucked away between the layers of sticky plastic. There's a little blue pen tucked into the coin slot. Behind the clear window, a picture of himself, arms around the lot of them, of Sal and Gareth and Rhodri. Marla, too. They're all smiling.

He licks the nib of the pen. Rests the card upon his thigh. Writes the words that will condemn him.

I'm so, so sorry.

He lowers himself to the floor. Crawls through the blood and the broken glass. Rests his head upon her chest, the softness of her nightie oddly pleasant upon his cheek.

And this is how they find him. Police Constable Wulfric Hagman, laid out upon the floor of the broken-down old farmhouse, snuggled up with the body of his former lover: his spectacles sticking out of her neck like a flag.

He doesn't protest when they cuff him. Doesn't offer a word in his own defence.

PART ONE

ONE

Transcript, BBC Radio Cumbria broadcast, 3.44 p.m., 10th June 1996
Conversation between Afternoon Show host Ricky Buller and Victoria Addison, running time 2 minutes 36 seconds.

RB: . . . you'll have to forgive me for cutting short Messrs Skinner and Baddiel, but we've just received news from Carlisle Crown Court where the jury has been deliberating in the murder trial of former community police officer, Wulfric Hagman. We're crossing live to our reporter Vicky Addison. Vicky, we have a verdict?

VA: We do, thank you, Ricky. And it's guilty. The jury has found Hagman guilty of murder after just four hours of deliberation. His Honour Judge Randall Rebanks has adjourned sentencing while reports are prepared by the probation services, but the man called a 'perfect gentleman' and 'gentle giant' by character witnesses is now facing a mandatory life sentence for the murder of his former lover.

RB: Extraordinary, Vic. This must be a huge relief to the family and friends of the victim. Can you remind our listeners about the circumstances of this brutal crime?

VA: This was a truly horrifying incident that shocked the quiet community in remote, rural Weardale. The court was told by Prosecutor Alyson Shipton that Hagman was guilty of a 'merciless and pre-meditated attack' on his former lover, Katrina Delaney – a physically disabled forty-year-old with whom Hagman had been briefly involved in an affair.

The court heard that Hagman had murder on his mind when he bore down on Pegswood Byre, the ramshackle farmhouse where the victim lived with her numerous children. The court heard that Hagman's victim had recently ended their relationship, and had begun dating a much younger man. The court heard that Hagman, a police officer with thirteen years of exemplary service, reacted badly to the break-up and conducted a campaign of stalking, intimidation and terror against the victim and her family. She in turn made accusations that Hagman had been taking indecent photographs of her children. His superiors at Cumbria Police implemented an immediate suspension. That campaign of retaliation ended in bloodshed in November of last year.

RB: The court heard that the mum – who had been a 'much-loved community arts worker' before mental health issues curtailed her career – was killed with a single stab wound to the neck . . .

VA: That's right, Rick. And that really is one of the shocking elements of this case – the murder weapon was a pair of spectacles – the edge used to slit this defenceless woman's throat.

RB: And we're led to believe that Hagman tried to take his own life – is that right Vicky?

VA: That's right, Rick. Indeed, it's the short, four-word suicide note that was perhaps the most compelling piece of evidence against him. After launching the attack, Hagman tried to take his own life by hanging himself with a length of bailing twine. In a remarkable twist of fate, the makeshift noose snapped under the weight of Hagman's sixteen-stone, six-foot-three-inch frame.

RB: And yet Hagman pleaded not guilty – is that correct?

VA: Yes, and that was seen as 'indescribably cruel' by investigators who had hoped that a guilty plea would spare her children the agony of a trial. As we reported in a previous bulletin, Hagman has barely spoken in his own defence and gave only halting, one-word answers when questioned about the murder – claiming to have no memory of the incident. His statement to the police, read out in court, brought gasps from the public gallery. He said he wished he could swap places with her, and that he would live with regret for the rest of his life, but that he had no memory of taking her life, having relapsed into alcoholism after several sober years.

RB: Can you tell us anything about Hagman's career?

VA: I can, Rick. PC Hagman was a respected and dedicated police constable based out of a tiny police station in the tiny market town of Alston. He first came into contact with Mrs Delaney when she moved her family into the abandoned farm property a mile above the tiny hamlet of Garrigill in an area referred to as the UK's 'last remaining wilderness' – a bleak, barren landscape scarred by centuries of mining and agriculture. PC Hagman was sent to move the family on, but the court heard that he took pity on her and her family, and friendship soon blossomed into something more. Hagman's marriage collapsed when news of the affair came to light. He was thrown out of the family home – a smallholding in the nearby Tynedale Valley. Prosecutors also said that it was 'a mercy and a miracle' that none of the victim's children were home at the time of the attack. It was implied that in the grip of his rage, Hagman could have easily set his sights on other members of the family.

RB: And we're led to believe that Hagman saw himself as something of a father figure to the children?

VA: That's the tragedy, Ricky. A neighbour claims that one of the children, who cannot be named for legal reasons, told her that of all the people in their life, Uncle Wulf was the only person with whom she felt safe . . .

To the Panel of the Oxbridge Access Scheme
Re: Financial Aid and Tutelage for Working-Class Students

07.11.01

I feel a strong compulsion to use the word 'esteemed' in my opening remarks. So there, I have. And you are.

Anyway, sob story, 101. That's what you do, yes? Weigh up whether I had it bad enough to qualify for financial assistance. Well, buckle up, Buttercup, because this one's got the lot. Poverty. Violence. Neglect. Death . . . can you imagine if they were four of the Seven Dwarves? Best to start with Mam, really. Everything did. Died with her, too.

The press should have had a field day with Mam. Monster Mother. Mum From Hell. The Face of Benefits Britain. Social Work Incompetence Contributed to Death of Tragic Mum. Oh, that one was actually printed. Incidentally, field day? I don't know where that phrase comes from. Maybe something to do with carnivals? Cuntry fayres? Yes, I spelt that correctly. Punch and Judy and coconut shies and merry-go-rounds and the stuff you see in books when you're trying to ease your way into another life . . .

But I digress. God, do you remember when everybody used to say that all the time? It was the same people who used to use their fingers as inverted commas. Yuk.

Sorry, I'm being too colloquial. Dagmara says you're probably looking for something that's all poetic and philosophical and flouncy. Soz. You're getting full Billy Elliot with me. And when I write, I write how I speak. I speak too much, according to Dagmara.

Soz again. Has anybody ever used the word 'soz' in their submission? I really hope you're wearing robes and mortar boards and drinking brandy while you read this on vellum scroll. I'd be devastated if you were an office worker on a PC. Not that I've got anything against office workers. I'm sure you look lovely. Enjoy your lunch.

Rambling, much? So, Press. Field day. Mam. Focus.

If you need to picture her, well . . . brace yourself. She was massive, by the end. I can't draw very well, but if I could, I'd sketch her as one of those big sows that win awards at country fairs. I mean, if you were to cobble together a mental picture of somebody who might just be evil, you'd make her look like this. You could hear her coming, at least. Floorboards would creak. The way her feet spilled out of her sandals, it was like watching Yorkshire puddings rise. Big everywhere. Arms like something you'd find in a butcher's shop. She'd tell us she'd been pretty once, but we've seen photos and she wasn't. Always sullen. Pouty. Sore. Always looked like she was trying to shit a ferret.

You'll want some fluffy stuff, will you? Some nice memories? I know she was vile, but there were moments when we really connected. Soz again. There's not a memory in my head that I want to keep. If you could reach in and wipe them all, I'd let you, though my brother would probably have to sign a consent form. We're twins. He's twelve minutes older than me. He's good at music and playing the guitar, and he's way cleverer than me, but he hasn't got the grades and I doubt you'd even look at his application. He's got a criminal record. I probably shouldn't tell you that, but I try to be honest these days. It's not easy when you can't remember what's real and what's not most of the time. Dagmara's helping me with all that. We meditate. It's not as embarrassing as you'd think. Dagmara makes you feel safe. She was my social worker, when I was young. Still is, actually. I see her three or four times a week and it's like taking a bath, it really is. She never stops. She just does what's right, you know, and if there's no right thing, she'll make the best decision she can in the circumstances. She was amazing for Jarod and me when we were little. And bigger. She's the one who told me that if I wrote to you fine people and told you a bit of a sob story, I might tick some sort of diversity quota and there might even be a grant in it. Dagmara's a bit cynical for somebody who's like the dictionary definition of a good person. She's a Socialist, which – full disclosure – I think I might be too. I'm getting very interested in politics. I want to know why everything is so dreadful. That seems like the sort of topic I might do for my PhD. Precocious? Watashi?

Anyway, I'm almost at the bottom of the form. So . . . my mam was a monster. She visited every kind of horror on me and my brothers and sisters. She still visits me in my nightmares, though they might be Jarod's memories, I can't be sure. For a little while, when I was eleven or twelve, she had a boyfriend of sorts. His name was Wulf. Wulfric Hagman. Police Constable, if you'll credit it. Fell in love with him like they were the stars of some ghastly opera. It was OK, for a while. We had Dagmara, too. She's my reference. I understand she used to help one of the panel when you were going through a difficult time? I say this purely conversationally.

Yes. Well. So. Wulfric is in prison for killing my mam. Stabbed her in the neck and shoved his glasses in the wound. Too much? I think the word is 'overkill'. Tried to hang himself from the hook in the kitchen. Poor sod was at death's door when the cord snapped. He came to think he was already in hell. Mam's body. All that blood. When they found him, he just kept saying he was sorry. She'd driven him insane, you see. Reeled him in, then turned. Made him her own little puppet on a string. Destroyed him. I mean, he was married, and he should have known better, but on balance, I don't think that means he deserves what she did. Of course, the word 'deserve' is worth a PhD on its own.

He pleaded not guilty because he couldn't remember what happened. Me and Jarod had to give evidence from a little room with a video camera. It was so intense. Dagmara was there. She always was. They asked me all sorts of horrible questions, and when I told the truth about what she did to us, all the barristers started getting shouty. The barristers even had barristers. Nobody can print my name – legal reasons. They all know Wulf Hagman's, though. I mean, if the press had been allowed to report what I'd said about her, it would have been different. They'd have called Wulf a hero for doing it. We did. Jarod and me were running away properly this time. It had been worse since Barry.

So, deep breath. I've told Dagmara and she'll tell Wulf when she visits him. She says he's starting to come back to himself. She's helping him meditate. Remember. She's got more time since she quit social work and started concentrating full-time on Weardy. That's the youth centre where she works. I help her. Jarod, too. I'd like to be a social worker one day, I think, though I doubt I'll be allowed when they see my file and all the reports. I don't look good on paper, which is a curious thing to write on an application form.

The night he came to the house, he was in his uniform. He'd been drinking. He was shouting her name. Begging her to tell them the truth, that he didn't take any photos of us kids. Telling her it didn't have to be like this. He put his boot through the door. She was in the kitchen skinning a rabbit. Yeah, I know. She was an OK cook, I suppose. Maybe that's something in the 'plus' column. She could make roadkill taste like venison. This feat was made considerably easier if the roadkill in question were a deer.

And, whatever happened next, she ended up dead, and he ended up swinging from a rope. I wasn't there, I know that, but I can see it anyway. I see it like a movie. I can pause it and rewind it and speed it up. Jarod can too. He remembers the exact same thing. We know we were at Weardy with Dagmara, but neither of us can even really remember how we found out what happened or what was happening next. We were off our heads by then, of course. She'd been grinding up the pills for months: feeding us our medicine on spoonfuls of jam. Can't stand jam, now.

So, that's my sob story, really. Dagmara let me stay with her for a while, and then she pulled some strings and an old teacher friend of hers said she'd start helping me catch up with the school I'd missed, and I liked learning and liked Dagmara, and even though Jarod was in all these different foster homes, Dag would drive for hours to make sure we saw each other all the time. She wanted both of us, but her bosses would only let her have one. Can you believe that? Like we're puppies. Jarod got the bullet in the Sophie's Choice thing. Said I had a better chance at being somebody than him. Wouldn't be talked out of it. I went a bit mad at fourteen and ended up in foster care anyway, but Dagmara helped me back on track. I've attached my CV (Weardy, and the newsagents, which went better than I expected) and my exam results and would like to draw your attention to the bits highlighted in luminous yellow and thruple-underlined. They are A-stars, my friends. Read 'em and weep.

I realize I've talked myself out of consideration, but I'd like to thank you for this opportunity to ramble on. It's been quite healing.

Yours,
Salome Delaney

PS. Wulf wanted to be a dad to me. I wanted to let him. Maybe that's what drove Mam up the wall, eh?

TWO

One year ago

Pain.

Pain beyond enduring. He feels as if there's a sizzling white flame devouring the flesh between his finger and thumb . . .

Barry realizes he can't see. He feels mummified, as if bound in layers of black ribbon. Thinks of spiders. Webs. He begins to shake. Can't feel it.

There's a rasp, against his cheek.

'That pain,' comes the growl at his ear, dry, scaly lips touching the skin of his neck. 'You keep that pain in your head, lad. You keep it front and centre. And you remember. Remember this feeling. You come back to this moment. This now. And you think of me, with my knife at the place where your skull meets your spine . . .'

A sharp, stinging pain. A bead of blood tadpoling down his neck.

The voice: 'And you thank your gods that you were given this second chance.'

The pain is climbing up his wrist – a bubbling agony: hot oil in a smoking pan.

'You have to change your ways, lad. You have to get better. Be better. Live better. Because right now, you're more trouble than you're worth. So be more. Be good. Be the best you can fucking be. Or I'll come back, lad. And I'll let you see my face. Because I swear, Barry lad, if you don't keep your demon in its cave, my face will be the last thing you'll see.'

He tries to scream. Can't. Pisses himself instead.

He feels wrinkled, serpentine skin against the orbit of his eye.

He tries to open his eyes. Can't.

'I swear, lad – we'll be face to face before the end. We'll

be eye to eye. And my face will be the last thing you see before the world turns black and red. Then it'll be dark for ever.'

He tries to move. Realizes he can't feel his legs. He's bound. There are straps. He's barefoot. Barefoot on damp grit, soft earth . . . There's a smell somewhere, above the chemical stench of burning skin . . . something floral, green; a bright, kiwi-sharp tang . . .

The voice at his ear: 'Uncle Wulf says hello.'

The blade at his wrists. A sudden, thudding impact.

Then the darkness oozes in like blood.

THREE

Nine months ago . . .

The hotel has the look of a stately home: a place of pomp and pageantry; of Doric columns and elaborate porticos; busts of Roman emperors; philosophers, industrial powerhouses with bald heads and luxuriant Darwin beards. Thirty-six bedrooms, apparently. Four-poster beds and blanket boxes stuffed with cashmere and Harris tweed. Suites to die for. A place of high ceilings and hand-cut flowers; rich men and well-maintained women hoovering up afternoon tea in the library. There should be liveried footmen; black-lacquered carriages and bustling, flour-cheeked maids. The best Marten Hall can recruit is the gaggle of teenagers stuffed into white shirts and ruby waistcoats, clip-on ties and name tags; all earning less per hour than the guests pay for a glass of average pinot noir.

Magda's drinking it in. Making memories. It's built in the Gothic style, according to the glossy brochure, though it doesn't chime with Detective Superintendent Magda Quinn's vision of such a word. She'd hoped for bat wings. Hoped for coffins and flickering torches. She fancies she'd fit in better in such a place. She has the look of a creature from Bram Stoker's dampest dreams: curves and cleavage, blood-red lips, lily-white face: deep, almond-shaped eyes and hair so sleekly black that it seems to shimmer as she turns her head.

She gives her companions a moment to digest the report. Lets them consider their options. She stands at the tall window frame, staring out across the rolling acres of landscaped, wooded garden: cherry blossom gusting in great blizzards across the bright, blue horizon: a bone spur of Hadrian's wall clinging to the curve of land beyond the tree line.

She's taken her shoes off and she can feel the sumptuous

plushness of the carpet as she squeezes it in her stockinged feet. She feels eyes upon her. Eyes where she wants them to be. She's good at distracting a certain type of man, is Magda. She thanks her God daily that such men tend to inhabit the upper tiers of every police force she has worked for. She hasn't slept her way to the top, but she's damn well used what she's got. She doesn't feel the need to apologize for herself. She has friends who spill their Chardonnay and give themselves all manner of indigestion if they dare admit to enjoying the male gaze. She has friends who call themselves bad feminists. Magda never joins in. She's a poster girl for taking a stiletto heel to the glass ceiling. She's done very well. Always been known as a rising star. Had been, she corrects herself. Had been, before . . .

'That's a very impressive presentation, Detective Superintendent.'

She turns away from the window. Seeks out the speaker. Callum Whitehead QPM. Retired at the rank of Chief Superintendent. An important man, if such a thing were not an oxymoron. Friends in high places: enemies behind bars and under concrete. He's at the head of the oval wooden table, his reflection shone back off the polished walnut grain. He's not in uniform. Could pass for one of the golfers: florid face, rheumy eyes; thinning hair still styled in the same savage side-parting as he had when he was young. He's wearing a maroon turtleneck under a smart jacket – his stomach straining against the folds as if he were entering his third trimester. He's got one eye closed so he can see what he's leering at. His reading glasses are on the table in front of him. He'd acquiesced to their use when Quinn had handed out the briefing documents. Within a couple of paragraphs, he'd thrown them off.

'Very impressive indeed, Magda,' he says again, dropping the use of the honorific. She's pleased. He's relaxing. He's older now. Hasn't got the clout he used to. He doesn't want to have to face all this again. She's taking it out of his tired old hands. She's making it all go away.

She sits forward. Lifts the briefing document and looks at the photo of Wulfric Hagman. He's hollow-eyed. Sallow.

There's mottling under his eyes: his face starved of sun. He looks greasy. Malarial. Sick all the way through.

'He's not a household name, Callum,' she says, gently. 'He's not a Nilsen or a Sutcliffe or a West. It's not going to be the media circus you fear. I can make it go away.'

Whitehead sits back. He's pushing seventy, now. Wiry black hairs standing out in his eyebrows and ears like spiders with rigor mortis. He considers her. Magda lets him. Fights the urge to preen.

'I'm not going to ask,' he says quietly. 'I want to, but I'm not going to ask.'

'Ask what, Callum?' She knows, but she's playing along.

'Whether he did it. Whether we got it wrong. I don't want to know. I do, I mean. But I really don't.'

Magda lets him prattle. She knows he's just twittering on to buy himself time to process it all. He's moving the pieces around inside his head as if playing solitaire. Imagining a conclusion where he's the only piece left on the board.

Beside Whitehead, there's a creak of leather as the other delegate shifts in their chair. They haven't spoken much. Just listened. Drunk it in.

'What is it you're asking for from us?' they ask. 'What can you promise?'

Magda acts as if she's making a difficult decision. In truth, she'd do anything for the opportunity to remove the stain from her perfect record. They haven't mentioned it. God, maybe they don't even know about it. Maybe they . . .

'You were optimistic once before. About Doctor Holloway, as I understand it.'

Magda gives a tight smile. It always comes back to the Dr Holloway case – the one and only time she screwed up. 'I was led by the science,' she says, shifting the blame the same way she did at all manner of internal investigations and disciplinary hearings. 'The postmortem showed evidence of foul play. We made the decision to release that information. It was all we could do, given the press interest.'

She stops. Forces herself to look at the memory. She'd gone on what the boffins had said. Gave heartfelt, oddly emotional appeals in front of lecterns and microphones and great big

Notts Police crests. Dr Holloway had been murdered, she said.
It was a cruel, calculating crime that had robbed the world of
a good father, a good man.

'Must have been quite a day when the real story came out,
eh? One might almost draw a line from that point to this.'

Magda takes a moment. Sips her water. Licks her lips.
Thinks of Dr Perry Holloway. He'd gone into the ground so
hard they'd half expected to find him surrounded by dinosaur
bones. Plunged 14,000 feet and hit the ground as if he'd been
in freefall from the moon. It was his sixtieth birthday, too.
Raising money for a local good cause. It was to be his two-
hundredth jump. This was the big one. He'd got nearly
eight thousand in donations from his colleagues and friends,
though the Bentley he'd driven to the airfield in had cost him
ten times that. Paid for it, and his other indulgences, with his
'specialist' reports. Gave psychological assessments away to
whichever social service, child protection agency or district
council cared to pay him. For a few quid more, he'd even
write what they wanted him to.

It all came out after he hit the ground; after Magda spoke
so eloquently about his decency and humanity. He'd been
responsible for writing scores of assessments about the
mental health of mothers who he'd never even spoken to.
Made decisions about their likelihood to harm their children
based, as far as anybody could tell, on nothing but good old-
fashioned prejudice. An action group was forming at the time
of his death, led by two MPs from different sides of the House.
They wanted answers. They wanted to know how many
children had been ripped away from their parents because
of his nest-feathering quackery.

Quinn was still digesting that bit of news when the results
came back from the lab. A pair of nail scissors had been found
in an inner pocket of his skydiving suit. They had been missed
on previous searches and were only discovered by accident
when a lab technician was sliding the garment back into the
evidence bag and felt something hard inside the lining.
The scissors were sent off for testing, but they went to the
bottom of the pile, sitting in somebody's in-tray while Magda
was leading a high-profile hunt for Dr Holloway's killer.

The results, when they finally returned, took the legs out from under them. There were fibres caught in the hinge: perfect fingerprints on the handles and blade. The results were inarguable. Dr Perry Holloway had sabotaged his own parachute. It was a suicide, not a murder. He was about to be outed: facing dozens of allegations that he deliberately misdiagnosed parents as having mental disorders, which led to them having their children taken away by social services. Parents with anxiety, with depression, with addiction issues: he declared them all to be potentially unfit to raise their children, pocketing a whopping salary for his trouble.

Magda hasn't tried to work out how much pain and hurt he caused, but she does take a perverse delight in looking at the crime scene photograph: the front of his head pushed through to the back and his insides reduced to a cold stew of jelly and meat and offal, all bound wetly in the Day-Glo prison of his skydiving suit.

The press had a ball. She found endless variations of her TV appearances: close-ups of her big wide eyes and heartfelt words as she eulogized a 'truly good man'. The internet scamps made clips of her speaking in such glowing terms about any number of historic bogeymen, from Caligula up to Farage. She hadn't seen the funny side – taking scant comfort in the number of viewers who took the time to comment on her cleavage.

'So,' says the smaller, quieter voice, 'if I'm reading this correctly, you still haven't given up on the idea that Hagman is our killer.'

'All lines of investigation are open,' she says smoothly. 'That's why we need to properly resource this operation. I'll need a team of six. Maybe seven. No shrinking violets. We'll have to liaise with Cumbria if we're going to get this Beecher on board. I want him as my deputy. He has a connection with Hagman's victims; I believe he's dating one of the children, Salome Delaney. I'll grease the wheels there. I can make it all work. I just need your go-ahead.'

Magda lowers her head, a penitent waiting to learn whether her soul is damned. She's fizzing on the inside. Guts churning; sweat slowly oozing up beneath her underwire and the elastic of her tights.

'And Hagman,' says Whitehead, after a moment's consultation. 'What if he remembers? What if it all comes flooding back?'

'I plan for all contingencies, Callum.' She smiles. She wonders if she's going too far. Wonders if it would seal the deal were she to crawl across the table on her hands and knees, little feline purrs in her throat, sensuality in every elegant roll of her shoulders.

'I'm sure you said the same before that shrink hit the deck,' he says, and his voice sounds more like the Geordie street copper he used to be. He toned it down when he joined the Lodge. When he joined the board of interesting little companies, hedge funds and brokerships; became vice-captain of the golf club, accepted a vice-chancellorship at the university. He doesn't sound like that man now. Sounds for a moment like the Geordie hard case of his youth, serving his time in a cold valley in the back of beyond: a scarred landscape of empty houses and disused mines. He sounds like the PC who put a beating on his colleague, Wulfric Hagman, one bloody night in 1995.

Magda's put it all together. Made educated guesses and intuitive leaps. Whitehead was first on the scene. Found his one-time mate sobbing over the body of Trina Delaney. Saw the ligature around his neck: the bloody glasses sticking out of his ex-lover's neck. Whitehead already despised him. Hagman had never been popular, never been respected. He was a soft sod. Wet as lettuce. He was the butt of every practical joke in the manual. They tolerated his weaknesses. But taking pictures of little girls . . . He didn't even pause. Just started beating him with fists and knees and boots. Messed up the crime scene. Added blood, added injuries, added mess. He'd cleared up the best he could. Called for an ambulance, called for back-up. Held Hagman's fractured skull together with his own bloody hands. The first detective on the scene had been a pal. A team player. One of the boys. They'd already selected Whitehead as Lodge material. He was made of the right stuff. Hagman never had been, that was clear – not now the stuff he was made of was leaking all over the floor.

The other officer had told him to leave it to him. It was all about safeguarding the chain of evidence now. About finding the kids. The conviction would be easy as pie, should he even pull through. Whitehead went with him in the ambulance. Was there when they started to undress him – placing each item in an individual polythene evidence bag. Saw them retrieve the crumpled Post-it note from the inside pocket. It even had a bloody thumbprint. It was an apology. Just a few scribbled words, but they'd been enough to constitute a suicide note. The story told itself. They put him away. Celebrated in the Howard Arms when the verdict came back. He got life, naturally.

They put him in a hole and didn't think of him again. Climbed the ladder. Did damn well. And then the letters had started arriving. Journalists. Writers. Bloggers. Podcasters. Whitehead hadn't known what half the bloody words meant. Some soft-hearted lawyer with a taste for lost causes was taking up his case. They'd already succeeded in overturning a dozen unsafe convictions. Hagman was cooperating. He was trying to recover his memories – working with the self-same old friend who had provided alibis for every other bugger the night he dragged himself to Pegswood Byre. Before he shed blood.

'She's always been a bloody nuisance,' grumbles Whitehead, leafing through the document. 'Bloody do-gooders. Bleeding hearts. She's probably only doing all these good deeds so she gets into heaven. I can't pick up the sodding paper without seeing her fat goblin face staring back.'

Magda tries to keep her own counsel. She knows they're talking about Dagmara Scrowther MBE. Can't quite bring herself to stay silent while somebody she admires is being so unfairly tarred and feathered.

'Read the Social Services report,' says Magda, and she has to change her expression so it sounds like a suggestion rather than an instruction. 'She put those kids back together. She's put half the valley back together at some time or another.'

'Fancies herself a copper, if you ask me,' remembers Whitehead, sneering. 'Blame shifting – that's the only way to explain it away. Knows she should have whipped those kids away from that woman and her midnight callers. Won't

be her that gets hauled over the coals though, will it? It'll be
muggins here.'

Quinn sits back in her chair. There's not much more to say.
They'll either give her the job or they won't. They'll give the
nod or they'll send her on her way. She isn't sure what she'll
do if they say no. It's down to this. She could have stayed
with Notts, of course, but once a halo's started rusting, there's
no way to buff it back to its original shine. Top brass hung
her out to dry. There was even a note made on her record –
she'd made a spectacular balls-up; done things in the wrong
order; trusted to luck and hubris when she should have done
things properly. They put her on Special Projects, after that:
a glorified data analyst, ploughing through spreadsheets and
analyses and cost-benefit reports. If she hadn't taken the call
from Whitehead, she might still be there. Instead, she's on
the verge of a new start, a new tram, a new investigation.
She's got the chance to put things right. All she has to do is
make sure Wulfric Hagman's appeal against Northumbria
Police dies a quiet death. Too many people have too much
to lose.

She's spent six weeks performing what she likes to call due
diligence: checking back through every spit and cough and
bloodstain to make sure the service can defend itself should
it succeed in gathering traction. Magda's found something
else. Found something better.

'Softly-softly,' says Whitehead, at last. 'No waves – not yet.
It's a useful bargaining chip. If they keep coming after us, we
can show our hand.'

Magda feels the mixed metaphors probing her back teeth.
Keeps her face neutral.

'Of course,' she says, as if no other course of action is
conceivable. She's one of them. She's made of the right stuff.
Knows the handshakes. Knows the currency of brotherhood;
of returning good turns, and bad.

'She'll give you hell,' says the other speaker, sitting forward
in their chair. 'Never even made her own mind up about
whether or not he did it, but she still says the conviction's
unsafe . . .'

'These names,' says Whitehead, looking at the papers. 'You

think Hagman killed *all* of them? They're all so . . . so bloody rotten. All such bastards.'

'That's the way they're selected, sir,' she answers, smoothly. 'That's why he does it. Bad people. Pimps, rapists, paedophiles, child abusers. Accidents and suicides, sir – whatever it takes to remove them from the lives of the people they hurt.'

Corrupt child psychotherapists too, she adds. Mums who make false allegations of paedophilia so they can score a point against a jilted lover.

'You'll have what you need,' says Whitehead, after glancing to his left and checking he's read the room correctly. 'Make the proposal through the official channels. You'll get the nod. You'll have what you need.'

Magda lets herself smile. Holds it for a second.

Looks at the two retired officers: such flimsy, pitiable old lumps of flab and turkey skin. Sees men long past their prime. Sees them as one might a portrait of some whiskered philanthropist: anachronisms, men out of time.

'Thank you,' she says. 'You won't regret it.'

She's very, *very* wrong.

FOUR

'Sal. You decent?'

She hears a muffled knocking: gloved fist on fragile glass. Hears some cursing. Hears the thud-thud-thud of a steel toe-capped boot banging on a gas canister. Hears the yelp as a Border Collie is briefly silenced beneath a private little avalanche of sliding snow.

'Sal. Sorry, dude, it's getting bad. You awake? Cock-a-doodle.'

Sal doesn't move. She doesn't want visitors. Doesn't want company. Doesn't want to be with people, or by herself.

'I'm coming in. If you've died in the night, I am going to be bloody furious. Sal! Howay, dude, I'm freezing here. Got you a tea.'

The sound is tempered by layer upon layer of cotton and quilt. Sal has fashioned herself a chrysalis of bedclothes, cocooning herself inside scratchy woollen blankets, snuggly jumpers and overcoats. She's still cold. She's got her arms around her knees, hugging herself close, chin tucked in: a child halted in the act of cannonballing into a swimming pool.

'D'you wanna build a snowman?'

Knobhead, thinks Sal.

Then: *Tea. Mmm.*

Tea might actually be worth waking up for. Throw in a Digestive biscuit and she could be persuaded to forego all further thoughts of suicide-by-stench until at least mid-morning.

'Might be tepid, like.'

Sal buries deeper into the sheets. If she could, she'd withdraw her head into her shoulders and her legs into her arse. She's been awake for ages but hasn't allowed herself to properly acknowledge it – preferring to repeatedly tell herself that she's still blessedly unconscious and, as such, should be spared the cruelties and responsibilities of wakefulness. Even with the nightmares – the convulsing, skeleton racking flickerpads of visceral, carnal horror that pour into and out of her subconscious as soon as she starts to doze – even then, she much prefers being asleep to being awake. She can't help thinking this is a sign of a life poorly lived.

'Smells like a folk festival in here, dude.'

Sal scrunches her eyes closed until she can see red. Grips her bedsocks with her toes, her knuckles around the seams. Braces herself for the pain. She feels grief settling upon every surface, pushing down upon her outline, crushing her like the snow that blankets the land beyond the tinny walls and plastic roof and cracked little window of the caravan.

''ck off.'

'What was that?'

'I said 'ck off.'

The bed shifts as Jarod plonks himself down beside her. Through the blankets, she feels him place his hand where he presumes her shoulder should be. 'I wouldn't move you, but it's not safe, mate. There's four feet of snow on the roof. I don't think it'll cave in, but I'm not risking it. You'll have to come up to the house.'

Sal has been staying in this little metal box for the past three weeks. Jarod's planning an advertising campaign promoting the space to tourists with a true taste for the oxymoronic. It's luxurious and basic: retro and ultra-modern; sumptuously furnished and yet surprisingly roomy. To Sal, it's a 1970s' caravan, propped up on bricks and tractor tyres. Its 'well-appointed kitchenette' consists of a camping stove, a plastic bucket and a cold tap.

'Not moving,' growls Sal from somewhere within the depths of the bed. 'Don't care.' She sounds petulant and toddler-ish: her voice a stamped foot and a moody flounce.

'You'll care if the roof caves in, Sal. And I will, too. I haven't actually sorted out the whole public liability insurance thingummy. So it would be awkward, y'know?'

Sal scowls into the hot, breathy air around her face. Her world smells of damp and wet wool; of last night's toast and marmite; of armpits and dry shampoo. She lets out a low growl, then tunnels upwards, using her head like a spade. The beads of sweat on her forehead cool instantly as she emerges into the bitter air.

'Oh, good,' smiles Jarod, as her face appears from the folds. 'It's a girl.' He angles his head torch towards her and frowns, as if reassessing. 'Sort of.'

Sal scowls up at her twin brother. She tries to think of something witty to say in return. Nothing comes. She's nearly forty-one years old, but the desire to give her sibling a dead arm remains as strong as ever. She just blows a raspberry and grips the sheets twice as hard.

'Here,' says Jarod, and he hands her a cardboard cup with a plastic lid. For a moment, she exudes the grace and demeanour of an injured Tyrannosaurus. She manages to extricate one of her arms from the bedclothes and awkwardly wraps her fingers around the cup warmth. She raises herself on one arm and takes a sip.

''nks,' mutters Sal, sipping at the lukewarm tea.

'Was that "thanks"?' asks Jarod, aiming his torch at the chaos on the floor beside the bed. He retrieves her glasses from the mess of books, wires, empty mugs and unopened envelopes that form a thought-provoking modern art install- ation between the bed and the sink. He huffs on the lenses, then wipes them on the hem of his padded shirt, sliding the arms into Sal's mass of black curls and hooking them behind her ears. She scowls again into her tea.

'I'm still here, then,' grumbles Sal, giving her living space a glare. Her nostrils become the barrels of a sawn-off shotgun. 'No carbon monoxide leaks? No passing bludgeoners.'

'Sorry, dude. I can advertise on Marketplace. Middle-aged Traffic Cop Seeks Passing Bludgeoner. Must be willing to finish the job.'

Sal licks the film on her teeth. 'I'm not a traffic cop. I'm a Collision Investigation Officer.'

'Same-same. Last I checked, you were a Family Liaison Officer planning on joining CID. More flip-flops than the Chinese army, Sal. I can't keep up with your changes of direc- tion. What was it you were going to be by forty?'

'Dead, according to Mam.'

Silence fills the small, frigid space.

Sal glances at the glass – at her frozen outbreaths forming a hard film over the thin, dirty pane. 'Going to be tears before bedtime, I reckon.'

'Aye, radio says it'll get worse before it gets better,' says Jarod, pulling a pouch of tobacco from the pocket of his waterproof coat and starting to roll a thin cigarette. His hands are filthy, the skin hardened by years of manual graft. There are cuts around the ridged white scar tissue of his mangled knuckles. 'Mental out there. Might end up worse than when the Beast hit. I could barely make it up the ghyll. None dead yet, but we'll be knee-deep by Wednesday.'

'People or sheep?'

'Sheep,' says Jarod immediately. 'People can fuck off.' He picks a stray twist of tobacco from his tongue. Looks at his sister and blows out a great lungful of thoughts still unsaid. 'I could use some help – if you're not too busy.'

Sal resists the urge to pull the covers back over her head. Jarod's right, of course. If the roof caves in, she doesn't fancy her chances of getting out alive. It's not that she doubts her ability to claw her way out of the snow – more that she doubts she'd have the motivation.

'Leave me here,' she groans. 'I've accomplished most of my dreams. I'm ready to hurl myself into the abyss.'

'You're not suicidal, Sal – you've had your heart broken. It's no different to grief, although when somebody dies, you can at least attempt to move on.' He closes his eyes for a moment. 'What that prick did . . . the way he just cast you aside . . .'

Sal swirls tea around her mouth. Glares at her brother. 'Bloody hell, Jarod – you ever think of working for a suicide helpline? Christ, you should just have let the roof squash me. Better still, drag me outside and lay me in a snow drift. Apparently, it's a very gentle way to go.'

'Stop saying things like that,' says Jarod quietly. He reaches out and squeezes her shoulder. Peers at her intently, their eyes perfect mirrors. 'You had the dream again?'

Sal nods. Closes her eyes. For a moment, she feels her twin softly moving through the contours of her brain.

'I'm sorry,' he says after what feels like an age. 'It'll fade again. It always fades.'

'It's OK,' says Sal, and she puts a clammy hand on her brother's bristly cheek. 'It's not your fault.'

He gives a twitch of a smile, just to show willing. Sal knows he'll never stop punishing himself for infecting their shared subconscious with terrible visions. Bad things happened to both of them when they were young, but Jarod endured the worst of it. He's pushed the memories down into some locked box inside himself. He keeps them there with medication, cannabis and twenty-hour days. But the monsters have slithered their way into Sal's genetically identical hippocampus. She endures night terrors by proxy. 'No more suicide talk this morning, yeah?' he asks quietly. 'Told you, you're not allowed to die until you're at least eighty, OK? That's that. And you're halfway, at least.'

'Whoop,' deadpans Sal, running her tongue over the film on her teeth. 'Not long now.'

Sal and Jarod have always had a preoccupation with the grave. They talk about death a lot. It's a coping strategy, according to Sal's most recent therapist. It's a reaction to the traumas of their childhood. Sal can't help thinking that her therapist gets a lot more out of their sessions than she does. She seems positively gleeful at the opportunity Sal's recent emotional downturn has provided her. Not many psychologists get the chance to probe the inner torment of the bloodily bereaved. Sal is a once-in-a-career kind of patient. She some-times feels a little put out that she has to pay the woman seventy-five an hour to have her great Jack O-Lantern head scraped out by the sharp metal spoon of the shrink's imposition.

'What time is it?' asks Sal, shifting her weight.

'Just gone seven,' says Jarod, without looking at his watch. He's peering at her in that way of his, looking into her as if trying to read something written on the lenses of her eyes. Sal makes herself go cross-eyed, just to make him stop. 'You OK?' he asks, for what must be the thousandth time.

'Never better,' says Sal, and her breath comes out through a rush of chattering teeth. The ensuing shiver causes the last dregs of tea to splash against the inside of the cup. She rummages around inside the bedclothes and wraps her hands around the chilly firmness of her mobile phone.

'Don't,' says Jarod, shaking his head. 'Spare yourself.'

Sal ignores him. Just because the advice is sound, she doesn't feel she has to take it.

'Anything?' asks Jarod hopefully.

She wrinkles her nose. 'Too early for him. But he'll be worried.'

'Aye, no doubt.'

'He will, Jarod.'

'I know, mate.'

Jarod looks away, and Sal can tell from the set of his shoulders that he's having to fight the impulse to say what he really feels about the love of her life, Lewis Beecher. It's been a month since he ended things. They were together nigh-on seven years. She'd committed. Properly given herself to him, to *them*, to the idea of family and love and silly bored Sundays having carpet picnics in front of a three-bar fire. She revelled in it. Her own childhood might have had all the tenderness and serenity of a fire in a rabbit hutch, but she was going to make up for that with all the isn't-this-jolly mumsiness she could channel.

He'd thought the world of her at first. The *real* her, or at least the closest she could get. The one that went through all that filth and grime and flame. The girl who found her mam dead in the kitchen. The girl who told a court that she was abused and that she hoped her mam was burning in hell. The girl who got away, and started again, and went to Oxford and got a first, then pissed about with festivals and peace convoys and politics until she scared herself. The girl who spent another decade trying to be a writer while working in a bookshop: big round glasses and fawn, floaty clothes: cats and biscuits and a Hufflepuff pen. She truly leant into the aesthetic. And then *her*. The woman. The proper grown-up who wanted to do something worthy. Something helpful.

She spent the evening of her thirtieth birthday filling out the application form to join the police. That's who Lewis met. He didn't know the broken little girl was still inside her until she woke him with her screaming on their first night in their new home. He'd held her. Stroked her hair. Accepted her. He loved her, he said. Loved her all the way through. There'd even been an engagement, of sorts, in the early days, though they'd never made it as far as picking a venue for a reception, let alone walking down the aisle. She fell in love with his kids too. Lottie and Nola were only two and six when she entered their lives. Nine and thirteen now. She mummed the hell out of them. Did the whole thing and did it like she was born to it; like she hadn't spent her own childhood with her face in the shit and her mother's fat foot on the back of her neck. Did it all with a smile and a story and a silly voice. She was there for chicken pox and mild concussions; fist-fights and first crushes; she made their costumes for World Book Day; painted their faces for Halloween; made scrapbooks of their days together; holidays and camping trips, West End theatre visits and little market towns. And they're not her children any more. The whole shape and flavour of her existence has been twisted. Ripped. She feels their absence like grief. She misses them so much it feels like her bones are shattering inside her skin. And this has been done *to* her. Done by the man she loves.

She thinks about him. Feels the sudden magnesium flash in her chest. Sees him. Sees five feet ten inches and fourteen stone of firm, meaty toughness. Sees the shiny round head and the rolled folds of muscle at the back of his head. Sees the goatee, with its bar-code of white stripes. Sees the glare – the hard eyes and the gritted teeth. Beecher has got a reputation as a hard man. He's dogged, ambitious: not a man to be crossed. Not many people see the real Beecher – Detective Inspector and third in command of Major Crimes. She sometimes wonders how much he's currently worrying that she will vengefully out him as a Liberal Democrat, a Radio Four listener and a fastidious vegan, notwithstanding the occasional brick of full-fat Wensleydale. She's made their separation easy for him. But what other solution was there? It was his house, not *hers*. They're his children, not *hers*. Of course she would have to be the one to leave. It was best for everybody, after all.

She hadn't made a fuss about the arrangements, being as she was primarily concerned with the utter annihilation of her heart. She didn't care about any of the practicalities. She just wanted it not to be happening. She wanted things to be as they were. They had their problems, but doesn't everybody? They'd come close to splitting up plenty of times over the years, but they'd always found their way through it. Not this time. He'd been deadly serious. She was too much. He wasn't sure he'd ever loved her. Didn't think he even liked her. Wasn't sure if he'd ever felt the way about her that he professed so fulsomely, so poetically, in the early days of their relationship. There wasn't anybody else, but he'd rather have nobody than continue with her. Sal had agreed to give him the space he needed to work himself out. She realized by the third day of their trial separation that it was possible the space in question was precisely five foot five and a little over twelve stone.

Jarod gives her a pat on the hip, as if she were a dairy cow entering the show ring at the auction mart. She's grateful for the gesture, however incongruous.

'Owt else?' asks Jarod, turning back to her.

Sal scrolls through her messages. Nola hasn't gotten out of the habit of sending her funny reels and links on social media. She opens up the latest missive and feels an instant prickling in her eyes as she reads the accompanying message: *Thought you'd find this funny xx.* Sal clicks the link and finds herself snuffling with laughter as she watches a hapless zookeeper disappear up to the shoulders in the back passage of a clumsy elephant. She snorts outrageously and plays it again for Jarod, who laughs the way she likes best: mouth open, head back: wrinkles gathering around his grey eyes. He's a handsome fellow, is Jarod. He's got the weather-beaten face of a man who works in the open air, but there's a certain crumpled fineness to his appearance: a lupine set to his angular features; his neat eyebrows – the smudge of stubble around his chin. There are faint blue tattoos beneath the grime and stubble at his neck and ears; Norse runes and indecipherable cuneiform scribbles, all rendered in mad whorls upon his scalp. They're enchantments, according to Jarod. Spells. They keep the worst of it away.

Sal never has to ask what *it* is. She was there, too.

There's a sudden creaking sound overhead, and Sal looks

upwards in alarm. She'd half thought her brother was joking, but the threat suddenly feels very real. Would it be the worst way to go, she wonders. She's seen worse. She's seen just how badly a life can end.

'Shall we?'

'I think we bloody shall,' agrees Jarod, standing up and putting out his hand as if she were a fine noblewoman alighting from a coach and horses. She rises from the bed still wrapped in blankets, her phone gripped in the same hand that holds the sheets around her like a mantle.

Jarod crosses to the little window above the sink as Sal shivers and curses and looks for her boots amid the carnage on the wet, mud-streaked linoleum. He stares out through his own reflection at the mile upon mile of perfect whiteness. She can almost read his thoughts. Jarod's a farmer. His sheep are grazing on the fell, their bellies swollen with the wriggling lambs that will soon slither from their mothers' bellies and into the savage chill of this angry, late-winter blitzkrieg of snow and ice and black, black air. He can't afford to lose any of the flock. Can't afford another profitless year. Can't get the tourist accommodation up and running until he brings in some money, and can't bring in any money until he's finished the accommodation. He's jacked in his hedgerow potions side-line: artisan glass bottles with pretty handwritten labels and a stick of something mystical resting in clear, cold lunar water. He used to sell them through the art shops. Lost that sideline when Wulfric came back and started helping him around the place. He lost suppliers. Lost friends. Suffered smashed windows and dead livestock. Nobody wanted to be associated with any business that the murdering bastard had any hand in. Nobody wanted the killer policeman anywhere near the valley – least of all hunkered down with his victim's son. The papers may never have named the pair of them, but everybody knew. Knew Jarod and Sal were Mad Trina's eldest pair. Knew what had been reported about her at the trial. Knew what Jared had shared about their mam in that newspaper interview, what must be four or five years ago now: that she was a monster. People didn't bring it up when they met in the queue at the post office. It wasn't an easy conversation to have.

'Is he in his room?' asks Sal distractedly, as she pushes her foot into her boot. She tries to keep the query light and inconsequential. Fails.

'Won't come out unless you want him to. Do you want him to?'

'I don't bloody know.'

'Neither does he.'

They stand and look at one another, both unsure what they actually feel – and how much of it they are ready to say. The man jailed for killing their mother has been living in Jarod's spare bedroom for almost a year.

It's an imperfect set-up now Sal is here. She and Hagman are polite to one another. Thoughtful, even. Sometimes they'll talk about politics or books. They steer clear of memories. Neither of them trusts their recollections – or their versions of events. Jarod doesn't believe Hagman is guilty of Trina Delaney's murder. Neither do the other brothers and sisters who were scattered like poisoned grain among foster families and cousins and family friends in the immediate wake of the slaughter at Pegswood Byre. Sal doesn't know what she thinks. If he killed her, she's grateful. If he didn't, then somebody she cares about has gotten away with murder. She doesn't like following that thought to its conclusion.

Sal straightens up, pushing her hand through her mess of curls. Her hair grows in perfect ringlets. With her pale skin and rosebud lips, she has the look of a toddler in an eighteenth-century oil painting. As a child, she was extraordinarily photo-genic. Mam took her to the art college in Carlisle to model for some of the students. She was the face of a local show shop's advertising campaign when she was four years old: pictured on billboards and hoardings playing with the buckles and bells on her gleaming leather shoes.

'I'll go build the fire up, get some eggs on, eh?'

Sal looks at her brother. He's watching her intently. She thinks he might like to give her a cuddle but isn't sure if she'll start to cry. She'd like to cuddle him, too.

'You're buzzing,' says Jarod, nodding at her hand.

'*You're* buzzing,' she says, as if it were a playground insult and he'd accused her of being the source of a bad smell.

'Your phone, dickhead.'

Sal pulls a face. '*You're* the dickhead,' she mutters, as Jarod smiles smugly and draws a one and a zero in the condensation on the glass. One-nil to Jarod.

The call comes from a number prefixed with 01228: the area code for Carlisle. The sensible thing to do would be to ignore it. She doesn't want to talk to anybody about anything. She presumes whoever is ringing will be disinclined to respect such parameters. She answers anyway. It could be Lewis.

'Hello . . .'

'Oh, thank fuck for that!'

Sal can't help twitching a little smile. Her boss, Sergeant Claire Graves, has a way of making her officers feel valued.

'That's quite an opening, Claire,' says Sal, and immediately wishes she hadn't.

'Aye, that's what he said,' laughs Claire, and she gives in to a cackle of filthy laughter that quickly becomes a rhapsody of coughs and wheezes. 'Fuck, I think I might have had sushi last night. Hope so. Can't think of any other reason I've just coughed up a jellyfish, can you?'

There's another creak overhead and Jarod, losing patience, takes his sister by the elbow and steers her towards the door. He shudders as he recognizes the tinny echo of Claire's voice. Jarod has never found the right woman to settle down with, but he's had plenty of full-bodied flings. He's even been in love a couple of times. What he shared with Claire Graves over the course of ten days in 2017 remains unclear. He has the look of somebody who can't work out whether they've experienced the most passionate love affair of their life or been a victim of a prolonged and complicated sexual assault.

'I'm on leave, Claire,' says Sal as Jarod opens the door, and she stares into the silence of the morning. Snowflakes fall in their billions: great fat flakes tumbling from a low black and silver sky. The snow lies upon the earth like a rind, mounded up in corners and in the protection of the low stone walls. The air is so cold that Sal feels as if a hand has reached inside her and closed its fist around her lungs.

'On leave, not on leave, it's all the same to me, love.'

'That doesn't make any sense, Claire.'

'What does, eh? I mean, we live on a big blue ball spinning through the eternal vastness of space. We used to be monkeys, for goodness' sake. Penguins are birds but they can't fly. I mean, it's all mental, isn't it?'

Sal starts laughing. Claire is a friend. She's tough and funny and a little bit unhinged.

'Weather bad out there?' asks Claire, her breath becoming rattly and liquid as she sucks upon her vape.

'No, Claire – this is the one spot in the North East where it's golden sunshine. I'm considering a picnic.'

'Ooh, a bit of sass! Love it! Lewis must have called you.'

Sal steps into the snow. Her leg disappears up to the knee. 'Bloody hell,' mutters Sal, and she pushes her way forward. Her feet find the hard ground beneath the thigh-deep covering. She starts to shiver. She's grateful for Jarod's hand at her elbow. 'He didn't call, no. I did get a video from Nola, though. A head up an elephant's arse.'

'My middle lass sent me that. Must be on the same algorithm. Jesus, what a world.'

The wind barrels down the gently sloping fell like an avalanche. Sal huddles into her blankets, phone pressed hard to the side of her face. The roar of the gale is merciless: a sound of ascending aircraft and passing steam trains. She can barely hear what Claire is saying. 'Say again, would you? It's insane up here.'

Claire raises her voice. She has four teenagers. She's yet to find a set of circumstances in which she can't make herself heard.

'. . . farm, out near Melmerby. Alston way . . . that's you, innit? . . . Seat Leon . . . wall's come down . . . under the snow . . . barely see it, but . . .'

Sal puts her finger in her ear. Winces as she tries to focus on the words. She's on leave. She's not supposed to be taking work calls. She sure as hell isn't meant to be attending any incidents. Had Claire said Melmerby? She feels something crackle inside her chest. Feels herself fill with static and fizz. But she's got nothing to do but sit and wait for Lewis to call. If she doesn't keep busy, she'll spend another day crying and writing messages that she'll delete before sending. She'll start to read and give up when the words become blurry and wet. She'll help Jarod with the animals and do nothing but get in his way. She might even make stilted conversation with her mam's killer. On balance, it might be better to be useful.

'Say that again . . .'

FIVE

Co-op Food, Haydon Bridge, Hexham

Dagmara hears her knees pop as she bends down to pick the sliced white loaf from the bottom of the special offer bin. It passes its sell-by date at midnight. There's a brown loaf closer, fresher and cheaper, but she hasn't reached that stage yet. Brown bread is for people who don't know how to enjoy themselves. That had been one of Cate's phrases, delivered in that soft, dreamy voice.

She straightens up sharply, before the memories can rise. She doesn't let herself think of Cate more than she has to. She'll talk about her, if it helps with a funding bid or she needs to tell an anecdote that will have the listeners clutching at their pearls. But she doesn't look too closely at the words. Recites them rather than feels them. It's too much. Even after all these years, it's too much.

'Made it through, eh? God, you're as reliable as Santa Claus.'

Dagmara recognizes the voice. It's Holly. Used to live in a bedsit with three sisters, an addict mum and a succession of pushers and pimps. By the time she was eleven years old, she'd witnessed every type of abuse and degradation. Dagmara was on the Child Protection team. She was one of the case workers. Formed a real friendship with the pale, malnourished waif with the scrubby blonde hair and the scabs on her top lip where the snot had run, and dried, and run again. Dagmara made her the promises her bosses told her never to make. Said she would do everything in her power to keep her and the sisters together if they had to be removed from her mum's care. Put an action plan in place that involved getting Mum off the drugs and the kids back into school. The boyfriend choked on his own puke in a disused garage on the Morton Park estate in Carlisle. Nobody had mourned. It was Weardy

that made the difference. Other kids. Other stories. Other sights
and sounds. Dagmara taught her how to play. To create. To
imagine. How to stare into the candle flame, and breathe.

'Eeh, you've barely changed, Holly! Gosh, you look absolutely
blooming.'

She does, too. She's pushing a stroller: plump baby all
wrapped up in a romper suit, scarf and bobble hat. Holly looks
fit. Looks well. There are points of colour in her cheeks: nice
gold hoops at her earlobes. She got an A-star in her Maths
GCSE, as far as Dagmara can recall. Works as a law clerk
now. Married to a big lovely lump of a chap. Little Gracie,
too, now.

'You always make people feel better,' grins Holly, reaching
past her to grab a packet of bagels. She drops it in her basket
and then frees her arms so she can give her a proper hug.
Dagmara gives her a full-bodied squeeze. Breathes nice
shampoo and sticky mousse.

'Quite exciting, isn't it?' laughs Holly. Her teeth are perfect.
White and neatly spaced. 'Gracie's been wide-eyed all the
way. I don't think I'll be out again after today; it's really
coming down, isn't it? Bet you've been out all day in it, haven't
you? Nothing slows you down.'

Dagmara laughs the compliment off. She's not comfortable
with praise. She wasn't raised with kind words, though she
knows how to dispense them. Knows how to weave a spell
with words.

'Did I see on the group chat that you're on the radio? You'll
never get through the snow!'

'Oh, nonsense,' scoffs Dagmara, squatting down to cluck
at Gracie's pink cheek. She hauls herself back upright. She's
relying on the stick today. There are new pains down her
side: hot, thudding soreness from her shoulder down to
her backside. She doesn't let it show in her face. 'Got
to head back and do a memory exercise with my pal, but I'll
put the foot down after that. Don't you worry about me.
Driven in worse, believe me. Farm girl through and through.
Haven't died yet!'

Holly laughs. Opens her mouth as if to say something
friendly, something jovial, something light. Nothing comes.

Dagmara gives her arm a squeeze, pudgy fingers patting the wet material of her navy-blue raincoat. 'Eeh, Holly – the roads you've travelled, eh? The mountains you've climbed. You're a bobby-dazzler, pet. Always been glorious – just lovely that everybody else is seeing it, too. Gracie here has a mam to look up to.'

Holly's manner changes. She tightens her posture. She looks self-conscious, pained. 'We climbed,' she whispers, trying to hide the depth of her feelings with a snatched, trembling grin. 'You pulled me up. All of us . . .'

'None of your nonsense,' says Dagmara, screwing up her face and sticking out her tongue. Holly laughs like she's twelve again. 'You're on the wall – y'know that, don't you? One of the shiniest stars on the Wall of Achievement. Told you you'd be up there, didn't I? With all the kids who people gave up on and who are living right, living well, doing good . . . you've more than earned your place, Holly. You're a bloody marvel.'

There's silence for a moment and they meet one another's gaze. Memories pass between them. Things witnessed. Things said and things sealed behind locked doors. They don't need to say anything now. They both know what the other is seeing.

'Bit of jam, eh,' says Dagmara brightly, stepping away. 'I can't spend another evening eating dry bread. Not a duck, am I?' She performs a passable impression of a damp duckling shaking its feathers. Gets a grin from Holly, Gracie and the trio of bored teenagers huddling by the crisps and trying to find a way to make a quid pay for three lunches. Dagmara doesn't know them. Doesn't know how she feels about that.

Well, I'll try and have a listen,' says Holly, looking as though she's having to work hard to keep her eyes from prickling with tears. Dagmara's used to such reactions from the people she's helped. She was there for them when they were in the pit of their own personal hell. She believed in them. Fought for them. Kept her word, apart from the one time when she let herself be talked out of doing the right thing.

'Won't be anything you haven't heard before,' says Dagmara, moving away. She grips the sheep-bone handle of her stick.

Picks her way through the mess of muddy, snow-flecked footprints. Grabs some milk and a bag of Revels. There's nobody
at the self-scan checkout but she refuses to use it. Damned
robots took somebody's job. She won't have any part of it.

She feels Holly's eyes on her as she makes her way into
the next aisle. Lets herself linger in a memory. Remembers
sitting in the Howard Arms with Police Constable Wulfric
Hagman. Remembers telling him about the evil, violent bastard
who'd been torturing a young mum and her terrified girls.
Remembers Hagman sucking his lower lip, sipping his pint:
awkward and uncomfortable in his scratchy blues. She
mentioned him by name. May even have given out an address.
She'd been drinking – so desperate and angry that her superiors
were going to split up the family. They couldn't let the kids
stay with Mum, no matter how much she was getting herself
together – not while the last boyfriend was still coming and
going as he pleased. And he'd listened. Listened, and drunk,
and let her vent. Three days later, the police found the man's
body, curled up on a mattress at the back of a dusty garage
full of old paint pots and empty crates. They'd put it down as
a drug death. Nobody asked questions.

She glances back. Feels eyes upon her. Feels the sting of
unspoken accusation. It joins the chorus of wordless accusations swirling around inside her. Finds its place among her
multitude of regrets.

Asks herself: *What do you truly believe, Dagmara? What
is it you're frightened of?*

She thinks of him.

Answers: *Everything.*

SIX

J arod leads them back to the main house. Sal scowls as they cross the wind-blown yard, picking her way across a miniature mountain range of frozen mud, concealed beneath a foot of fresh, thick snow. Jarod can just make out the footprints he left half an hour before. Can see the tread of the quad. He whistled for Tips and feels a genuine pang of pleasure as she emerges from behind the old milking parlour and bounds, soggily, towards her humans. Jarod watches Sal stuff her hands in her pockets. She doesn't want to touch Tips. She's cold and uncomfortable, and sometimes the thought of certain types of physical contact makes her start to hyperventilate and see things that are neither memory nor imagination. She can't wear shiny lining against bare skin. Can't have water on the back of her neck. Needs to hold the seam of her sock beneath the toenail of her big toe. Can't think about wet wool without squeezing her thumbs inside her fists.

Jarod ducks beneath the rotten wood awning and pushes open the split wooden door. Wipes his boots on the proddy mat. Slips out of his boots and hangs up his coat. He hears Sal do the same. There's movement upstairs. The old house is a chorus of creaks and groans and sighs: old timbers and ancient stone settling and shifting as if the old building is trying to grind itself into the earth. It's sat here since the early nineteenth century. Belonged to the same farming family until a few years back. Jarod Delaney owns Hagman's Farm, now. He never expected to. Doesn't believe in ownership and has never wanted the responsibility that comes with the role of custodian. Uncle Wulf had insisted, even if 'insisted' isn't a word that seems to have any business in describing the grey, stooped, crook-backed killer who's busy making his bed in the spare bedroom.

Jarod refastens the elastic band that holds his hair back from his face. Wipes his wet, dirty hands on his jumper.

'Five,' mutters Jarod, stepping over the collection of dirty boots and cluing his way to the staircase. Each wooden step groans as it takes his weight. He's joked about having them tuned – would like to see if he could play 'Chopsticks' with his feet.

His bedroom's at the top of the stairs. There are charms and pendants around the black door: the uneven stone walls supporting lopsided shelves that display old bottles and animal skulls; smooth stones and corn dollies bound with sashes of richly coloured ribbon. He takes the key from the ribbon around his neck and slides it into the old lock. At night, he locks himself inside – slides the key out on to the landing. Wulf lets him out when he gets up to make the day's first pot of tea. They don't speak about their routine. Neither knows precisely what he fears, but they both feel more comfortable knowing that their respective monsters are behind a locked door.

He tugs off his shirt and throws it on to the bare mattress. It sits on a divan bed at the far end of the small, low-ceilinged room. There's a proddy mat on the bare floorboards: rags and ribbons and unwanted clothes shredded and repurposed as multicoloured matting. Dagmara showed them all how to do it when they were young: rags of silk and cotton and tweed all twisted into one another with the little bone needle. There's no fire in the grate –just dirty water, charred papers, blackened pine cones.

He catches a glimpse of himself in the mirrored door on the open wardrobe. It's been a long time since he truly noted his scars. Most of his body is covered in faded blue tattoos: whorls and swirls and woad. They fail to cover the scar beneath. Here, now, he has the look of a battle-scarred Viking: the ink shimmering where it smudges into the lumps and ridges and keloids of scar tissue.

He pulls a shirt from the wooden clothes horse wedged up against the windowsill. Looks out through the small, square windows at the gathering snow. The world looks wrong, somehow, as if all the colour has somehow bled away. He sits down on the wide sill. There's an overflowing ashtray and a coffee pot holding a posy of dead flowers. He rolls himself a cigarette from the leather pouch in his pocket. Rolls, twists, licks, lights, breathes.

He'll take Sal up to the crash site on the quad. It's not a problem. She doesn't even have to ask. He's got the sheep in, but there's a wall that needs looking at and the mini tractor was making a nasty coughing noise last time he turned the engine over. There's a loose fence post to sort. Feed to stock up. Needs to check his account and see what he's working with: which debts to save for another day and which to outright refuse.

'We good, Jarod?' shouts Sal, from downstairs. 'I can walk, like. Strong, independent woman, remember . . .'

Jarod smiles around a mouthful of smoke. He loves having her here, despite the circumstances. The years when they were apart were the longest of his life. He could still feel her, in the moments before sleep claimed him, but for those years of travel and drugs and self-discovery, he almost learned what it was to be a single entity rather than half of a whole. He'd slept better; he remembers that. The nightmares have been hitting harder since she came to stay. Some nights he doesn't dare sleep, such are the horrors he witnesses in his dreams.

He doesn't rush himself. Takes his time. Dagmara showed him how to centre himself. Showed them all. All he has to do is summon the image of the candle flame and listen to the gentle melody of her voice. She keeps the worst of the bad memories away. Even when he was off the grid, Dagmara found ways to check up on him. Even on the beaches in Thailand, Dagmara would track him down. She'd help him meditate. Compartmentalize. *Breathe . . .*

He gives his attention to the far wall, with its looping garlands of bunting and its framed charcoal drawings: trees and serpents and skulls. There's a yellowing page from the *Tynedale Mercury*, hidden behind dusty glass. Dagmara had framed it for him. Told him he was doing something that mattered, something of worth. He was being a man to be proud of. He was being all he could be.

He extinguishes his cigarette on his palm. In his pocket, his phone sounds an alarm. He's due his pills. Due a phone call with Dagmara, too. Can't seem to face either. Can't seem to find himself since the nightmares started up again. It doesn't seem fair, somehow. Just because he's living with the man convicted of killing his mam, he doesn't see why it should upset his equilibrium. He pictures Barry, laughing in his face, imitating the word. Sees Mam, too: mouth twisted, pig-nose puckering with disdain. She's handing Barry a lighter from her cleavage. Telling him there are pincers in the kitchen. She wants to watch him hold Jarod's tongue to the flame – to see if words will appear, like text in a speech bubble, as his tongue begins to blister and burn.

'I'm leaving!'

He kicks off from the mantelpiece as if diving into the shallow end of a pool. He locks the door behind him when he pulls it, too. Leaves the words on the wall, garlanded in dead men's clothes.

My Mum Was a Monster
10 November 2019

The son of a murdered Tynedale mum has made an emotional appeal to the parole board – and begged them to set her killer free.

And he stunned authorities when he declared: 'I know he didn't do it!'

Jarod Delaney, 36, spoke to the panel on behalf of convicted killer Wulfric Hagman, 57, who was a community police officer when he brutally killed his ex-lover, before trying to end his own life.

Hagman was convicted of murder in 1996. His victim's children gave evidence during the trial, but their identities were kept anonymous and their testimony was given behind closed doors, with the press controversially banned from attendance.

Delaney revealed that he now lives at Hagman's former home in rural Tynedale – Hagman having granted his victim's family the deed to the family farm.

He said: 'He was the only man in our lives and he did the best he could in circumstances that nobody else can begin to imagine. That creature wasn't a mother. She was ill, yes: she was mentally unwell; psychotic . . . He should have called in his colleagues; of course he should. But he believed her when she said she was sorry. And he really did love her. Loved us: me, my sisters and brothers. When she grew tired of him, it was like she was making up for lost time. Let the real monster out. She was hell-bent on destroying him, just because she'd allowed herself to be vulnerable in front of him and hated that he'd seen her weak.'

The victim's son continued: 'I've stayed in contact with him throughout his time inside. I've written. Stayed in touch. Watching what prison has done to him just breaks my heart. He's no danger to anybody. He's served his time. He should never have been locked up in the first place.'

In the wake of the brutal killing, a Serious Case Review was conducted by the many partner agencies who had been in contact with the victim's children in the months before her death. She was an alcoholic and addict, and had previously been diagnosed as suffering from schizophrenia. She was prone to bouts of extreme violence, and her children confirmed reports made by Child Protection workers that they had been subjected to sustained violence. Hagman, they said, had been the only stability in their lives.

Few details were reported at the time of Hagman's jailing, due to the gagging order, but his case has been taken up by a number of campaign groups – including those who believe he was right to try to end the cycle of violence. He was convicted on the evidence of a scribbled suicide note left at the scene, and a statement given to a colleague immediately after being found cradling his victim's body.

The hearing was told that suitable accommodation had already been offered by one of Hagman's supporters, but his long-term goal was to return to his home in the valley – alongside his victim's son.

The man added: 'People are waking up to what went on. A lot of solicitors and campaigners and journalists are taking a look, and I can promise you there are going to be a lot of red faces among some old boys in blue. I'll be supporting him in his campaign to clear his name.'

The parole board deferred their decision for a further six months amid concerns that Hagman had not yet fully accepted his culpability for the brutal stabbing at Pegswood Byre,

Garrigill, in 1995. At the time of the murder, he had been suspended and was under investigation for making indecent images of a child . . .

SEVEN

Sal has her face pressed against her brother's back, doing her best to leech all the warmth from his body. Tips, the rather feckless Border Collie, seems only too pleased to follow her example – huddling his sleek, wet body in behind her. In their colossal one-piece coveralls, squished in tight on the back of a too-small quad bike, crunching over snow into the disappearing grey-black wilderness, they look like a novelty circus act, or the stars of an award-winning short film.

Sal's grumbling. Chuntering on, as Mam used to say. *Nowt worse than chuntering on*, according to Mam. *Nowt worse than being a mardy-arse. Nowt worse than being a bloody martyr.* She had a lot of sayings like that, did Trina. Gave out a lot of advice. Got upset when she didn't take it. Got upset if she did. Ended the same way regardless. Ended with Sal on her knees; all snot and blood and tears, having her face stroked by Mam, sobbing, so sorry, so sorry . . . *You know how I get, my darling, my baby, my Salome . . . I won't again, I promise, I won't again . . .*

'You chuntering, Sal?'

She doesn't reply. Just carries on scowling into the damp fabric, listing all the things she dislikes. Snow's currently top of the list. Stupid, stupid snow. And stupid Weardale. Stupid bloody planet. Can't even do global warming right. She hates the cold. Can't think properly when she's mummified like this: all fleeces and coats and waterproofs. Of course, that's not to say she likes the sunshine. She hates it when it's too hot. Can't stand the wind. Rainy days can piss off, too. Maybe Lewis was right. Maybe there are literally only twenty minutes in any given year when she's satisfied with the temperature.

'Wiggly bit coming up, sis. Slippy as owt by the gate.'

Her arms are wrapped around his waist. The wheels of the quad bike throw up waves of dirty snow, soaking her legs well past the knee. The clouds press down low upon the landscape:

just a small patch of daylight visible between the bank of grey cloud and the pristine whiteness of the land. The snow has smoothed down the lumps and bumps of Weardale: thrown a soft astrakhan fleece over this craggy, scarred landscape. Sal thinks of funeral shrouds. Thinks of a cloth laid out upon the newly dead.

'You all right?'

Sal squeezes Jarod around the middle. He pushes the quad further up the incline. She huddles against him, not wanting to look up. She can smell sweat and petrol. She feels sick.

She feels the quad slowing. Jarod gives her a little dig in the ribs and nods across the vast expanse of blurry whiteness to where a solitary blue Land Rover is parked up, a little lopsided, against a bank of wind-blown snow. 'Yonder,' shouts Jarod. 'That's Mason Bewley's car. You never said it was Mason Bewley.'

Sal scrunches up her face. The car looks as if it's made up of millions of tiny pixels. Smoke is billowing upwards from the exhaust. The cloud of sparkling grey air makes her think of old fantasy movies: great serpents breathing out wreaths and ribbons of enchanted smoke. Mason Bewley? She can't place the name.

'Do we have a problem with Mason Bewley?' asks Sal, rummaging around inside her too-big all-in-one and attempting to retrieve her notebook and phone without removing her waterproof mittens. She clambers down from the quad and steps into thick, perfect, knee-deep snow.

'Wanted our place when it were up for auction. Weren't happy it went to me. I'll come back for you, eh? Hour long enough?'

Sal doesn't push him for more details. Her brother can be a little funny around certain people. He sometimes struggles to know who to be. She has no doubt that part of him would be overly friendly around Bewley: chatty and warm to the point of mania – talking over him, keeping things light, doing his damnedest to keep the unpleasantness out of their interaction. The other part would want confrontation, a reckoning. As the eldest of the children, albeit by only twelve minutes, he was always the peacemaker. He kept things bearable for the others. He was a barometer for Mam's moods. As an adult, long since orphaned, he still can't deal with atmospheres of awkwardness or of building temper. Sal may be his twin, may share near-identical DNA, but their closeness isn't built upon any similarity of character. Sal doesn't mind confrontation in the slightest. According to Lewis, she actively seeks it out. According to Lewis, there isn't a happy space that she can't spoil with her temper.

'An hour? I'll be dead. Do a lap, come back. If I'm dead, cut my head off and put me down a mine shaft. I want to be an archaeological conundrum.'

Jarod isn't really listening. The wind is blasting down from the peaks, whipping the snow into helix patterns. Occasionally, the top of a barbed-wire fence pokes out from beneath a drift. Somewhere nearby, a crow emits a low, mournful croak.

There's movement up ahead. The passenger door of the Land Rover opens in a series of awkward jerks, pushing against the slope of snow that's blown against it. She can just make out a fluorescent coat. Then the door closes again, yanked shut with a definite air of 'sod that'. Sal stamps her booted feet through the snow, seeking the grip of the road. She can't quite get her bearings. There's a bad turn here; she knows that. There's a farmhouse a little further up the hill, just past the bridge. She wonders if the waterfall is frozen. She remembers standing behind that perfect cascade of icy water: her and Jarod and a couple of the little ones, grubby in vests and pants and welly boots: leaping from the slimy rocks into the pool below.

She's a few feet away from the Land Rover when the door opens again. This time, she recognizes the bulk of PC Paul Torrance. He's wearing a fleecy hat and his face is pink and greasy, like sausage meat left out on a warm counter.

'That you under there, Sal?' asks Torrance, squinting. Sal's features have essentially been reduced to a pair of snow-rimed spectacles and a stray twist of black curly hair. The rest is all overalls, boots, padded shirts and muddy gloves.

'No,' grumbles Sal. 'I'm a rogue Jellybaby.'

'Teletubby, I was thinking,' smiles Torrance. He's a dark-haired, bright-eyed chap in his early thirties and would be quite handsome if not for his strangely shaped lips: two moist, purple slugs oozing their way across the space between nose and chin. He always seems to be doing battle with an excessive amount of spit. He has an unpleasant habit of sucking saliva through his teeth when he's thinking. It doesn't happen often.

'Where's the patrol car?' asks Sal, sheltering from the wind behind the open door.

'Way back. Couldn't get near. Mr Bewley here was good enough to pick me up. Vehicle's down the way there. Wouldn't have seen it for days if we hadn't struck lucky. Or unlucky, depending on your point of view.'

She tucks herself into the blast of warm air. The inside of the battered old vehicle smells of sweat and sheep, roll-ups and petrol. She glances past Torrance and gives a professional nod to the man in the driving seat. He's fleshy and round: probably sixty-ish. Wispy curls of toffee-coloured hair curl out from under his sodden flat cap. There's a dog-end, long since burnt out, clamped in the thin line of his mouth. The stubble at his pink neck has worn a hole in the collar of his flannel shirt. Sal recognizes him at once.

'Mr Bewley,' says Sal, pulling down her hood and shaking out her curls. 'I'm Sal Delaney, I'm a Collision Investigation Officer. I appreciate you hanging on with my colleague here – as you can imagine . . .'

Bewley wrinkles his forehead, a deep ridge appearing between his eyebrows. 'Salami, is it? Trina's eldest girl? Aye, heard you were a copper. Who'd have thought it, eh?'

Sal gives a tight smile. Of course he remembers her. Of course he knows who she is. Everybody knows who she is. She gives him her most professional smile. 'The old nicknames never die, do they?'

'Salami Bloody Delaney,' he says again. There's something about his gaze that makes her feel as if she's being paraded at the auction: as if he's assessing her muscle tone and the brightness of her eyes – trying to decide whether she's worth a bid. 'Been an age, hasn't it? You well?'

Sal ignores the enquiry. She gives her attention to Torrance, who's waiting expectantly for an explanation.

'Salome,' she says tiredly. 'Kids called me Salami.'

'You're called Salome?' asks Torrance, with the air of somebody who went to school with sixteen other kids called Paul and who thinks of the name 'Dan' as a bit bloody exotic. 'Seriously, Salome? Do people know?'

'It's not an infectious disease, Paul,' says Sal tiredly. She looks past him to Bewley. 'I understand you've reported an abandoned vehicle?'

Bewley has a strange little smile on his face, as if he's replaying a memory that makes him tingle. He was probably one of Mam's 'gentleman callers'. Stuffed a few quid in her pocket for five minutes of huffing and puffing and not having to bother the wife.

Bewley removes the dog-end from his lips. Winds down the window and flicks it into the snow. He flicks his tongue out, the tip worrying at a stray hair that's worked its way into the corner of his mouth. 'Did I hear that sick bastard is living with your brother?'

Sal holds his gaze. Pretends she hasn't heard. 'You'll have to forgive the skeleton crew, I'm afraid, Mr Bewley. In an ideal world, we'd have a team here from Carlisle, but as you can probably guess, nobody can get through, so it's left to PC Torrance here to do his best, and to daft buggers who can't say "no", like me. Could you just talk me through it, please?'

Bewley looks at Torrance: an old-school doctor checking in with the husband about whether or not he's allowed to examine the wife.

'I can give you the background, Sal . . .' begins Torrance, warming his hands on the blowers.

'From Mr Bewley, please,' says Sal, with her most apologetic smile.

Bewley scratches at his stomach. Shrugs. 'Nowt to tell, lass. Came to put some hay down for the flock and saw the wall were down again. Hasn't been back up more than a few months – you might even have been here for that. Prick in a Subaru went through it, showing off to his girlfriend. Smashed the front end in – the car, not the lass. If he weren't wearing a seatbelt, he'd have ended up down the falls. Airbags saved the both of 'em. Didn't do no favours to me bloody wall, mind. Had to get stonemason in from Middleton, which weren't bloody cheap. Anyway, snow were already mad and there were black ice under the tyres. Weren't hard to see what had happened.'

'And you found a vehicle – is that right?'

Bewley shrugs again. 'Couldn't see it from the road, but owt that had gone through the wall weren't coming back out under its own steam. Plodded down, like you do. Couldn't just bugger off, could I? Anyway, there it was, half buried, half in the little ghyll. You'll need a crane to get it out, I reckon.'

'Black SEAT Leon,' interjects Torrance. '2008 reg.'

'You've been down?'

'Secured the scene best I could,' says Torrance, looking like a man who expects to receive a bollocking a mile on from every fork in the road. 'Only got here myself through a bit of good fortune – followed a snowplough up from Brampton. Couple of gritters doing their bit, too. Hasn't done the paint job on the patrol car many favours, like . . .'

'And the vehicle's empty?' asks Sal.

'Wouldn't be sitting here if it wasn't,' scoffs Bewley. 'Three kids and a widow are sat howling in the back, but we thought we shouldn't tamper with the evidence. Jesus, where do you find 'em, lad?'

Sal lets him chunter. Feels the heat of his glare. He's got his reasons for hating her. She can't, in good conscience, hate him back.

'Vehicle registered to one Ann Kelly, of the Police House, Humshaugh. I don't know how to pronounce it.'

'Pretty place. Twenty minutes from here usually. In this weather? You put a call in?'

'Can't get enough of a signal to make myself understood. I don't really know what they expect you to do in these conditions.'

'My best, I suppose,' says Sal, looking past Bewley to the endless whiteness beyond. 'You may as well get going, Paul. I'll get some pictures, give it a once-over, and then we're in the lap of the gods until the weather changes. Jarod'll pick me up in a bit.'

Bewley wrinkles his nose at the mention of her brother. 'He didn't come and say hello. Pity that. Plenty to ask him. Still happy there, is he? Not looking to flog it on? Seems odd to me, hunkered down in a knackered old pile like that, only Wulfric Hagman for company . . .'

'I know that name,' says Torrance brightly. 'Community police officer based at Alston, wasn't he? I suppose he was my predecessor.'

'Not really, Paul. It was thirty years ago; also, he hasn't pre-deceased you.'

'And he's living with your brother, is he?'

Sal's never sure how much of her background is a source of gossip among her fellow officers. Those closest to her know what she grew up around, and what happened to her mam. As for those passing acquaintances and nodding-terms interlopers, she doesn't know whether they've Googled her, read the court transcripts or dipped into the files on the database. She knows that she would have done if the roles were reversed. She has always suffered from a desperate need to know the truth about things – no matter the consequences.

'Good to see you, Paul,' says Sal, stepping out of the slightly warmer air afforded by the shelter of the car door. 'Remind me to thank you properly for bringing this into my life.'

'Sorry, Salami,' says Torrance, with what he seems to think is a boyish grin.

She nods, acknowledging the attempt at charm, then slams the door closed and begins her laborious trudge through the deep snow. She can just about make out where the stone wall is supposed to be, though the snow is so thick that in places she can't be sure whether she is walking on road, grass or empty air. She pulls out her phone and starts to video her progress, limiting her curses as she stumbles and slips. The fresh snowfall has all but obscured the maze of footprints left by Bewley and Torrance on their brief trips down to the abandoned vehicle. Sal takes a wider line, trying not to disturb anything of evidential value. The very thought makes her feel like laughing. This was a fool's errand, a piss-take. It'll be days before this can be done properly. Any tyre tracks or skid marks are buried under four feet of snow. She looks back the way she's come and sees Bewley struggling to get the old Land Rover moving. The engine roars as he puts his foot to the floor. She wonders whether he would appreciate being told to put it in second gear. Decides he probably wouldn't.

She goes through the motions. Takes photographs of the wall and the half-buried constellation of displaced bricks. She videos the entire panorama: a full 360, showing the sharp bend in the road and the sudden dip beneath. The snow makes the landscape unreadable: the video looking like a home movie shot inside a golf ball. She's good at her job and doesn't like to jump to conclusions, but it's bloody obvious what's happened. Somebody's come down the hill too fast, skidded, gone through the wall and buggered off. They're either home safe or hunkered down with some local farmer. She got out of bed for this!

She trudges on into deeper snow. She isn't even sure that this is part of Cumbria Police's territory any more. It all gets a bit vague out in the valley. She could well be on Durham's turf. They're welcome to it. Welcome to the whole bloody . . .

She stops when she sees the unmistakable hump of a snow-covered SEAT Leon. It's gone into a snowdrift at a decent speed and taken out a couple of old, spindly trees, the mesh of dirt and roots and snow all providing a perfect camouflage. It was pure luck that Bewley found it.

Sal keeps shooting footage. Occasionally, she takes static photos. She squats down atop the compacted snow and looks at the scarring on the trunk of the closest tree. She pulls herself forward and the ground seems to lurch. She tries to get her bearings. She's maybe fifty metres from the road but she can't even see as far as the field. The ground slides away sharply to her left, disappearing down to where a little river is frozen hard as iron.

Sal grabs hold of one of the tree branches and shuffles herself forward until she can see into the car. Takes a quick glance and gathers up all the little details. Opens a mental file. Windscreen smashed in. No airbag. Gearstick in neutral. Handbrake off. Broken glass. Blood.

She shuffles back out and around to the rear of the vehicle. There's snow on the back windshield and rear window, and she takes care to photograph both in situ before she wipes the snow from the glass with her sleeve. She peers into the gloom. There's a child seat in the back of the car. An empty child seat: all empty raisin boxes and Fruit Shoot bottles. There's a scrunched-up Happy Meal box in the footwell. A kit-bag. An empty bottle of bubble mixture. Sal feels a little tremble just behind her heart. Thinks of Nola. Of Lottie. Of the daughters she's no longer allowed to claim as her own. Could there have been a child in the vehicle? Has some frantic parent climbed from the wreckage and set off with their freezing child to look for shelter? Sal wishes she had some back-up. Wishes she had her proper equipment. Wishes that . . .

There's a flapping of wings from nearby: a baleful croak as the wind momentarily stops its assault on the land. Sal looks around instinctively. A little further down the valley, maybe twenty paces away, a big black crow is regarding her with that peculiarly corvid air of combined sorrow and menace. It pecks at the ground in front of it: knife-like beak breaking through the snow like a fork through a pie crust. It lets out another croak. Stabs again.

'Get,' shouts Sal. She doesn't like crows. Too clever by half, Mam said. 'Go on, get.'

The bird flaps its wings. Lifts off and sinks down again. There's something comical about its movements. It looks drunk. Looks delirious. Looks sated.

Sal drags herself away from the vehicle. Picks a path down the valley. Each step seems to take her into deeper snow and soon she is sodden and shivering, the cold seeming to eat through to the bone.

She manages to hold on to the branches of a low-hanging tree as she slips and stomps down the steep bank. She feels her energy levels dissipating. Each step becomes harder than the last. She's breathing hard: a burning tingle in her chest. The sweat on her cheeks seems to freeze each time she exhales. And she's still got to get back to the road. She feels the weight of her own misery settling upon her. She'd like to just lie down, to be honest. Like to make an eiderdown of the deep, delicious snow.

The crow caws. Lifts off. The daft lump can barely fly. It only gets a few feet and then drops back down to the snow.

Only then does Sal see the curious pink tinge to the snow that she has displaced on her trudge down the bank. Silently, she rubs at the top layer of snow. Jerks her hand back as she sees the first spots of red.

She pulls out her phone. Concentrates on doing things properly. Films her last few laborious paces through to the spot where the crow had stopped to feed. She brushes away the loose flakes. Looks down at the carrion upon which the crow had been feasting.

The face is almost gone. The flesh has been stripped back to the bone. Both eyeballs have been plucked from the sockets and all of the soft tissue below the scalp has been torn free and consumed. The neck has been torn open: frozen pink and purple twists of trachea and tongue are visible through the frozen ridges of the wound.

Sal makes sure she doesn't shake as she focuses the camera on the corpse. She's seen worse things. Not many, but she's seen worse. It's a man; that much is obvious. She wants to rub the snow away from the body, but she knows she can't risk destroying whatever evidence might be preserved beneath the frost. All she can tell is that it's a man. Youngish. She thinks he might be wearing a denim jacket.

To her left, the crow lets out a throaty caw. The wind ruffles its feathers. Sal finds herself staring into that black, black eye. It's almost hypnotic. She has to shake herself. Has to force herself to focus on the little strip of gold that hangs from the bird's beak. Sal takes a photo. Pulls off her gloves and uses her quivering fingers to enlarge the picture on her screen.

She looks at the thin golden chain and the pendant that hangs, limply, at the base. It's cylindrical: silver and gold. Letters are picked out on the sides in a Hebrew script. He used to hang it on the bedroom door when he was fucking Mum. He told them about it once, sitting there at the kitchen table, bare feet up on the wood. Told all his new pals about the necklace that protected him: engraved with the names of his three personal angels. It kept him safe, he said. Kept him on the side of the angels.

Sal looks down again at the faceless man in the snow.

Squats down and feels herself grow light-headed, her stomach heaving, a strange pins-and-needles prickling in her feet.

She knows this man. Knows him, and hates him in a way that goes all the way through to the bone.

She glares at the lipless, gurning skull. For a moment, she'd like to take a rock and smash his bones to powder.

She lets out a low, ragged breath. Squats down and stares at the ragged edges of the wound at his neck. There's a strange smell rising from the earth. Something chemical. Something wrong.

The bird tries to fly again. It flaps its wings twice. Screeches. Caws. Gulps and totters, spirals like a downed Spitfire. It hits the snow and lies there, half buried, twitching: black feathers falling like flakes of ash.

Sal breathes deep. Catches that faint trace of acid in the air. Looks again at the wound, then back to the bird that feasted upon his flesh. She straightens up. Could there be a child? Could there be somebody else beneath that snow, their face ripped away by sharp, eager beaks?

Another croak. Another shriek.

She looks down into the whiteness of the disappearing valley. Sees the sad, black pile of frozen feathers, like the remains of a campfire. Another, further down. Three birds . . . four, all dead or dying: bellies and throats eaten away: entrails and gizzards oozing sloppily from the sizzling wounds in their feathers and flesh.

EIGHT

Hagman twists the papers into long, thin cigarillos. Ties them around one another in a crude approximation of a Palm Sunday cross. His movements are as gentle as if he were tying a toddler's laces. He drops the crosses into the cold black grate.

His eyes fall upon a random line of text, staring up as if trying to catch his attention. He feels a surge of guilt, as if caught in the act of pretending to be Santa Claus. Can't help but read the proffered lines: . . . *accused the defendant of taking indecent images of her sleeping children and informed his superiors.* He looks away.

'*No, Wulf, lad. Bloody no. Not again. You'll get it wrong. Make it worse. Just bloody leave it, lad.*'

He's made up his mind. He can't face it again. Can't face the questions and the answers and the lies. It might take him all day, but every damn page is going on the fire. He's giving it all to the flames.

Even as he wills himself not to, he glances down again. Wishes, again, he was a stronger man. Sees another line: this one a caption to accompany an evidence exhibit. Fig. CCWH0186: a picture of the broken door lock. He can't remember smashing it open. Can't remember being there. But he knows he was. He was arrested there, covered in her blood. He left a suicide note. He begged for forgiveness. He tried to end himself – the actions of a guilty man. He doesn't blame the jury. If he'd been on the jury, he wouldn't have believed the man in the dock either.

'I'm bored here, Wulf. Attention, please. Ms Dagmara Scrowther MBE. And you pronounce that "mzzz" – the way a wasp would say it. Important person, lots of friends, making time to help and being roundly ignored . . .'

A real voice, this time. Not an echo, but a real, slightly Geordie, increasingly pissed-off voice. Female. Soft, but with an edge – the kind of voice that can perform all the voices when reading bedtime stories. Can do the witches and the dragons just as well as the princesses.

Wulf twists another sheaf of pages. Witness statement, this one: . . . *clearly intoxicated – he begged me to take him up there to see her but there was no good going to come of that.* Grabs more, wringing and twisting the pages out as if pulling a bird's neck. Keeps going until half a dozen diagonal crosses have covered the old black metal. He takes the box of matches from the pocket of his padded shirt and enjoys the simple rasp and magnesium flash of flame. Holds the flickering red flower to the closest paper and savours the soft transference of heat and light. Enjoys the moment. He likes this ritual. It's soothing. There is comfort to be had in routine.

'Are you nearly settled, Wulf? I'm seeing more of your backside than I'm comfortable with.'

Hagman turns away from the big black metal range. Looks at the disembodied head on the old, age-blackened kitchen table. He'd forgotten she was there.

'Nearly done,' he says, reaching into the black-lacquered coal bucket and selecting a bushel of bone-dry sticks. He places them one by one into the flickering flame. If the kiss of the fire pains him, he does not let it show.

'Wulf, I swear . . .'

He gives the head his full attention. Smiles an apology. In his V-neck pullover, button-down shirt and padded plaid overshirt, he has the look of a kindly grandad. He has what he likes to call an 'upside-down head': completely hairless on top but luxuriously hirsute around the chin and jaw – his badger-tail beard neatly coaxed into a Spartan wedge of thick bristles. There's something fundamentally amiable about him: a general air of perpetual mildness. He talks softly and has a tendency to leave big spaces in between his sentences so he can properly choose the apposite words to convey his true thoughts. He's rarely afforded the opportunity to complete such declarations – other people leaping into the gap with their own anecdotes long before Hagman has finished his point. He's not given to complaining, though he has a range of facial expressions that engender spontaneous sympathy.

His big brown eyes and quavering lower lip put people in mind of a toddler scolded by a grandparent. He makes a perfect poster boy for the wrongfully convicted. It's no wonder the people at the Juris Project are so desperate for him to let them help. He looks every inch a man broken by a cruel, corrupt system.

'Sorry, Dagmara. You were two minutes early.'

The floating head lights up in a warm smile as Hagman takes his seat at the table and gives her his full attention. He's comfortable with most modern technology but finds these 'face-to-face phone calls' give him little wispy moments of anxiety. Dagmara's face fills the whole screen of the laptop, and in the gloom of the dark, smoky kitchen, his imagination invariably hands him visions of the horrific. Every time his eyes fall upon the laptop screen, he imagines that he is again awakening to an act of frenzied brutality: a player in a blood-spattered Jacobean tragedy.

'Bad out there, I presume,' asks Dagmara, in her soft Northumberland accent. 'Radio said it was bloody awful.'

'Jarod's been out. No casualties in the flock as yet, but there's something going on. He took Sal out on the quad a bit ago. Called in by that Claire. Hope nobody's in too much trouble. No bugger should even be out.'

Dagmara sucks on the information as if it were a boiled sweet. She nods to herself, plucking a single strand of long, red hair from the corner of her mouth. Dagmara's not far off sixty but her great fox-fur mane doesn't betray a single strand of white. There's something of the jolly Irish baby about her: pale skin atop a palimpsest of some pale blue tracery: blotchy limbs and angry fists; cherry tomato cheeks and busy blue eyes.

She nods again, in total agreement with herself. 'Weather like this, there's always somebody going to end up dead in a ditch. People don't know how to drive for the conditions; that's the trouble. In Scandinavia, they put on winter tyres. They take courses on how to save their own lives. We can't even get people to clear the windscreen of snow before they're doing sixty in their cul-de-sac.'

Hagman listens to the pleasing crackle of the fire taking

hold. It matches the tone and timbre of Dagmara's voice perfectly.

'She's all right, is she?' asks Dagmara, as she comes to the end of her rant about imbecile motorists. She worries about Sal. Dagmara worries about everybody.

'I think so. We don't really talk about anything like that. There's that distance, you know? Not like with Jarod. I don't know how much to lay at her feet; that's the truth of it. I mean, if I tell her everything, if I properly lay myself bare, then maybe I'm just unburdening myself to somebody who then has to carry it on my behalf. It's like forgiving yourself, isn't it? The arrogance of that astounds me.' He stops, aware that he's been monopolizing the conversation with his ramblings. He feels guilty at once. Tells himself to shut up and keep it light.

'Could you turn your light up, Wulf?' asks Dagmara, squinting out from the screen. There's only one window in the cramped, low-ceilinged kitchen and the old nylon curtains are still drawn across. The light comes from the fire and the wind-up torch that hangs from a lethal-looking hook on one of the chocolate-coloured beams overhead. They were once used to hang game. Hagman can't look at the hooks without visualizing dead grouse, dead pheasants. He feels the sudden acid lump in his throat as he pictures a shimmering, headless rabbit hanging above him, dripping greasy blood from its skinned haunches to puddle upon the cold floor.

'If you mean "put another log on the fire", I can do that. The light's not going to get brighter.'

Dagmara peers past him. He can feel her drinking in the rest of the room: sifting, filing, assessing. She has spent her working life having to make life-or-death judgment calls on people's suitability for being a parent, being a husband: being locked up or released. In forty years as a social worker and the guiding light behind Weardale Youth Initiative, she's seen it all, heard it all, and got more right than wrong. She was awarded an MBE in the Queen's penultimate birthday honours. She didn't tell anybody, but word got out. She can tell a lot about how somebody is coping with their reality based on whether the picture frames hang straight and whether there

are as many knives in the knife block as the last time she
checked. Dagmara's intelligence is fierce and keen. She intim-
idates people without meaning to. She's short and round and
friendly and has made a career out of being underestimated
by people who mistake pleasantness for weakness. If her
brain were a fist, it would be at the end of Mike Tyson's wrist.
The *Cumberland News* and some glossy lifestyle magazines
featured her story, and she appeared on *BBC Look North*:
rolling her eyes at the slick anchorman's sentimental introduc-
tion and looking at her watch throughout the interview –
eventually telling him she couldn't be long as she was taking
a group of autistic, disadvantaged LGBTQ teens for a game
of ten-pin bowling. Her steadfast refusal to alter a single
scrap of her aesthetic went down wonderfully with viewers
who adored this crumpled, red-haired community champion
in her blue sweatshirt, covered in dog hairs, toddler snot and
Jammy Dodger crumbs.

Dagmara reaches over for her mug, using her other hand to
steady herself. Hagman glimpses her hands. They're chapped
and red: dirt ground into the knuckles. She's always liked
working outside. He doubts any members of the board that
oversees her charity's spending would be as willing to roll up
their sleeves and muck in with the workmen and landscape
gardeners. She's never been too proud to get her hands filthy.

'Burdock,' she says, pulling a face. 'Good for the digestive
system but bloody horrible for the tastebuds. It's one of Jarod's.
Bottle was nice but the contents tasted like a vegan's bathwater.
I won't be having another.'

Hagman gives her a smile. Scratches at his beard. It's irrit-
ating him. Getting itchy. He wants to shave, suddenly. Wants
to feel the sting of the cold wind on a freshly shorn chin. He's
fizzy. Hot. He can feel bugs moving between his muscles and
epidermis.

'I don't think he's doing any of that any more,' he says,
picking up a random sheaf of paper and tearing it into a neat
twist. He thinks it might be Barry Ford's statement – the one
that did as much as his own confession to put him away. He
doesn't want to read it again. Knows it off by heart.

'At least he's stopped the potions,' says Dagmara distractedly, looking away. Her phone is ringing somewhere in the house. 'I'll let the machine get it,' she mutters. 'Probably another poor bugger on their uppers. I need a stiff drink before I can tackle them, though I sit here feeling like a nasty sod for not making it my first priority. I think it might be getting a bit much for me, y'know, Wulf. Not just the getting old, the getting tired – it's what's coming through the door and the state they're in. God, it's getting worse, Wulf. If somebody had told me in 1997 that the world would look like this by now . . . Jesus, we wouldn't all have been singing "Things Can Only Get Better".'

Hagman's only half listening. He's looking past her at the great lopsided mosaic of photographs and pictures on her kitchen wall. She likes to keep pictures of the children she's helped over the years. They go back a long way. Some of the images show polyester sweatshirts, big glasses and junior perms; in others, the kids are in shell suits, spiked hair or floppy curtains of fringe. They work up to the present day: flabby, hollow-eyed, sun-starved faces, summoning up a smile for the camera. The pictures are all laid out around Dagmara's favourite oil painting. It's by Caravaggio. It shows the Seven Acts of Mercy. Everybody who goes to Weardy knows them by heart. They're rules to live by. *Bury the dead. Visit the imprisoned* and *feed the hungry. Shelter the homeless. Clothe the naked. Visit the sick. Refresh the thirsty.*

Dagmara isn't a particularly religious person, but she likes the simplicity of the message. Do these things, and you'll be a good person. Don't do them, and you're not much of a person at all. It's a message she's spelled out to countless colleagues, clients and angry-faced delinquents over her many years trying to help people. The print was a gift from an old friend, Dagmara had told him, when Hagman asked about it on one of the first home visits the governor permitted him ahead of his impending release. She hadn't offered up much more. For all that she knows about everybody else, Dagmara isn't naturally forth-coming about her own personal life. She's never had a partner, to Hagman's knowledge. Never had kids. He's occasionally wondered whether there mightn't have been something romantic between Dagmara and her old social worker colleague,

Cate, whose picture sits on the bookshelf in the living room beside fresh flowers and a framed photograph of a bright-eyed, smiling girl with long hair and a floppy hat, smiling through a collage of falling blossom. He hadn't asked any more than that – wary of spoiling the arrangement.

Dagmara had been willing to put him up. She had the room, after all. Her little bungalow had two spare rooms and she'd be glad of the company – even if the company in question happened to be a convicted murderer. It became a permanent arrangement upon his release. Moving over to Jarod's hadn't been easy for either of them. They'd come to be something akin to husband and wife.

'Coming down bad,' says Dagmara, glancing out of her kitchen window. The roads are still passable on her side of the valley. Hagman has no doubt she'll make it to her radio interview this afternoon. Her little Saxo is so light it fairly skims over the drifts, and he is aware from painful experience that she knows how to get more out of the little engine than even its manufacturers would have thought possible. She only lives a stone's throw from her youth centre in Haydon Bridge. From her bedroom window, she can see its reassuring shape: the play area and the Think Tank, all the way down to the Memorial Garden and its haunting spray of specially selected black and white blooms. She did a lot of the grunt work herself: she and Jarod exhausted themselves laying sleepers and digging trenches, erecting walls and placing every monochrome stone in the rockeries by hand. Dagmara tends to the garden's well-being as if to a sick child. Hagman has no doubt that the heated lights will be on already, protecting the delicate bulbs from the snow. She'll have hell to pay at the next budget meeting. Sometimes, Hagman thinks she just does it for fun.

Hagman jumps as a stick snaps in the heat of the fire. He jerks around in his chair, shoulders set, fists up. Takes a breath. Holds it. Counts to three. Breathes out. Feels the tension bleed from his body.

'You OK, Wulf? Is that . . .?'

Hagman realizes that in jumping up, he's knocked the laptop and changed her view of the room. She can see what he's burning. The side table by the range is covered in great sheaves of legal documents, court transcripts, witness statements and forensic reports.

'Wulf, I thought you said you were going to . . .'

'Not again, Dagmara,' says Hagman, crossing to the draining board and locating a relatively clean glass. He turns on the copper tap and a gout of water spurts into the deep sink to the sound of screeches and wheezing from the pipes beneath the floor. Hagman winces as he shuts it off. Makes his way back to the table, sipping gently. Even all these years later, his throat is still a constant point of fire. He broke his hyoid bone the night Trina died. His voice is still low and gentle, but there's a pained rasp to it. 'It's not a decision I've taken lightly. I just can't. I can't hear it all again. I can't face it all again. And the kids shouldn't have to, either. There's nowt to be gained, is there?'

Dagmara bristles. Clucks her short, powerful arms like a damp chicken. 'How about clearing your name, Wulf? How about proving that you didn't do it and spent twenty-three years in prison for something you didn't do.'

'We don't know that . . .'

'That's why we keep going, Wulf. You're getting somewhere. Last time we tried, you remembered things, didn't you? There are other ways to go deeper. Even if we unlock a little – even if we just lift the blind and peer into the locked rooms. You want to know, don't you? I mean . . .'

Hagman holds up his hand, asking for a moment so he can choose his words. He doesn't get the chance to find them. He can hear barking across the yard. He hears the murmur of a nearing quad.

'Jarod,' says Hagman unnecessarily. He crosses back to the window and opens the short, scratchy curtains. He watches as Jarod brings the quad to a halt by the old silage shed across the yard. He stomps his way briskly through the deepening snow, grumbling at Tips to stop snorkelling through the thick covering of white. Hagman watches him struggle with the locked door and thinks about running outside to help. But he's not dressed for outdoors, and by the time he gets his boots on, it'll probably already be sorted, and sometimes Jarod is grateful for help and sometimes he looks as if he wants to smash Wulf's face in for daring to imply he couldn't cope. So he sips his water. Watches.

A moment later, Jarod stumbles awkwardly out from behind the crumbling, paint-chipped black door. He's carrying old cardboard boxes, dismantled and pushed flat. Hagman turns back to Dagmara. She's cleverer than he is and always presumes she'll be able to offer an explanation or advice. 'Jarod's come back and taken some old boxes from the silage shed,' he says deliberately.

'Bloody hell, Wulf, your diary's going to be riveting tonight, isn't it?' says Dagmara, pulling a face that suggests she has rarely heard anything as tedious. Then she breaks into a smile. She likes winding people up, from time to time. She's found that most of the people she deals with can only really express themselves through gentle teasing and the occasional outright fight.

'Should I go and . . .?'

'No, he'll be grand. Probably preserving evidence, I shouldn't wonder. Tracks. Prints. All that jazz. God, worst possible weather for it, isn't it? Maybe it'll be good for Sal, eh? Get her out of herself? Is she still talking to his girls? They must be so bloody confused, Wulf.'

'She'll get herself right,' says Hagman, hoping it's true. 'She's good at all this. She'll probably get a pat on the back for going out in this. She's on leave; I told you, didn't I? That Claire told her she was making everybody miserable and sent her home. Bit different to our day. Progress, I suppose.' He sits back at the table and hears the sound of the quad disappearing up the lane, the snow snatching the roar and rumble in its dead fist.

'Are you really going to stop it all?' asks Dagmara, softening her expression and holding his gaze. They're as close as they were all those years in the visiting room at HMP Franklin. He wishes they could hold hands. Wished it then, too.

'None of it really matters,' he says, with something that might be a shrug. He despises what it makes him. Hates his weakness, his ceaseless fear. Wishes he could tell Dagmara what it feels like to be locked out of your own thoughts. He just doesn't think he can demonstrate extremities of emotion any more. He's cried himself out. He's shouted and screamed and pummelled, and none of it has made any difference.

There's a growl from outside: a big engine, huge tyres pushing through drifts of snow. He recognizes the engine. Land Rover Defender, 2002, Heritage model. That's Bewley's car. Christ, he can't handle Bewley. Not today, not ever. 'Bewley,' he says quietly, and he closes his eyes. 'And Jarod's not here – no, no, I'm not talking to him now . . .'

He hears a door slam. Hears the clunk of a gear change. The silly sod's trying a three-point turn on the narrow lane by the gate. He stands up, retracing his steps to the window. Looks out just as Sal runs past, face flushed, glasses spattered with snow. She comes through the door like she's been slung by a trebuchet.

'Wulf . . . fuck, did Jarod, . . . he came back, yeah, I saw him . . . oh, hi, Dagmara, sorry . . . there's been . . .'

Hagman stands back. Silently, he hands her his glass of water. Watches her gulp it down – her breath emerging in ribbons of steam.

'It's bad, is it?' asks Dagmara from the screen.

Hagman holds his breath. Waits. Feels Sal look from one to the other, assessing her audience; asking herself who knows what, and who told the truth, and which of their lies they can still remember.

Her words come out in a rush. 'There's a body near the crashed car, up by the waterfall's edge. His face is gone but I don't know if it was the acid or the crows.'

'Acid?' asks Dagmara, looking up. 'What's happened, Salome? Are you OK? Jarod?'

'The body,' says Sal, and there's a moment when her lip trembles: a solitary wavelet upon a still lake. Then she blinks back the tears and takes control of herself. 'I've called it in but lost the signal. I need the laptop, I'm really sorry – it's going to be a bloody nightmare . . . for us, for them.' She looks at Hagman, her eyes full of apology and unspoken regret. 'For you.'

'For me?' asks Hagman. 'Why?'

'The dead man,' says Sal cautiously. 'It's Barry Ford.'

NINE

'Oh, that's the best one yet! Carrots! God, my sides are sore. Eeeh, you're off yer head! Quick as bloody lightning, Hank. Four snowmen! And one goes, "Can you smell carrots?" Cos their noses are carrots! So they can smell them! You get it, don't you? That's so good I think I've tiddled!'

They're laughing again. Laughing like he's proper funny. Laughing like he's said something brilliant. Laughing like he's clever. Laughing like he's not a total tit. They're nudging each other and looking as though they're about to split open like unpricked sausages: giggles and belly laughs slithering out like eels. They're looking at each other, all mischievous and conspiratorial, as if they're doing something they shouldn't be – as if they're all being proper little devils.

'Not like that one, Nola?'

She hears her name but doesn't look up. She's got her head in a book. It's a glossy, cheaply-made thing she bought off the internet. It's called *Evil Among Us: A Memoir of Murder and Betrayal* and is written by 'the award-winning journalist who counted the killer as a friend' and who had found himself 'at the heart of the grisly tale'. It's about the murder of Salome's mam, and she feels sort of bad for reading it – albeit not bad enough to stop. Anyway, she's not really reading it right now, but it serves as concealment of sorts. She holds her hardbacks like a Victorian debutante might carry their parasol: a pretty tool to deflect unwelcome glares.

'Nola, I've told you – stop ignoring Hank. You missed the joke.'

Nola slides her eyes over the lip of the book. She manages to read a line of text while fixing her mother with a dead-eyed glare. 'What joke?'

Hank gives a proper guffaw at that, throwing his head back and opening his mouth so wide that Nola reckons she could probably fit the top twelve inches of a traffic cone down his gullet before his jawbone started creaking. Hank always laughs with his mouth open. Sometimes there's a string of spit joining one of his crooked incisors to his spitty lower lip. She can see his fillings. Can see whatever he's been eating stuck in his back teeth. Dad doesn't laugh like that. Doesn't laugh much at all. Dad's got a nice crinkly smile: his blue eyes going a sort of bright forget-me-not blue when he's happy. She isn't sure she's ever heard her dad laugh. But she knows what he looks like and feels like and smells like when he's feeling good about the world and his place within it, and he doesn't ever feel the need to show the world that he's half a steak bake impregnated into his molars.

'Don't be rude, Nola. Hank's trying to make your sister laugh, that's all.'

'Give over, Jasmine.' Hank's chuckling to himself. He doesn't mind. It doesn't matter. Nothing matters really. So what if his girlfriend's eldest daughter thinks he's a proper tit? He'll win her over. He's good at wearing people down.

'Did you not get it, Nola?' asks Lottie, from the rug. She's lying on her tummy in front of the open fire, turning herself a fetching shade of broiled-lobster rouge. She's eleven now but she acts younger. Looks younger. She's little, with brown hair in messy bunches and half-chipped, mismatched nail polish on the nails of her fingers and toes. She's wearing one of Mam's T-shirts: a washed-out black number with a 1990s Indie band picked out in faded pixels on the front. It stretches down to the floor when she stands.

'Shall I put another log on?'

Nola gives her attention back to her book. She's agreed to stay in the living room rather than retreat to her bedroom, but she'll be damned if she's going to involve herself in any of their stupid games or laugh at their little private jokes. It's all pretend, anyway. It's all one big fat stupid lie.

'Hank, babe – shall I put another log on?'

Nola raises her eyes again for a moment. For a fraction of a second, she locks eyes with Mam's boyfriend. His name's Harrison Grosvenor, but he's gone by 'Hank' since university. Mam had introduced him as such. She'd said it as if they

already knew who he was, or what he was to Mam, or the
reason he was in her house, mid-afternoon on a school day,
wearing suit trousers and a crumpled shirt, sockless in brown
brogues. 'Girls – this is Hank.'

Lottie had acted as if it was all perfectly normal. She'd
shown him her best toys and took him into the little garden
to explain which plants were hers and which were Mam's,
and to show him all the places where she had hurt herself in
the past few months: the sites of scrapes and grazes and
concussions all marked out in her mind with invisible crosses.
She was holding his hand when they came back in. He'd given
her a fiver and some warm toffees with chocolate centres.
Nola wasn't going to make it easy for him. Not for Mam
either. She thought Hank was a prat. A pillock. What was the
other word Dad used when he wasn't allowed to swear? A
wazzock – that was it. Yeah, Hank was a prat and a pillock
and a wazzock. But he was a prat and a pillock and a wazzock
who kept staying over, and waking her up for school, and
giving her and Lottie lifts to places; picking them up
and buying them little treats; letting them ride in the front seat
of his fancy Swedish car with the cream leather seats and not
saying a word if they dropped ketchup on the upholstery or
let crumbs of chocolate melt into the immaculate white
stitching. He didn't get wound up about the same stuff that
Dad did. He didn't tend to get wound up at all.

'I'll leave it,' says Jasmine, rearranging herself in the
armchair. Until Hank tells her to put another log on the fire,
she'll leave things be. 'May as well be talking to my blooming
self.'

Lottie lifts her head and pulls a face, directing quizzical
nostrils at her mother. 'What is it you're asking, Mam?'

'Nothing much,' says Jasmine, swatting her hand at the air
as if trying to subtly snatch back the words. 'Just ignore me,
my little Chicken Dipper. You warmed through?'

Nola watches as Hank moves with surprising speed, from
his place at the far end of the sofa. In one burst of energy,
he's on the floor beside Lottie, pressing the back of his hands
to her forehead, to the back of her neck; taking her pulse with
his thumbs. He's got his spectacles right down the end of his

nose and is speaking in a foreign accent. It might be Mexican, but Nola isn't sure. She just knows he's cringe and ridiculous, and he shouldn't be here.

'Oh my goodness, she's a hot tamale. She's peri-peri. She's a spit-roast chicken with a magma glaze. Quick, Mum – throw a glass of water on the fire or she's going to explode!'

Lottie's wriggling and squealing, giving little peals of laughter. 'Stop it!' she's laughing. 'Hank! Hank, stop it!'

Jas is laughing, too. This could be a nice memory, given time. They're hunkered down in their little white-painted cottage: the living room door barricaded against the achingly cold air and the fire churning out wobbling waves of scorching heat. It's a cosy living room, erratic and untidy. There are lopsided paintings covering the places where children's fingers peeled off or scribbled on the lurid patterned wallpaper, and the dust and cat hair on the hardwood floor is almost as thick as the imitation sheepskin rug. There are empty yoghurt pots and Fruit Shoot bottles lined up on the mantelpiece, and certificates of achievement folding and flopping over the little ceramic ornaments and the grimy Balkan glassware that Jas started collecting on a whim one weekend in 2013 and which now contains a whopping three specimens.

'Hank, I'll wee, I'll wee!'

'She doesn't like it,' mutters Nola under her breath, as Lottie kicks and writhes. She's still laughing but she's got her teeth locked together at the back and there's a bit of temper in her eyes. 'Mam, she doesn't like it.'

Nola yanks her head away and forces herself back into her book. Let them prat about if they want. Let them have their lovely day.

'Doesn't like it?' asks Hank, sitting astride Lottie's tummy and pining her hands above her head with one hand so he can tickle her armpit with the index finger of the other. 'Nurse, Nurse! The patient is fighting it! We need a hundred and fifty micrograms of ketamine and a Thermos of Ritalin. Stat!'

Lottie's laughing again now. She's getting a bit hysterical, truth be told, but Nola will be damned if she intercedes again. Mam brought Hank into their lives and she can deal with the consequences. She's the one who winds him up the most. She seems to want him to be cross. Nola doesn't understand it. He's got scary eyes, and sometimes he looks as though he'd like to hurt somebody. Mam, probably. He plays rough, according to Mam. Doesn't know his own strength. Never means any harm . . .

'That me or you, love?'

Hank stops what he's doing at the sound of the sudden low buzzing. Hank works as some kind of promotions and publicity specialist for a rally car team. He's away for days at a time – followed by a damnably long spell of doing nothing but hanging around the house. He's not officially moved in, not yet, but he's here whenever Nola is and more when she's not. He still has a flat a few miles north of Newcastle, but as far as Nola can tell, Mam has never visited. It's in a bad signal zone so when he does stay in his own place, she can't contact him. She doesn't like that. Mam has a tendency to work herself into a lather when there's nobody around to derail her thoughts of catastrophe, abandonment and betrayal. Nola knows from Dad that he and Mam were never what he refers to as 'an easy fit'. He would never say anything outright derogatory about his ex-wife, but Nola has pieced together a surprisingly accurate picture of their lives together based largely on the things he has let slip and half admitted. *Hard work*, apparently. *Difficult. A lot to take. A lot of woman. A bit much.* Hank doesn't seem to find her hard-going, but then Nola can't see why he would. She's better-looking than him. Just as clever. She makes nicer dinners and her jokes, when she makes them, are actually funny and make some kind of sense. She can't understand why Mam even wants a boyfriend. Dad had Sal for seven years and, in the end, it was all for nothing. Why even take the risk? And why risk it for some stale cheese sandwich like Hank?

'It's mine,' mutters Nola, noticing her phone buzzing away in her lap. She's still wearing her pyjamas beneath her massive fleecy hoodie. Lottie got up early to go and play in the back garden with Mam and Hank, trundling great orbs of compacted snow up and down the little patch of garden. She wore her onesie and gloves and pulled the flaps right down on her hat, but she was still frozen through within half an hour – retreating to the living room to thaw out and warm up with a mug of hot orange squash and a great bowl of chocolate porridge. Nola had been offered the chance to come out to play. She'd nearly said yes – only giving her traditional monosyllabic grunt of disinclination when she realized Hank would be playing, too. The snowman they've built in the garden is a lopsided, muddy affair. Hank's dressed him in a high-vis jacket, a Burberry scarf and an old cowboy hat from one of Lottie's dolls. His face is Ray-Bans and a courgette. The snow is coming down so thickly that the whole edifice could be completely obscured within another few hours: the lumpen outline of the snowman transformed into a great white termite mound. Mam took some pictures and they're already up on Instagram, hashtagged 'familytime' and 'snowday', 'sohappy' and 'snowjoke'. She hasn't tagged Nola in the pictures. Hasn't tagged Hank either. There's not much about Hank online. He doesn't do social media. He always asks to be cropped out of any photos that Jasmine decides to show her 400 followers.

Nola picks up her phone and glances at the screen. It's Dad. She has to fight the urge to smile. She doesn't want to be the kind of pampered princess who wants to be front and centre in her Daddy's thoughts. Nor does she want Lottie to get all giddy and grab the phone. She silences the call and lets it go to voicemail. He hangs up without leaving a message. A moment later, she gets a text.

> **Don't go outside. Too cold and the roads are too dangerous. Stay warm and keep Lottie out of mischief. I've put twenty quid in your account in case you need to pay for movies. Just tell Mam they're free. Love you. Dad x**

Nola glances over the lip of her book. Fights her smile. Feels good, for a second; feels like a kid who's just got a hug from their favourite grown-up. It doesn't last. She catches sight of her reflection in the blank TV screen. Still too short. Still too fat. Still round and squat and puggish: snub-nosed and with a thatch of kinked red-brown hair. Still got stupid massive boobs that make her feel like she's carrying a baby in a sling.

Still needs braces on her teeth. Hank's looking at her with a
funny little expression on his face. He's sitting on the rug,
blocking the heat with his back. Lottie's rolled herself out of
harm's way and is panting, red-faced, unsure whether to laugh
or cry or wet herself.

'Boyfriend, is it?' asks Hank, licking his teeth. He's wearing
some kind of branded leisurewear: tight joggers and a stretchy
long-sleeve vest. She can see the shape of him under the material. 'Can't cope a day without you? Pining, is he? Bet you've
got them all falling for you. God, at my school we'd have
given anything for a looker like you – even with the old
pit-pony legs. Fine legs for a table, that's what my nan would
have said. Same as your mam's. Footballer's legs. He likes
them, does he? Your bloke?'

Nola feels a strange little trilling sensation in her chest,
as if a wasp were trapped inside one of her lungs. There's a
sweaty patch at the nape of her neck, where her hair gets
all knotted if she doesn't straighten it. She's suddenly very
aware of herself: of her unshaved shins, the sticky place on
her thumb where she picked up the honey pot for her toast.
She feels the hairs rise on her arms and wants to squeeze
her fingers around her wrists until the blood seeps into fat,
crescent-moon welts. There's a low buzzing in her ears. She
gets like this sometimes. She feels like she's caving in. Can
feel her heart trying to stop. She knows there will be tears.
Knows she'll get the taste again: the bitter, chemical belch
that rises from her gut and fills her mouth with the whisper
of cold iron.

'Not talking again, Nola? Such a lovely name, isn't it? No-la.
No-la! It's like it bounces on your tongue. I like the "L" bit.
It flicks off your palate, doesn't it? Hits your teeth . . .'

Jas laughs without seeming to find anything funny. There's
a gleam in her eyes, as though the lenses were pebbles viewed
beneath a clear mountain stream. She's put her make-up back
on after coming in from the garden. She looks good. She's
put some weight on since meeting Hank. She feels squishier
now – all cleavage and round hips; hair cut in a ruffly bob,
and her green, cat-like eyes accentuated with dark pencil.
There's little evidence of the fragile, lank-haired waif who

looks out, dead-eyed, from the handful of framed family photographs that stare down wonkily from the walls. Nola can't help but feel pleased that she at least looks like her mam for the first time. One of her first memories is of old ladies at a bus stop, squeezing at her thick thighs and marvelling that such a bonny big lass could have emerged from such a dainty dot of a thing. She remembers Mam smiling at that – a rare grin of genuine pleasure splitting her features. Nola logged the knowledge away, absurdly pleased to have discovered something that made Mammy smile.

'Are you not answering Hank, Nola? Nola!'

She holds her hands in fists. Tries to concentrate on breathing. What had the guidance counsellor said? Name five things you can see, four things you can feel, three things you can . . . what, what else was it?

She sees spots dance in her vision. It feels as though there are bricks being laid out on her chest. The world tilts. She feels like she's falling off the edge of the world. Desperately, she tries to unball her fists. Glances out through the square window at the endless whiteness beyond the glass. Imagines the cool of the thick, deep snow. Cools herself with the vision. She untwists her fingers and rummages in her pockets for her headphones. She knows she'll get a dirty look for being rude, but she doesn't care. She starts scrolling through her phone, looking for the playlist that she'd made with Sal. It's all the music that gives her 'the feels'. It's mostly the music that Sal introduced her to: weird Indie bands from the 1990s and the kind of classical music that, in Sal's words, makes your feet tingle and your bum pucker. She picks something loud: a track by Hole. She remembers Sal telling her that the lead singer used to be married to Kurt Cobain. When she'd asked her who Kurt Cobain was, Sal had mimed shooting herself in the head. She'd got a telling-off from Dad.

A message flashes through as she's scrolling: loud, jangly guitars thrumming into the centre of her head. It's an alert from Weardale Youth Initiative, affectionately known as Weardy by its members – a message from Dagmara to all her little rascals.

Hello all! Hope you're doing OK with all of this snow. It's bad but we've got through worse. Just remember to be the best versions of yourselves, OK? There'll be scared grown-ups, and you know how useless they can be! So let's have our proper heads on, shall we? Keep our temps, mind our manners and generally pretend that we're all lovely people! Me and the band are here if you need anything. And if you're going to do some homework, just make sure it's not maths! I've never seen the need for it. Take care, D xx

P.S. I'm on some radio thingy this afternoon at 3. There's a link. If you want a mid-afternoon nap, this should put you right to sleep!

Nola realizes she's started breathing again. She's OK. She's held it together. Nobody saw. It was just a horrid feeling, but it's gone now. She wonders if she could call Sal. She can't work out whether Dad would mind. She doesn't know the rules. Sal was her stepmum for seven years. She did parent evenings and sports days, pick-ups and drop-offs, doctor's appointments and wet beds, nightmares and tampons. And now she's just . . . *gone*. Over. Out the door. Living with her brother and the man who killed her mam! Other people's lives always seemed so much more interesting than her own. She types out a quick note to herself and sets her alarm. She doesn't want to miss it. Dagmara's awesome. Nola might not be an actual bad girl, not per se, but she didn't mind people thinking it now and again. The girls at school, the popular crew, the Hermiones and the Alicias and the Naomis – they'd be too damn scared to go along to the community centre where the angry little social worker from the telly was keeping the bad lads and the bad girls on the straight and narrow.

Nola hadn't known any of that when she first went along with Sal, who was helping out one wet Saturday. She'd just got chatting to the first pre-teens she came across, giggling over squash and biscuits and painting faces on hard-boiled eggs under the expert gaze of a bright-eyed goblin in dungarees. It had come as a shock to find out she had spent the day with a group of 'troubled' youngsters. They were, according to Naomi's mum, 'juvenile delinquents'. They were also some of Nola's best friends and she loved being a part of the chat group. Dagmara doesn't really know how to use modern technology, so she doesn't see most of the filthy, funny, sweary chat that the others indulged in and which Nola takes great delight in reading under cover of darkness.

'Nola. What are you listening to? Is it that one I heard you playing the other day? Was it Bowie? Never got into Bowie, really. What's the deal? You a fan?'

Nola sees his lips moving. Pretends she can't.

'I am trying, Nola,' says Hank softly, his manner deflating. 'I'm just trying to make you laugh a bit. Lottie thinks I'm funny, don't you, my little Pot Noodle?'

Lottie grins, pleased to be the centre of attention. 'Funny-looking,' she says, as if she hasn't made the same stupid joke a thousand times before.

'Funny-looking, am I?' asks Hank, pretending to look offended. 'Come here, I'll show you who's funny-looking . . .'

Mam hauls herself out of the chair. She grabs a log from the stack in the fireplace and makes to open the door of the wood burner. Nola is about to tell her to stop – to remind her how the metal handle will be. She opens her mouth . . .

'Fuck! Fuck I've burned my . . . shit, that smells like bacon. Fuck, there's skin gone! Hank, there's skin gone!'

Nola watches as her mam pushes past Hank and towards the kitchen, clutching one hand with the other. She hears the rushing of a tap; curses and expletives.

Hank stays where he is. Glares after her, his hands in fists. Sometimes he really looks at her as though she's disgusting.

He walks into the kitchen. Closes the door.

Nola covers her ears as the banging and the shouting begin.

TEN

Sal snatches her wet sleeve across her face, smearing the icy tears that leak from her half-closed eyes. There are snowflakes in her eyelashes, fluttering like tissue paper in the periphery of her vision. She's scrunching her face up, scowling into the wind as it lashes at the space between her scarf and her hood. Ahead, the world is just formless grey. As she trudges through the knee-deep drifts, she feels as if the horizon is evaporating – as if all ahead is ashes and smoke.

Dagmara hadn't believed her at first. Had just kept saying, 'No, no, can't be right, no' – little meaningless sounds emanating from the disembodied head on the dark old table. Wulf hadn't said a word. He'd just stood there, looking gormless and sad – looking like he did when Trina told him that she didn't want him coming over any more; that she found him pitiful, found him pathetic, found him suffocating; that she was wrapping herself around Barry now and he made her feel the way a real man should. That revelation led to murder in 1995. Now? He's too broken to even summon up the energy to be aghast. Instead, he'd started fussing, clucking over her, boiling kettles, warming porridge, trying to wrap her in towels and blankets. He'd acted as if she hadn't spoken the dead man's name; hadn't voiced the name of the very bastard who'd helped cage him for all those empty, bitter years. Dagmara had to shout at him to stop his fussing and to let her speak. All she could do was repeat what she'd seen. A car accident. Barry in the driving seat. He'd gone through the window. Dragged himself thirty yards. And then somebody had poured acid down his throat.

There'd been no time to absorb the enormity of it all. She'd already called in the discovery of the body. From the moment she made the call, every single moment of the investigative timeline had to be able to withstand forensic scrutiny when the case eventually came to court. Even given the extreme conditions, she fancies she can't really justify popping home for a bath and a mug of cocoa at the start of a murder investigation.

'Jesus, this is fucking horrible . . .'

She mumbles to herself as she trudges towards the spindly black tree that she fancies is around a hundred yards from the site of the body. She's unravelling blue-and-white tape behind her as she fights through the snow – under orders to secure the crime scene. She pauses for breath and looks ahead and behind her. Glares into the fleecy, grey-white air and feels like the last person alive. The absurdity of the task she's been given suddenly strikes her as bitterly funny. She finds herself grinning madly, her lip catching on the zipper of her all-in-one. She thinks of the picture she must make; a colossal Jellybaby fighting her way through a blizzard to seal off a square mile of rapidly building snow. She's feeling the burn of it all in her calves now. She's exhausted. She bites down, crushing her back teeth together in the one place where they meet. There's a popping sound by her temple. Her jaw was broken when she was eleven. Her teeth grew in crooked. She's got a nice smile, but the hinge of her jawbone is improperly aligned. Sometimes it affects her hearing. She gets bad headaches. Sorting it out is on her to-do list. It's a long list.

She pushes forward, feeling a perverse urge to laugh. She feels ridiculous. Each footprint is filled at once with a wedge of shadow. She feels like she's looking for a piece of straw in a stack of needles.

Unbidden, an image swims in her mind. She spent four days on a career development course, learning the best and safest ways to safeguard evidence in any weather. At the time, the notion of collecting physical specimens in a blizzard or monsoon had seemed laughably improbable. Today, she's glad she listened. She can visualize the lecturer: all six foot six of him, Scottish and gentle with a big red beard and eyes like a scolded spaniel. He'd spoken with such gentle earnestness, with such heartfelt sincerity, that the words had drifted inside her and taken up residence. She's not got a photographic memory, not quite, but her powers of recall are extraordinary.

'We don't get to pick our crime scenes,' he'd said, looking uncomfortable and discreetly clammy in a blue three-piece suit. 'Crime Scene Investigators have to make peace with that. Crime scenes are presented to us in the extreme cold, extreme hot, pouring rain, snow. We have to adapt. We have to think fast. I've had situations where there have been tiny blood droplets visible – and rain coming down like somebody has upended a lake. They have to become priority number one. Same with snow. We were able to place markers over the top of the minute blood spots to protect them from the snow. Then we could continue processing the scene through our normal protocols. However, shoe impressions and tire tracks in the snow can be easily destroyed by additional snow. The natural thought would be to cover these impressions with something like a cardboard box to prevent them from being filled in by the additional snow. However, the brown cardboard is likely to absorb enough heat from the sun to melt away any impression that may be under the box.

'Every single decision you make will have consequences. I sometimes wish I didn't know that. The pressure can be pretty intense. Even getting photographs of footprints or tyre impressions is made next to impossible by snow. You're trying to photograph something that is made up of clear particles. You get small mirrors reflecting back at you. Always be sure to record your reasons for your decisions and circumstances for breaking your standard protocols for documentation in your notes or your evidence management software. You will have to be able to defend yourself later in the courtroom as to why you made the decisions that you made when you made them . . .'

She'd Googled him after the course. He had two Queen's Police Medals to his name for bravery. She'd sent him a friend request on Facebook after the course. She'd got a message back from his wife and another from his boss. Apparently, he was well and truly spoken for.

She hopes she's doing him proud. Lewis, too. She'd like to see any of them make a better job of it in these conditions. They'll be here soon. There had been talk of sending up the helicopter, but the pilot had taken a look at the sky and told the Assistant Chief Constable that he wasn't in the mood for suicide. Patterdale Mountain Rescue team has made two all-terrain rescue vehicles available to Cumbria Police. According to the last update, the science officers, medical examiner and the nearest available detective sergeant were probably still half an hour away.

'Die, you bastard,' mumbles Sal, as she wraps the garrotte of police tape around the trunk of the birch, pulling it as tight as her gloved hands will allow.

The last of her energy seems to bleed out through the soles of her feet. Tiredness is spreading through her body like an infection. She puts her back against the tree. Feels the world spin. Wipes the tears from her eyes and tells herself it's just the wind. She's not weeping. Not crying for Barry. That would be perverse, wouldn't it? To cry for the bastard who, who . . . who did such terrible, evil things, who . . .

She forces herself to stop. To grab a hold of her thoughts. She needs to think like a police officer. She's already told the duty CID sergeant the particulars of the discovery. She's sent across photographs and her initial calculations on the speed of travel and the little she has been able to discern from the vehicle. She's photographed the dead birds. She tramped to the crest of the little incline where the road wound round the river. If the vehicle had skidded there, it could indeed have gone through the wall. There was every possibility that the death was an accident. But the acid? It had to be murder. She'd told the detective sergeant as much in her first breathless report. She'd heard him audibly roll his eyes until she explained that there were obvious signs of use of some acidic substance and that must mean third-party involvement . . .

He'd cut her off quite quickly after that. Told her to sit tight. Await instruction. She'd been so annoyed with herself and pissed off with the snotty sergeant that she hadn't even told him she suspected she knew the ID of the victim. And once she realized she hadn't made that clear during the initial call, she began to think it might seem decidedly suspect if she then dropped it into a follow-up briefing. So maybe she shouldn't say anything at all. But then, when the identification came about through different channels, and the link to Sal's family became instantly clear, wouldn't it seem even more bloody suspect if she had acted surprised when news of the victim's identity first broke?

Sal gasps for breath, as if there are boulders laid out on her chest. She feels the sweat freeze on her body. She's famished, suddenly: absurdly ravenous. She hasn't eaten. Hasn't snatched more than a few sips of tea. She'd be shattered even if this were a routine case. But it's not the physical ailments that cause her eyes to glisten and her chest to come in sharp, staccato bursts. Memories are rising like floodwater – swirling whirlpools of fetid ooze and sludge, bobbing like boiling soup; spitting up gobbets of undigested pain; unhealed trauma, memories hidden behind locked doors.

'Fuck,' she whispers, wrapping her arms around herself as she begins to shiver. 'Sal, you've seriously fucked up . . .'

Sal feels almost grateful to be able to focus on the procedural fuck-up instead of addressing any of the other questions that are slithering around inside her head. She can't do anything about any of that now. But not telling the sergeant about her connection to the dead man? Not giving them a steer in the right direction? That was going to look bad. It was bad.

She swears again, unable to think of a better idea than the terrible one that's been propelling her up the hill and through the snow. As her energy fades, so her resolution wavers. She'd promised herself she wouldn't call him. Wouldn't check in to see if he was doing OK. Wouldn't recriminate. She would keep her head held high and she would let him come to the conclusion, in his own good time, that he was a fucking moron for allowing himself to lose the one person who loved him so deeply and perfectly that it was all she could do not to bite his neck and consume him while he slept. Jarod had frequently counselled that her poetic imagery was always a little carnal for mainstream tastes. But Jarod hadn't gone to Oxford, had he, so Jarod could . . .

'Bugger it,' says Sal, and she calls the man she loves most in the world – hating him, and herself, with equal gusto.

She presses the phone to the side of her face, huddling into her coat.

'Sal,' Lewis says tersely, after four rings. 'You OK up there? Shivering?'

She finds herself warmed by the sound of his voice. Scowls at herself for her weakness.

'You heard?'

'Yeah, I think I'm going to be running it. Just need the nod. Makes sense, anyway. Course, might be nothing.'

Sal concentrates on breathing. Lets her gaze drift back to where Barry lies, forever frozen in his agony, sightless eye sockets gazing up at the underside of a blue tarpaulin weighted down with rocks.

'. . . so aye, if there's owt in it, which there might not be, like.'

There's a pause. Sal wonders where he is. Who's around. What he's wearing. Whether he shaved with a new razor and nicked himself in that little sensitive place below his left ear.

'You doing OK up there? I can get an update on the estimated time of arrival. You've got Elsie, I think. Good copper, Elsie. You met her, I think . . . that do at the Gosling Bridge . . .' he trails off, not wanting to rake over the coals of their shared memory.

'I know who it is, Lewis,' says Sal so quietly she can barely hear it herself. She has to say it again. Has to say it so loud that it sounds as if she's cross.

'Oh, right,' says Beecher, his voice studiedly neutral. 'You find a wallet? You haven't touched him, have you, 'cause they get so bloody shirty about that, these boffins, y'know . . .'

'I recognized his necklace, Lew. It's Barry Fucking Ford.'

She wonders whether he'll make the connection or if she'll have to spell it out. He makes it at once. Lewis Beecher is a good detective. He's not as intelligent as Sal, but he's often twice as clever.

'Trina's boyfriend,' he growls, lowering his voice. 'Little fucking weasel. He's the victim? Report said signs of an acid attack . . .'

'The necklace he's wearing,' she says, picturing its neat tumbles and twists. 'It was Mam's. She gave him it. Said it was the only nice thing she had and that none of us bastards

deserved it. He made her 'appy. He made her feel alive. So
he could have it and that were that.'

Sal pauses for breath. She hears the echo of the words still
clanging inside her skull. Her voice changes when she talks
of her mam. She does her voice perfectly. She has her manner-
isms. Mam once found her entertaining her brothers and sisters
by staging a full music hall performance in character as
Monster Mother, perfectly recreating all of Trina's pet phrases
and ferocious drunken outbursts. She'd put on one of Mam's
coats. Put on her bobble hat and found a pair of her weird,
upside-down glasses with the sharp cat's eye frames.

*'Been there, ain't I? Seen it, love. Got the T-shirt. Mam
died when I was six years old. Dad abused me. Pregnant the
first time I kissed a boy, though maybe I was kissing him
wrong, eh? Don't fall in love, that's my motto. Treat your
heart like a dog treats a ball, that's what I say . . . oh, my
Salome, the face on her; cold as a witch's tit, always got her
face in a book, which is better than having to look at it, I
suppose . . . Honestly, she can sour milk. That pout. Makes
you want to take your foot to it, don't you think . . . but you
can't, can you? Not these days. Social will whip them off you if
you so much as cut their nails right to left. Still, I always tells
them, you can report me, but I can do a lot of bastard harm
before the blue lights turn up, you see if I can't . . .'*

She'd had them all howling. They'd thought Trina was too
drunk to find them, huddled together in the least cold bedroom:
cardboard and plastic taped over the empty window panes:
torchbeams swatting wildly at the graffiti-daubed walls like
searchlights seeking enemy aircraft. The kids sitting in a neat
curve, like dentures. Jarod. Ichabod. Marla. Rhodri. Gareth –
only a nose poking out of a chrysalis of blankets. And Mam
– unborn Cassandra and Artemisia swelling at her belly . . .
Mam, standing there in the doorway in her dressing gown and
wellingtons, gut hanging over her corduroy flares, watching
the show with a look on her face that Sal's never quite been
able to decipher. Looking back, she thinks it might have been
a look of indecision. She's often wondered whether her mam
was making up her mind whether or not to kill her. Standing
there, watching her eldest daughter make a fool of her. She'd

heard the whole performance. Even came in and laughed along. Acted like she was part of the game. Acted like she could take the joke. Then she opened the gin. Drank herself bitter and angry and vengeful. What followed, best forgotten.

'Sal?' The air has changed a little. He's moved to somewhere quieter. His voice is softer when he speaks again, as if they were lying together, nose to nose, talking about the future, about how it feels to be her, to be him, to be them. 'Sal, you can't be sure. You can't make assumptions. You've been waiting for that prick to come back into your life for years, so as soon as you saw the necklace, maybe you . . .'

'It's him,' she hisses, angry that he would doubt her. 'Give permission and I'll go back and find his wallet.'

Lewis lets out a little laugh. 'Give *permission*? My God, did that word stick in your throat?'

Sal chews on her cheeks. She suddenly wants the day to unwind: to go back to the bleak, empty coldness of this morning. Things were dreadful then. But they were better than this.

'Right, I phoned you for a briefing when I heard you were at the scene, and you informed me of your suspicions as to the identity of the victim. I'll feed that into the log and disseminate it as required. It won't be more than a phone call or two before the name is doing the rounds, and I'd give it about thirty seconds before somebody types that into Google, or, heaven forbid, finds it on our own database, and then I should imagine your phone is going to get busy. Where's Wulfric?'

'Home,' says Sal, her voice soft. 'Jarod's, I mean.'

'And he knows?'

'I just blurted it out. I couldn't keep it in.'

'I understand,' says Lewis, and he clearly means it. She can hear his mind whirring, weighing up the options for protecting operational integrity and keeping the wolves from Sal's door. He never said he didn't love her any more. He just said they couldn't be together. 'His reaction? Genuine?'

Sal fights the urge to snap at him. She knows he's always going to think like a police officer. That's why he's never said that he believes her, or Dagmara, about Hagman's innocence. He's been keeping an open mind ever since he and Sal got

together. And while he is willing to admit there were faults
in the initial enquiry, he's not so convinced about Hagman's
decency that he's comfortable with him still being a part of
Sal's life. By the end, he was pretty much all they argued
about. Moving back in with Jarod, with Wulf . . . her inner
psychoanalyst occasionally wonders whether it had been as
much to piss Lewis off as it had been about anything else.
Dagmara would have taken her in. She could have stuck it out
in a Premier Inn for a fortnight while she found herself
somewhere new to rent. But her heart had been broken, her
happiness ground to powdered glass beneath Lewis's merciless
heel. She wasn't making good decisions. She wanted to crawl
into the darkness – to be cocooned in sorrow and pain and
regret. The only place to go had been home.

'Look, hang on, Sal. Give me two minutes; I'll ring you
back.'

Sal doesn't get a chance to reply. For a full minute, she just
stands and stares, snowflakes and icy air collecting in her
eyelashes, cold gnawing through to the marrow in her bones.
She jumps when the phone buzzes in her hand.

'Barry Ford,' says Beecher, without preamble. 'Not much of
a record. Couple of vehicular offences, years back . . . arrested
over a domestic disturbance at . . . yes, well . . .'

'It's OK,' mutters Sal, knowing that Lewis has no idea how
best to approach mention of her own past. 'I was there.'

'Then nothing between 1994 and 2009, when he was
arrested for grievous bodily harm on one Terrence Ruckle,
date of birth second September 1980 . . . released on bail,
no further enquiries . . . then, here, Thursday last week, four
nights ago . . . nine-nine-nine call made by one Ann Kelly,
reporting that her granddaughter's boyfriend had stolen her
car . . .'

Sal lets her gaze linger on the distant smudge of whiteness
where the vehicle hangs suspended over the frozen stream.
She sweeps her eyes to the right – to where he lies, frozen
and torn beneath a tarp.

'I'm on his Facebook now,' mumbles Lewis.

'Changing your relationship status?' asks Sal. 'Poking
anyone?'

'Nice-looking lad in the profile pic,' says Lewis. 'Reddish-brown beard, tattoo on his neck, decent head of hair, a big old mess of tattoos on his chest and stomach. We have two friends in common. Dagmara Scrowther and Jarod Delaney. This just gets better . . . Relationship status: "It's complicated!" Pics here of him sitting with his arms around a nice-looking girl – sorry, young woman. Blonde hair, dark eyebrows, a bit of a Mumsy sort . . . name of Leanne Whittle. And, yep, recently separated, loads of broken-heart emojis and inspirational break-up tunes. Two kids . . . studying at university, mature student . . . she's twenty-seven . . . got a weird-looking dog . . . apparently, it's a Shar Pei called Rosco . . .'

Sal feels like she's drifting above it all. Feels like she's drawn some delicious green herb deep into her lungs and it's made everything muffled and far away. She stares across the thick snow, squinting through the swirling fractals of spiteful ice. She can see Jarod. He's waving. Pointing. A little to the right, a bright-red rescue vehicle emerges from the fog.

'I'm going to tell Elsie to go and see this woman, pronto,' says Lewis, in the voice he uses when he's made up his mind about exactly what's going to happen next. 'Scene's secure, isn't it? Those bodies will be arriving with Elsie. This young lass, she's got kids. May be in need of a Family Liaison Officer.'

The tail of the sentence hangs just above Sal's reach. She can't be sure but she feels like she's missed something.

'What's the name, again?'

Lewis repeats it.

'You said something about an FLO.'

'Yes, I did,' says Lewis, getting impatient. 'Because I see the value in an FLO in this type of situation, but because of the difficult weather conditions I haven't many options but to second a traffic collision investigator who happens to have done lots of excellent FLO duties in the past, like maybe . . .'

'Oh,' says Sal, and it feels like there are bats swooping around in her head. Why would he be doing this? The last time they spoke, he was telling her that it was over; that he felt like he was losing his mind every time they got into a fight; that they were both too broken to be able to heal themselves while still together. It had sounded like the sort of social media psychobabble that she had done her damnedest to convince him of during their actual relationship. She was always pointing out potential new diagnoses, new syndromes, new conditions, different types of divergence and quizzes inviting him to think of ten different ways to spot a narcissist. She'd always had insecurities, and having Lewis reaffirm his devotion every time she began to worry that he might not be in love with her but actually clinically insane, she'd been indoctrinating him into her own twisted view of love, and of what to do with it. She'd finally convinced him, he said. They were planted in toxic earth. They'd never bloom.

'Well?' asks Lewis, and again she wonders where he is and what expression he might be pulling. 'Is that good?'

'But won't there be a conflict of interest? I mean, I knew the victim . . .'

'We don't know he is the victim yet. And it's the valley, Sal – everybody knows everybody. It's a way in.'

'A way into what?'

Lewis whispers something that she can't make out and realizes that it wasn't meant for her. He's not alone. 'I'm so sorry to have dumped this in your lap,' says Sal. When she doesn't know what else to say, she tends to apologize.

'It's going to be OK, Sal,' says Lewis, suddenly giving her his full attention. 'You can do anything, you know that.' He's said it to her thousands of times – invariably holding her gently by the arms and staring earnestly into her eyes. It had been all she could do not to laugh in his face. Even so, she bristles at this sudden display of concern. She's not his any more. He's not hers. So really, he's just a superior officer talking to her as though she's seven.

'I know the job, Lewis – I've been a bloody FLO half my career.'

'I didn't mean that,' he says softly. 'With Hagman, I mean. It will be OK.'

Sal feels like she's been punched in the stomach. She pictures his face – the certainty of what was to come. 'He didn't do it,' she says fervently. 'He didn't kill Trina and he didn't do this. I swear to you.'

'You know where he was on Thursday evening, Sal?' asks Lewis quietly. She can hear him tapping at a keyboard. Hears him let out a long, slow breath.

She casts her mind back. She'd watched a movie in the kitchen on her laptop, then read a book in the caravan. Jarod had been tinkering in one of the barns, head in the guts of some great behemoth of farming machinery, legs sticking out like they belonged to a magician's assistant. Was Wulf out there helping? Or was he pottering in his room the way he'd pottered through his sentence: a small man with small needs – a life of word searches and Sudoku: bland, easy food; books of gentle fiction and self-improvement; perhaps a podcast about wildlife or one of the painters he came to appreciate while inside. He tells her about it, when she shows interest. She's careful not to show interest very often.

'He'll tell you. He'll come straight out and bloody tell you. For an ex-copper, he is so shit at duplicity.'

She hears a little chuckle escape from Lewis's mouth. It's one of the best noises in the world.

'I'll ping the info over now. Let the techs do their job. Conditions like these, we can't do things properly, but we can still do our best. If you can get access, help Elsie knock on some doors, but if it's a no-go, get yourself to the girlfriend. I'll send a couple of PCs, too, if they're not all slipping on their arses. It's like policing a fucking cartoon, Sal.'

He's already hung up before she gets a chance to thank him. She's grateful for that kindness. She still can't hang up on him without saying 'I love you'.

She pushes off from the tree, making for the distant shape of her brother. Pushes back through the snow, moving through the same trench she dug with her shins on the outward journey. She's nearly close enough to shout to Jarod when she sees the sudden flash of something incongruous poking out from the disturbed snow. She bends down, wincing into the wind, and pushes the little drifts and eddies away until she can see what has caught her attention. It's dark green and bulbous at the bottom; a thin neck protrudes from the bowl. It's an old, slightly misshapen bottle. She fumbles with her phone. Snaps off a picture with the bottle in it and then manages to wrestle a polythene evidence bag from one of her pockets. She scoops up the bottle and a good handful of snow. Holds it up and peers at the curious object. She recognizes it at once. There are the remnants of a cork clinging to the lip, some globules of red lacquer dribbled like wax down one side. There are scraps of some indecipherable label on the bottle, little black-rimmed holes peppering the surface.

She opens the bag. Breathes in. Catches the chemical tang of acid.

She's seen bottles like these in the kitchen at the farmhouse. Jarod keeps everything he finds that interests him: old shoes, bleached-white skulls; colourful feathers, curious stones, old bottles, to colour the light from the kitchen window. Wulf sometimes cleans them for him, just to be nice, wiping a shammy over the smooth glass like a butler polishing the silver.

The thought is already there, pecking away inside her head. It's insistent and unstoppable.

What if Wulfric did this?

And then, insidiously: *What if he did it all?*

ELEVEN

Dagmara breathes. Centres herself. Focuses on her core. She sees inside herself, the way she has learned. Visualizes the still, flat surface of the misty silver lake where she feels at peace. Draws in a cool, clear breath of good air. Forces out a long, slow lungful of memory and pain, spinning into nothingness like flakes of ash.

'That sound level's OK, yes? You're comfortable.'

Dagmara opens her eyes to the jolly, toothy smile of an impossibly young intern at the radio station: some sneakered girl in rolled-up dungarees, lanyard worn like a crucifix. Her name's Daisy. She's so sweet it must hurt her gums.

'Sorry, did I startle you? You're OK, yes? You have your water? We're out of sparkling but I can give it a swish with a swizzle stick . . .'

Dagmara nods. Puts some effervescence into her expression. Makes Daisy feel fascinating. 'Went a bit Frank Zappa there, didn't I?'

Daisy's smile stays in place while her eyes register absolute blankness.

'He was a sixties legend . . . bit of a stoner,' explains Dagmara, in the patient, mildly disappointed voice she uses upon teenage offenders who've taken more than their share of Jaffa Cakes from the snack tray. 'I'm doing him a disservice there. I could lend you an album.'

'Great, great!' says Daisy, clutching her lanyard and moving back towards the door. 'That would be so great. We're recording it as if it were live, yes? But it's not. So, you know, if you swear, we can bleep it! Anyway, best of luck. She's lovely!'

Dagmara doesn't get a chance to reply. The door closes and she's alone in the little booth, headphones clamped over her fiery red hair so that the ends stick out from her cheeks like mutton-chop sideburns. There's a microphone in front of her. Then a bare wall. She feels like she's waiting to see a prisoner.

Knows the feeling too damn well. For twenty years, she fought
to bring Wulf back to life; to help him clear his name, or, at
the very least, to give him a chance to be more than just the
bent nonce copper who went mad and killed his girlfriend,
as certain red-top papers and lurid websites had taken to
calling him. She'd almost rather be back there now. Would
rather be anywhere than in this cramped, cold space, smelling
the staleness of her damp, still-grubby clothes; the mud on
her hiking boots; the shit under her nails from cleaning out
the budgie cage; the ointment she rubs on the backs of her
wrists to keep them from breaking out in psoriasis. She can
tolerate the itchiness but the red skin makes the criss-
cross wounds on her wrists stand out like twin Xs on a
treasure map.

She can't quite believe that she made it in; that the little
one-litre Citroën had made it up the land and found the groove
that led to the Brampton road. It had taken two hours and
plenty of three-point turns, but Dagmara knows how to drive
in the most hellish of circumstances and there's nothing in the
valley that she hasn't managed to overcome in the past. She'd
made it to the Radio Cumbria studios half an hour ahead of
schedule. She'd achieved more than the presenter, who was
having to conduct the show from home and talk to her guests
down a slightly unreliable phone line.

She pats the pocket of her jogging trousers. Feels the bulge
of car keys, club keys, house keys, phone. Wonders if she
should try Wulf again. Whether he's done something daft.
God, the look on the poor man's face. On Sal's, too. So much
unspoken; so many unsaid thoughts and pushed-down memories unspooling into the air in swirling helixes of vanishing
calligraphy. She knows what's going to happen next. She
knows what the police will think. What they'll do. All that
will happen to good people as the result of the death of one
very bad man.

'Barry,' she mutters, and she has to fight the urge to wrinkle
her nostrils. She'd like to spit. Would like to smash her size-
four walking boot into the glossy orange wood of the little
console table. Then she'd like to go piss on his ashes, squatting above his urn like a cat above a litter tray. And so what

if he hasn't been cremated yet? She'll hold it in until the
service is done. Build up a real bastard bladder-full . . .

'Breathe,' she says again. Tells herself to be mindful. To
see the lake. To feel the coolness, the peace.

Dagmara has done a lot of work on controlling her baser
emotions. There was a time when she would flip tables at
Child Protection conferences: slam whiteboards down and
rip up committee agendas like a circus strongman tearing a
phonebook in half. She's a lot more at peace with herself
these days. She thinks before she acts. She takes her time.
It's better this way. Better for everybody.

A song begins to play in her headphones: the final bars of
'Season of the Witch'. Dagmara smiles, enjoying a sudden
flicker-pad of memories. Thinks of Cate. Thinks of the vibrant,
soulful young woman who taught her a new way to live, then
died at the hands of a drug-addict dad she'd given one chance
too many to. Sees her in her swishy skirt and little purple top:
astrological signs painted in concentric circles around her belly
button, swaying her hips and beckoning her forward through
the flickering light of the fire; sinister, sensual lyrics blaring
out from the stereo of their broken-down campervan. She tries
to hold the memory; to put her hand on Cate's cheek, to kiss
the tip of her nose, to whisper something silly, cheeks touching,
smiling into one another . . .

'. . . oh, what a classic! There's something just so, I dunno,
so deliciously spooky about that one, isn't there? Reminds me
of Kate Bush. Reminds me, thinking on . . . did I ever tell
you all about how she scared me with all that weird dancing?
"Wuthering Heights" on *Top of the Pops*. I was behind the
sofa. I spent half my life back there, to be honest. I had a
little stash of those chewy chocolate eclairs. My brother found
out when he saw his first Dalek. Dived for my hiding spot
and had himself quite the feast. I hope he's listening. I haven't
forgiven you yet, bro!

'Anyway, enough about me. I'm about to chat with a truly
inspirational member of our community – indeed, a very
special person in general. I'm joined by Dagmara Scrowther,
an actual MBE, don't-cha-know! Do I call you Your Ladyship
now, Dagmara? I can curtsey.'

Dagmara's careful not to sigh into the microphone. Tells herself that this is important – it's part of the job. Raised profile means raised awareness and raised awareness should, in turn, mean increased funds. And increased funds means helping more people. And there are always more people who need help. It's the dispiriting metric of necessity.

'You can call me whatever you want,' smiles Dagmara, playing along. 'I've been called a lot worse.'

'Oh, I'll bet, I'll bet.' The presenter's voice is a little too loud. It's not the headphones. Dagmara knows her well, and even in close proximity, her voice is too loud. She sounds giddy. 'And that rather leads me on to the point . . . the people you've helped over goodness knows how many years . . . the bad lads and bad girls you've steered on to the right path – are there moments when you actually total it up? When you calculate how many lives you've, well, if not exactly saved, then certainly improved?'

Dagmara winces. What a load of absolute tripe. Out loud, she says: 'I don't think I'd put what we do like that, I'm afraid. It all sounds very grand. Really, we just give people a place to be themselves. That's what it's all about, really.'

'Oh, come on now,' laughs Judith, not buying it. 'You're being your usual self-effacing best. But you have been a saint to some of the most, shall we say – troubled? – troubled youngsters in the region.'

Troubled, thinks Dagmara. As a euphemism, it falls a little short. 'We're all troubled in some way or another,' says Dagmara, merry enough. 'We all have different challenges. Almost anybody can become a better person. That's all anybody's trying to do really. Become the best version of themselves. Some of our kids have been dealt bad hands. Some have made poor decisions. Some are just doing their best to survive. But the twenty-first century isn't a very nice time to be young, in my humble opinion. Nobody seems to know what to do, or what to be, so working out who to be is twisting them inside out. We – the team and I – we just try to give them a place to be young, and safe. That shouldn't be such a hard thing for people to achieve.'

Dagmara comes to a stop. She realizes she's been talking from the heart. Reins herself back in.

'Strong words there, Dagmara, and I'm sure we'll have lots to discuss when we come back. We shall be talking about Dagmara's involvement in one of the region's most notorious murder cases: the brutal slaying of a much-loved single mum by her policeman lover. But first, here's the mighty Tom Jones with the all-time classic, "Delilah" . . . don't go away . . .'

Dagmara sits back in the uncomfortable chair. Closes her eyes. She doesn't give herself more than a breath or two before she's rummaging in her bulging pocket and checking her messages. There's a text from Wulf, at last. He's *OK*. He's sorry if he scared her. He's just sitting. Thinking. *Don't worry – will be fine*.

Dagmara gives a little growl. God, he can be such a bloody martyr! She wonders whether he's wrapped himself in a shawl and ripped the big toe off his stockinged foot so he can properly look the part as he festers and broods in his rocking chair. He's not even any good at feeling sorry for himself. Always so bloody accepting, so gracious, so sickeningly magnanimous. He's only breathing fresh air because she forced him to stop sitting on his backside looking all sad-eyed and guilty. Years of writing letters to him, for him, drumming up interest, publicity, seeking out lawyers and case workers. He'd still be inside if she hadn't lit the fire under him. And now Barry Ford's going to spoil it all. Going to get people sniffing around, asking questions, making accusations: raking over the dead coals looking for a spark.

She can't even work out why she keeps doing it, why she keeps helping him, why she keeps making sure his life is the best it can be. Wulfric Bloody Hagman. Still the lumbering, moon-faced kid with the watery eyes and the wheezy chest. Still the lad whose dad got dragged under a harvester one cold September day; just the lad from the sheep farm on the high land over Alston, bookish and crap at sports; the farmer's lad who had to become a man overnight. She's never bought it. He's just a jug-eared, snot-lipped eight-year-old who's been poured into a grown-up costume: a soft sod who thinks the

world should be something it's not, even after twenty-odd
years in prison.

No fight in him. No fire. Only ever interesting when he had
a drink and even had to go and balls up that one small act of
social disobedience by turning into a full-blown alcoholic
within a year of his first legal pint of bitter. Couldn't stand a
bad atmosphere but took on a job where he spent his life in
the firing line for other people's pain. Married the first girl he
kissed. Blind to the possibilities, he was. Never could see what
was staring him in the face. An innocent, hard as that might
be for others to believe.

But that's how she's always seen him: an orphaned lamb
being bottle-fed in front of the fire: a bit fragile, a bit point-
less, but unceasingly adorable. She's known him the best part
of fifty years, and he's still the same daft lad who ended up
with split lips and bleeding knees when he tried to fight off
some big kids who had made fun of her red hair. He'd been
her Sir Gawain, her valiant knight errant, demanding the insult
be remedied forthwith. He'd been an impressive sight, right
up until the moment he got punched in the mouth and fell on
his backside, his face a mask of incomprehension. She can
still picture his look of acute surprise. That wasn't how the
story was supposed to go. He was supposed to see them off,
to earn respect and admiration for his courage, his fearlessness.
He was supposed to be David slaying Goliath. He learned a
lesson that day, though it didn't change him. How the hell
he'd thought he was cut out for the police force she'll never
bloody know.

'And we're back. What a voice, eh? Anybody out there ever
thrown their knickers at Tom Jones? Don't be afraid to text
in – you know who you are. Now, my special guest is Dagmara
Scrowther, a former social worker who runs an award-winning
youth initiative for disadvantaged teens and who has helped
change countless lives across the North. Now, Dagmara, I
spoke before the break about your part in the campaign to free
Wulfric Hagman, which is a name many of our listeners will
be familiar with. Just for clarity – how did you and Hagman
first come to be friends?'

Dagmara lets her thoughts drift. She's answered so many

interview questions that she can go on a sort of autopilot. But she feels twitchy today. She isn't sure she can trust herself to say only the things she permits herself.

'We were friends when we were kids,' says Dagmara, as if it's not much of a story. 'His dad farmed about half a mile from my dad's farm, and in an area like the Dale, there are so few kids to play with that you sort of become one another's brother and sister by accident. Wulf was just this nice, friendly lad, really. Stuck up for me when some morons were making fun of me. Came to my place when he had a row with his mum – I'd do the same when Dad was yelling. It was all very normal.'

Yelling? Dagmara disgusts herself with the euphemism. God, what she wouldn't give to tell the truth.

'But you went in similar directions, professionally – is that right?'

'Well, it was a bit of a shock when he chose to be a police officer, but he was always really interested in helping people and he really wasn't cut out for farming, so maybe it made sense to him. I didn't know what the blazes I wanted to do, but I was fortunate enough to be born with a brain that works a certain way and had parents who were glad of the chance to rent my room out, so university was the best place for me. UCL from 1979 to 1982. Time of my life, really, but my goodness, I realized how little my life, and my experiences, actually meant to anybody outside our world. I mean, I felt like a character out of a nineteenth-century novel who'd just been air-dropped into modern life.'

'And that was when you became politically active?'

'It's when I started giving a monkey's about the world, I suppose,' says Dagmara with an audible shrug. 'I joined a lot of societies. I went on marches. I think I may have bought a beret, for which I can only apologize. I definitely wanted to make the world a better place, but, looking back, I was so sickeningly pious and I had so much to say about everybody else's choices. I'm not really very proud of the person I was then. I think it might have just been a case of showing off. It made it hard to be friends with Wulf, too. He was a proba- tionary police officer, and I was on picket lines or chaining

myself to railings and calling the police officers "pigs" and
"fascists". We made for unlikely friends. But somehow, we
just kind of rose above that. Stayed in touch. Wrote to one
another. And when we managed to make our way back to
where we were from, we just stayed clear of the politics and
whatnot.'

Dagmara wonders whether people are tuning out. Who
would care about this? Who would give a toss about this daft
old woman and her unremarkable friendship with a hapless
young copper? She can hear the presenter asking herself the
same question.

'You ended up working in social work, yes?'

'Eventually. I was in London long after I finished my degree,
working with charities and shelters and community groups –
learning to see the nuances and the subtleties and working out
how to be an actual help rather than just feeling good about
making the attempt. I was twenty-six when I came back up
North and took a job with the county council in social care.
It all went from there, really.'

'And that's how you came into contact with Trina Delaney?'

Dagmara grips the sides of the desk. Takes a moment.
Breathes. Thinks about the woman who would become a
symbol for so many different campaigns. To the right-wing
press, she was the ultimate benefits scrounger: a mum of eight
who inveigled endless hand-outs from a succession of different
local authorities and whose kids were little more than feral
delinquents roaming the bleak wildness of the valley. To others,
she was an innocent victim: a mum troubled by mental health
problems and a survivor of hideous traumas. She was the mum
who tried to bring her children back to a simpler way of
life; who took possession of an empty farm and set about
raising her offspring in the old ways. She didn't want them
to go to school – to be pumped full of erroneous or irrelevant
information. She wanted them to learn about crop rotation and
weather patterns, hedgerow potions and the phases of the
moon. And she became a victim of a system designed to make
people like her illegal. Dagmara knows the truth. She knows
precisely what Trina was.

Her pocket buzzes. It's Wulf. She knows, without looking,

that he's listening. Wonders how many others are, too: how many people are chewing their nails and wondering whether she's going to drop them in it.

Sod it, she thinks, and she wonders whether or not the sentiment will be chiselled on her tombstone someday. *Tell them the bloody truth.*

She looks at her phone again. Jarod, now. He needs to see her. He's unravelling. Can't tell up from down and when he's in his own head and when he's not. He'll remember all of it, soon. This might be her last bloody chance.

'She was evil,' she says. 'Whoever killed her, they did those kids a favour . . .'

TWELVE

L ewis Beecher stares at the phone for a full twenty seconds after he's ended the call. He can't seem to bring himself to move. This moment, this now; this is the best it's going to be for a while. Here, in his underpants, shirt and tie; sitting at his desk in the converted attic of his neat terraced home at the nicer end of Dalston Road, Carlisle.

He realizes he's squeezing the phone in his palm, gripping it, throttling it. He's holding on too tight. He's sweating under his tight, crinkled shirt. Window open, snow in the air and he's still oozing with perspiration. Itchy, too. He thinks he's done the washing wrong. Thinks he should probably buy an iron when he gets the chance. Reminds himself to Google what all the other dials on the tumble dryer mean. Wonders whether he's lived his entire life wrong for the last forty-five bastard years . . .

'Well played, Lew. Remind me never to play poker with you.'

Beecher turns. Detective Chief Inspector Magdalene Quinn stands in the doorway. She's wearing a towel. Her long, dark hair hangs over her unblemished skin.

'You look like you should be holding a snake and eating an apple.'

Quinn makes an impressive flickering motion with her tongue. Hisses. Grins. Puts her head to one side and softens her face. It looks as if she's practised the gesture in a mirror. 'Salome. Is she OK?'

Beecher swallows. Closes his eyes. Wishes. Prays. *Stay strong. It's cool. She's just freshening up, and you're just, well, sitting here in your pants, you silly twat . . .*

'Masterstroke with the FLO idea,' continues Quinn, licking her lips. 'Must be awful up there, poor lamb. Don't you think?'

Beecher opens his eyes. Gives the smile she's waiting for. Drinks her in as she makes a show of noticing the impropriety.

Laughs at him, bedraggled. She seems to be lingering – deliberate in the way she moves the towel. She's slim-waisted but there's a pleasing curviness at her shoulders and hips. There's a tattoo of a robin on her left flank. It almost veils the twisted scar that runs from her ribs to her pubis. She'd told him the story long before he first saw the wound. She'd been interviewing a mum accused of force-feeding a fatal dose of painkillers to her two children. It had been all tea and biscuits and earnest conversation, all friendly, and then she just picked up the knife she'd stashed behind a cushion on the sofa and opened Magda's guts like a tin of peaches. She died twice. She was back at work within the year.

Quinn rubs her forearms. Nods at the window. 'Snow's blowing in. I've got goose pimples over here.' She moves her long hair aside like the curtains of a stage. She smirks. 'Nipples like bullets.'

'Don't,' says Lewis. 'Please.'

He nudges the mouse of his computer and the screen lights up. He looks into the face of Wulfric Hagman. The picture was taken when he was booked in at Brampton Police Station in 1995. He's a mess. There's crusted blood in his nostrils and a purple bruise around his left eye. There's an ugly red wound at his throat; bruises behind his jawbone. There's nothing in his gaze. He looks like he's dead already.

'Keep her out of harm's way, Lew,' says Quinn, walking towards him. She stands by his side. He closes his eyes again as he catches her scent. 'She was meant to be as far away from all this as either of us could manage, right? She's in Collision Investigation, for God's sake. And being off on leave? Well, that's about as good as we could wish for. Just bad luck that they got him within a stone's throw of her brother's place.'

He laughs, unable to help himself. 'They? You think this was his old friends? I thought you were going to put your money on this being Hagman.'

Magda looks at him with disappointment, as if he's a schoolboy who's given a silly answer. 'Lewis, I am trying to prove that Wulfric Hagman is responsible for at least eight murders. I am trying to suggest that he's a self-appointed executioner-in-chief, Lewis – an Angel of Fucking Death. He selects his victims with meticulous attention to detail and has managed to stay undetected for so long because he camouflages his crimes as accidents and suicides. I don't think it really fits the profile to have him suddenly bump off the man who put him away, and to do it five miles from his front door – to brutalize him like that . . . the acid . . . no. No, that's not right.'

Lewis wants coffee. Wants a cigarette. Would consider heroin if the offer were genuine. Wants air. He's spent nearly nine months churning himself to pieces, keeping secret from Sal what he'd first learned in a briefing with the Case Review Unit over in Newcastle. Detective Superintendent Magda Quinn had reopened the investigation into Trina Delaney's death. The investigation was still in its infancy, but she needed help from Cumbria CID to fill in some of the gaps in the case history. She had been unaware that Trina's eldest daughter, Salome, was now working for Cumbria Constabulary. Nor did she know that Sal and DI Beecher had been in a relationship for the last seven years. It had been an awkward conversation on both sides; the tension broken when Magda had given in to a fit of somewhat unprofessional giggles at the absurdity of the situation. He'd joined in. It had been a bonding moment. Over coffee, Magda had laid out the bare bones of what she already knew, and what she suspected. Wulfric Hagman had *abso-fucking-lutely* killed Trina Delaney in 1995. They had a new witness, in the shape of his former padmate at HMP Wakefield, Troy Holland. They spent nearly six months sharing a cell. He'd found Hagman polite, courteous and utterly harmless, right up to the moment Holland started telling him what he'd done to be locked up. Hagman hadn't made much comment at the time. But Holland woke that night to find Hagman sitting on his chest, forcing wads of tissue paper down his throat, eyes ablaze with righteous rage. Hagman was mumbling names and dates: the people he'd hurt, the bad people he'd wiped out. Holland had to bite his thumb down to the bone to get him off him. The witness statement from the guard confirms Holland's version of events, and prison records show Hagman was indeed treated for a gash to his thumb that required nine stitches and a tetanus shot. Hagman was already out by the time Holland spoke of what had happened. He was facing another long stretch for his campaign of violence against his wife and children and was hoping to shave some years off his sentence. He gave Quinn everything: what he could remember and what he'd managed to scribble down in the hours after the attack.

Holland had Hagman responsible for the deaths of at least three other people before he was sent down. He managed two while in prison in Full Sutton and another in Wakefield. One accident, two suicides. He'd rattled them off like football scores. Two or three more, since coming out. Quinn had identified a pattern and had sufficient pull with the top brass to be allowed to chase down more intelligence. They're falling over themselves to give her what she wants. Hagman's case has been getting a little too high-profile of late, with the rumours of wrongful conviction spreading. If the doubt that they locked up the right man sticks, it's going to look bad for a lot of people with shiny buttons and fat pensions. Hagman has been under intermittent surveillance for months. Lewis has heard rumours, of course. Heard she wasn't above feeding her witnesses the lines they need to say. But effective coppers always attract spite.

It was only as Quinn began to talk about how good it would feel to catch a genuine serial killer that Lewis had to explain the complexities of Trina Delaney's murder, and the impact it had on those who knew her. Nobody grieved Trina Delaney, he explained – not even her kids. Her own social worker and one-time friend had branded her 'evil personified' during Hagman's trial. The press had barely been able to report any of it to protect the innocent children involved.

Beecher didn't know how to explain it all. Sal saw Hagman as something more akin to a saviour. He slayed her dragon. He was, and would forever be, Uncle Wulf. Beecher couldn't have predicted, that terrible day when Magda briefed him on the Hagman case, that within the year, he'd choose to break Sal's heart, kick her out and drive her to the place where his prime suspect had set up home. That Hagman had gifted the house to her brother was just an extra little knot in the maze of spider silk: another thread for the new breed of campaigning journalists to pull at.

Looking back, Beecher thinks that day, nine months ago, was when the darkness flooded in. Until then, Beecher had never truly permitted himself to think too deeply about Sal's childhood or what she endured in the years before they found one another. He'd be there to listen if she ever chose to talk about it, but he never pushed. He didn't want to think of those things. Not at home. Not in the place where he got to stop being a police officer for a little while. Until that moment, he'd never even read any of the books about the murder. Hadn't listened to the podcasts. Hadn't opened the case files.

That night, he couldn't help himself. He waded through every last scrap of information he could find. He'd grown so angry that he'd found himself tasting blood. When he woke, the whole world seemed misshapen, malformed. He'd felt his certainties bleeding out of him; had felt himself filling with shame for every raised voice, every unkind word, every accusatory or cutting comment. He didn't know how to be with her any more. Should he wrap her up? Coddle her? Cocoon her in kindness and nurture? Or stay aloof? Pretend not to know? Pretend not to be aware to his very core about the things that happened at that house and why she could never bring herself to think of Wulfric as a bad man. He'd thought himself to a standstill. Talked himself out of love. And then he'd told her it was over. Over and done. She'd gone to her brother. Gone to Wulfric Hagman. And now, *fuck* . . . she was slap bang in the middle of it all.

'Here, look,' says Quinn, reaching past him and taking control of the keyboard. She opens the file on the desktop. Half a dozen files pop open. 'Focus, yes. We are investigating the murders of eight individuals . . .'

'Suspicious deaths,' mutters Lewis. 'Deaths that were put down as Accidental, Suicide or Open at Inquest. The deaths of horrible bastards, if you recall.'

'Horrible bastards have the same rights as everybody else, Detective Inspector.'

Beecher feels the fight go out of him. Wishes he hadn't invited her to stay over after their debriefing. He had a spare room, he said. An empty house off Dalston Road. Warm. Heating's been on all day. Come back, have a drink, get some sleep – we can discuss the investigation. He's got no reason not to take her up on her obvious invitation. But to do so would be to accept – what? That it was truly over. He shivers, suddenly.

'We'll catch him,' she says, smiling. 'We'll put him inside. She'll understand. For now, it's damage limitation. In many ways, the storm's a blessing. Let her have a day or so more thinking of him as Uncle Wulf. He hasn't harmed anybody he cares about before.'

'Other than Trina,' mumbles Beecher.

'He despised Trina, Lewis. I've explained this.'

On his desk, his phone buzzes. He looks up. It's Nola. He isn't sure he can face it now. Can't tell more lies. The call dies. Something inside him does, too.

'Uncle Wulf,' chuckles Magda. 'Bet he's doing his nut right now. So careful for so long – and then this on his doorstep.'

'It'll kill her,' Beecher mutters.

He knows what Sal will say and think and do. Knows it the way she can forecast his typical responses with such uncanny accuracy. It might not stop her heart, but when she learns that she's been deceived for nearly her whole life; deceived by a man she holds up as a flawed hero . . . he fears something might snap. He's always been afraid of what will happen to her when the prison warden in her mind unlocks the cages.

THIRTEEN

Dagmara stumps her way down the driveway. She makes a pleasing print: big wide bootprints and the occasional stab of her walking stick. She lets the snow land on her face. Enjoys it. Always likes to let the elements kiss her as they wish. Hopes to die with her face upturned to gentle rain.

She tries to keep some distance between herself and her fears. Keeps herself bound. Doesn't dwell. Too much to do. Too many people to see.

She catches a glimpse of herself in the glass of her neighbour's big black car. Decides she'll just about pass muster. Perfected the role of the slightly dotty bag-lady, with her big boots and baggy overalls, her hair like autumn leaves, all blubber and pudding. She makes people smile; she knows that. People always feel better for drifting into her little bubble. She doesn't think she was particularly pretty, but there was a time in her youth when she turned a few heads, even if the heads in question most likely contained words like 'Boudicca' and 'Bilbo Baggins' and 'troll'. How had Cate described her? A face like a drawing of a cheerful Brussels sprout. It had been one of their little in-jokes. They had lots of them. Shared everything. Two peas in a pod, they said. Thick as thieves, in the office: mentor and mentee and sisters-in-arms, fighting the good fight in a dangerous world. God, she'd been naive. They were still accusing her of that on her last day in the office, turning over a desk and slamming a monitor against a filing cabinet, and making one of the most spectacular exits the office had witnessed in an age. They're still accusing her of naivety today. Forty years of dealing with every manner of family, holding hands and wiping tears and taking the gobbets of righteous spit and hearing those fucking words, over and over: interfering bitch . . . baby-snatching cunt . . . bastards, lying fucking bastards, you're not taking my baby . . . and

Dagmara listening, forcing down the words she wanted to say, wanted to scream: *Look after them, then, you fucking animal!* All that, and still they say she doesn't know the youth of today. She's served her time. Done so much for so many. Got herself a big old shiny star on the local notables page and an entry in Wikipedia. MBE, don't you know. Take it easy now. Step aside. Let somebody else take the strain. You've got too tight a hold on what is becoming quite a sizeable charitable organization, and given your insistence on answering questions about your friend Wulfric Hagman, participating in these interviews, spearheading this new campaign, it does seem something of a distraction . . .

She boots the tyres of the Citroën. Apologizes at once. It's a good car. Hasn't let her down. It's grubby inside and out and looks slightly absurd with the wedding cake slab of snow on its roof. There are scrapes all down the near side. One of the headlights doesn't gleam as brightly as the other. There's a clunking noise when she turns left. But she's a bloody good driver. When you get a call at two a.m. from a terrified single mum, and she tells you he's here again, he's screaming, *he's got a knife* . . . you learn to put your foot down and get through the bollards on two wheels.

'Oh, shut up,' she snaps, as her phone starts buzzing away in the front pocket of her top layer. She rummages around. Finds some humbugs and a plastic toy. There are dried-up daisies amid the fluff: little posies from any number of tiny princes and princesses: knights errant and maidens fair, trying to win the heart of the sun queen. Or something. She often loses sense of the games she plays with the under-nines. She loves their imagination. Adores being invited into their worlds of story, adventure and play. She's been inside so many minds over the years. Carries the weight of so many other people's inner worlds.

'Oh, bollocks,' she grumbles, as she answers the call, almost dropping her walking stick as she bundles her way into the cold, cramped interior. The car looks as though it's been built around an overflowing skip. Every manner of bag, box, file and crate, all spilling over with charity shop bags, food-bank deliveries, toys for the crèche, the church . . . a few bits and bobs for an abused mum starting out on her own for the first time – bits and bobs rustled up with a quiet word, a well-placed Facebook post; a WhatsApp grenade or two. She's got a three-piece suite and a gorgeous pine cot arriving in a day or so. She needs to ring one of her lads to sort the delivery. Busy busy, always pushing on, trying, being the best she can be . . .

She rubs her scar tissue. Wonders what she was about to do.

'Hello, Dagmara . . .'

The tinny little sound trickles out of the blocky old mobile phone in her hand. She takes a second to compose herself. Puts on her best Dagmara voice, breathless and helpful and brimming over with *joie de vivre*. It's bloody exhausting sometimes.

'Violet,' she says. 'Oh, goodness, if you could see me now. I look like a garden gnome making a dash for freedom. It's mental here. Can I say" mental"? I won't say it. A little change can change the world, eh? Are you well? Your Gracie was practising for her Grade Five last time we spoke. Did she do well? Such a talent!'

There's a pause, as the Knightsbridge-based lawyer mentally recalibrates their approach to conversation. There is, after all, an art to speaking to Northerners. 'Dreadful, isn't it? We saw it on the news. Must be absolutely terrible up at the farm.'

'Oh, they'll hunker down, light some candles, make an adventure of it like we did in the old days. It'll be a story to tell.'

'Won't it just,' says Violet, a little too pointedly. The 'story' is a sticking point in their back-and-forth negotiations. As far as Dagmara is concerned, publicity is helpful if it promotes Wulf's appeal, but if they let the fox into the hen house and cosy up with the documentary team, they'll have no control. They could come out of it looking like dithering fantasists, or, worse, woolly liberals. She doesn't want the kids to have to face it again. Violet is more open to the idea. It is, after all, expensive work running an organization designed to overturn unlawful convictions. And they are helping Hagman for free. Dagmara knows that 'free' can be damned expensive.

'Barry Ford,' says Violet, drawing out every syllable. 'We're having difficulty.'

Dagmara keeps the smile on her face. Makes a noise that suggests she's worrying over nothing. 'Always was a bloody difficulty,' she says with a grunt. He is what the youngsters call a 'problematic thought'. She rather likes the phrase. Thinking of him always makes her feel emotionally wrung out. He was such a nasty little shite when he was little: not explosive or outwardly naughty but sadistic from the moment he could pick up a pair of nail scissors. Mam and Dad were terrified of him. They were one of those families: three-bed semi, two children, golf clubs in the back of the people carrier. The sort who put on a good show, then went to town on one another behind closed doors; a house of violence and silent screams; hands across mouths and the rough scrape of the carpet against his cheek. Mam screaming in his face, *it's your fault, your fault, your fault* . . . Dagmar made allowances for the atrocities he would commit against animals while he was working the worst of the hate out of his soul. He'd have got free of it, too, if not for Mad Trina. For that monster, that—

'Dagmara, are you there? I'm getting concerned. The discrepancies our investigator highlighted in the timeline, the absence of the phone call from the log, the witness statement that got buried, Trina out on the moors in her nightie, shouting for Barry; then there's Whitehead's inability to make it that distance in the time he says . . . there's a lot to talk about, Dagmara, and Wulf seems to be going very cold on us.

'If Barry does change his statement, if he admits he said what he said because he was terrified of Whitehead, that's a real turbo-boost moment for the case. So we need Barry asap. Hayley, our investigator, has been going through his recent business history, his profile on LinkedIn, all of the social media stuff – it doesn't chime with the man she spoke to. She said he was genuinely frightening. She made the pitch, passed on a card and a note, but he just stood staring at her, sizing her up. So if we're pinning our hopes on him, we'll really need those soothing horse-whisperer skills, yes . . . let's get every-body together again, see if we can't finally push through the barrier . . . as I say, we've looked into a different specialist, an expert in memory retrieval – give you a break after all those years trying to hold their minds in the palm of your hands . . .'

Dagmara feels her heart beating faster. Forces her temper down. Her face twitches, as if she's working her way into ill-fitting skin.

'We'll get there, my love,' she says, as brightly as she's able with her throat so dry. She rummages in the footwell and finds a bottle of Lucozade with a dribble of something yellow inside. She decides to take the risk. Either she's struck lucky or she needs a diabetes test.

'Dagmara, could we perhaps get a date in the diary, then? And loath as I am to push Sal at such a difficult time, she's adamant that she's spoken before about the pictures; remembers telling somebody else how her mum made it all up, swore she'd hurt her if she told the truth, but she can't remember: it's all just a blur, like so much else. So we need a fresh statement. God, for a brain so sharp, there's an awful lot that's decidedly out of focus.'

'Will you forgive me, Violet? I've got to get the mean machine out of the snowdrift. Don't give Wulf any more headaches now and let me do the softly-softly with the twins. You're asking them to open doors that are shut for a reason. Do you know how many years I've been helping them to make space for it all inside their heads? And if you start trying to persuade them to give up their anonymity, I swear, this whole thing is over – you understand?' Dagmara surprises herself. She sounded like a social worker again.

'Dagmara, this is the situation we've talked about – we were wondering, perhaps if we came up to see you all . . . perhaps even doorstep Whitehead. We're hearing some really troubling rumours about the Masons angle, though so much of that seems like urban myth really, but then, so did Jack the Ripper . . .'

Dagmara can't bear it. Ends the call without a goodbye. Lets out a long, eloquent stream of powerful, deep-down invective. There are words in there that may be eighth-century Norse. Those who see her at Weardy would be aghast. Those who knew her as a social worker would have smiled at the sight of her back to her best.

She sits and shakes for a moment. She notices that she's got her hands around the steering wheel. Her walking stick is across her knees digging into her stomach. She can't feel it. She's wearing a lot of layers.

'Fuck it,' says Dagmara, and slams the Citroën into second gear. She's out of the drift in one great roar: a spume of snow arcing out in a ghostly rainbow behind the black snow tyres. She'll make it. She'll get there. And then she'll sort it all out.

In her head, Cate's voice:

He stabbed me. He's stabbed me, my love . . .

FOURTEEN

Jarod watches Sal make her way through the thick snow: a blurry figure lost in a great swirl of ghostly petals. His vision splits. Fragments. For a moment, he's looking at himself through a kaleidoscope of spinning, twisting shapes. He feels like a giant fly: his vision magnified and splintered into endless perfect cubes. For a moment, he sees himself through her eyes. For a moment, he is inside her head: the hot haze of her pain searing his own nerve endings as he drifts within her consciousness.

She knows, he tells himself. Knows, deep down . . .

He shakes his head. Blinks. Returns to himself. He has been losing himself more and more in recent weeks. There had been a mix-up with his medication: the pharmacy at Hexham General made their standard cock-up over his repeat prescriptions. He'd missed four days. The withdrawal was an agony unlike any he'd known: zapping, vibrating darts of scorching agony ripping through the centre of his brain. It had been harder than coming off cocaine. By the fifth day, he began to wonder whether it mightn't be a good idea to push on through. To let the last of the antidepressants and antipsychotics leave his bloodstream. He was beginning to feel . . . alive. Memories long since dormant were beginning to resurface. He saw parts of himself as a great dragon asleep upon a mound of gold coins and glittering treasures. In his head, he saw its tail flicker. Saw it begin to wake.

He hates that he's deceiving Sal. She's still falling for the performance. Wulf, too. He's no doubt Dagmara will see through it, but he's doing a good job of keeping her at arm's length. The snow has been a Godsend. He'd agreed to help with some renovations to Cate's peace garden at the youth centre. He isn't sure he'd have been able to keep up the act. Dagmara has always been able to read people. She knows what's written in people's hearts. Knows what they're worth.

'You heard?'

Jarod balls his hands. Forces himself back into this moment, seals himself within his own skin.

'Say again?'

Sal comes to a halt a few paces ahead of him. There's snow on her glasses, tears in her eyes. The rectangle of skin between hood and scarf looks wind-slapped and sore.

'You heard. They told you. Barry.'

She fires the words like bullets. She's short of breath. He wishes he'd brought her a hot drink. Wonders if that's what the other version of himself would do: the one that he's still pretending to be. He doesn't want to lay it on too thick. Needs to get the balance right. It really does have to be the performance of a lifetime.

'You're sure?' asks Jarod. His words are lost in the wind, and he has to lean forward on the quad and shout the words again.

Sal doesn't reply. She just stares at him, looking lost and hurt. For a second, she is Little Sal again, with curly hair and rosebud lips, big eyes and a friendly smile. She's standing in front of him, nose mangled, lips smashed: misshapen triangles of swollen bruises turning her face into a patchwork of purples, blues and blacks. She's trying to be brave while he dabs TCP on her cuts. Picks the bits of broken glass out of her hair. Her lower lip is wobbling. She's asking him when it will end. She's whispering it, lips against his ear, blood smudging against his cheek: *When will it end, Jarod? She's going to kill one of us. One of them. Please let me tell Dagmara. She wants to help. Anything's better than this . . .*

'He's wearing the necklace. Right build. Car registered to his girlfriend's grandparents. I couldn't search for a wallet, and he's got no fucking face, so, y'know, hard to say anything a hundred per cent . . .'

She falls silent. Shakes her head.

'Lewis has put me on as FLO,' she shouts. 'Supporting his family. Can you believe it?'

Jarod isn't sure what she wants him to say. Should he be pleased? Disappointed? Amazed? He remains studiedly neutral.

'Are you OK with that?' he asks.

'It's just mental,' shouts Sal, throwing up her hands. 'I mean, look, Jarod – my head is disintegrating over here. I haven't thought about Barry Fucking Ford more than half a dozen times in ten years! I don't let myself think about all that horrible shit. And then, what, three times in a month, and one of them just happens to be when I'm looking down at his dead body!'

Jarod puts his hand up, patting at the falling snow. 'Three times in a month? When were the others?'

Sal looks exasperated, though whether it's with herself or him he can't be sure. 'I told you, Jarod. When I was at Weardy, just before Lewis and me . . . ended.' It pains her to say it, he can tell. He wonders what it would be like to feel such delicious agony as a broken heart. Since he stopped the drugs, he feels things more keenly, more deeply, than he ever imagined possible. Every nerve ending in his body feels intoxicated: high.

'Tell me again,' says Jarod, with a hangdog smile. 'My memory . . . the weed.'

'I was helping Dagmara set up for art club, so it'll have been a Saturday. They have that hippy with the flowery dungarees, showing them how to do flowers and stuff – like when we used to go – and it was . . . what was her name? Oh, look, that doesn't matter, OK? Point is, Dagmara was talking to a couple of carers about the success stories over the years – you know the spiel she gives when she's applying for funding or chatting with the mayor or whoever. This is Cassie. She was into drink and drugs and blowjobs in exchange for Pokémon cards when she started attending and now she's first viola in the Northern Sinfonia and runs three community groups of her own . . .'

'You're babbling, Sal,' says Jarod gently. 'Just breathe, OK? Just go slow.'

She squeezes her eyes shut. Tears freeze upon her cheeks.

'She mentioned Barry,' shouts Sal, stomping closer so they are almost nose to nose. His reflection swims on the mirror of her glasses, inverted upon the lenses of her eyes. He stares into his own tiny likeness. Sees the miniature reflection split apart. In Sal's eyes, he sees the thing that awoke within him when he stopped taking the pills. It's all hair and teeth: gore-encrusted tusks and scrimshawed bones.

'Go on,' he mutters, out of breath. He blinks. Forces himself to concentrate.

'I don't know how it came up, but she started talking about this lad who really went to the dark side. Lovely kid, underneath . . . that's how she described him. Lovely kid who liked to set fire to people's hair, eh, Jarod? Lovely kid who put his cigarettes out on a little girl's skin because it made Mam laugh, yeah? That lovely kid.'

She's sobbing now, the words coming out in staggered gulps. He can barely make out what she's saying.

'Model citizen, now. Stepdad to three lovely kids, running a maintenance crew for the council, giving back to the community – workshops, activism, getting kids off the streets. Real fucking hero, yeah? I genuinely wondered who she was talking about. She had to mention his name in passing before I twigged. I mean, Jesus! Are you sure I haven't already told you this, Jarod? I must have – you told me to have it out with her, and I said there was no point because she's Dagmara and she's never bloody wrong . . .'

'That's not fair, dude,' says Jarod, and he surprises himself with the vehemence with which he says it. 'She won't have known you were listening, that's all. It'll just have been some spiel for the visitors. You know she goes on to autopilot. And I won't have said to have it out with her – just maybe talk to her. Bring it up, like – ask what he's up to and, more importantly, how she knows.'

'Aye, how does she know?' grunts Sal. She shivers. Glances past him to where the lights of an all-terrain vehicle are flashing on and off, casting an eerie yellow light into the gauzy grey sky. 'How long has she been in contact with him? And for why?'

'The other time,' says Jarod, his voice soft. 'You said there was another time.'

'Wulf's court documents,' she snaps. 'I didn't read them. Didn't even want to look at the boxes they arrived in. But just knowing they were there – well, he flashed into my head. I mean, I punched it back down like I was playing splat-the-rat, but just for an instant, I thought about him and Mam. And I thought about Wulf. What Mam said he did to me. He was just there, in my head, for a nanosecond, but it was like somebody had dropped acid into my brain . . .' She stops. Whips off her glasses, mumbling to herself.

'Acid?' asks Jarod. 'Poor choice of words, Sal.'

She shakes her head. 'That fucking necklace,' she mutters. 'Wish I'd never seen it. Should have kept my mouth shut, too. It's one thing we're good at in this family. Keeping our mouths shut.' She sniffs. Hardens her gaze, pulling herself together. 'Have you told the others?'

Jarod shakes his head. Their siblings are living their own lives, for better and worse, far from the valley. Sal and Jarod are the only Delaneys intent on staying here. The others want to put as many miles as they can between themselves and the site of their nightmares.

'Figured it wouldn't look good for you if I started blabbing,' he says. 'No need to stir it all up again for them until we really have to. It might all huff and puff and fade away, y'know? It could just be an accident. Could be suicide. Could be not very much interested in catching his killer – especially if he's still the evil wee shite we know him to be. And yeah, it's close to our front door, but so bloody what? He could have been on his way to settle a score with Wulf or me, for all we know. Or you, for that matter. Or he could have been off joyriding and decided to look at his old stomping ground – remember the good times.'

'And Wulf?' asks Sal. 'You don't think he could have . . .'

Jarod's face crinkles into a frown. 'Wulf? Jesus, he can't get the top off the marmalade without a tea towel, Sal. He hasn't got the fight in him to clear his own name. He's not about to pour acid down anybody's throat, is he? He's almost a recluse.'

He can see Sal digesting his words. He fights the urge to wrinkle inside his skin. There's a burning pain at the back of his neck, like sunburn but on the inside. He wants to stroke the scar tissue there: to run his finger along the ridged and puckered line. Jarod has many scars. This is the only one that shames him.

'Will you run me back up?' she asks. She looks around. 'And where's Tips?'

'Didn't think you'd want paws on your crime scene,' says Jarod, smiling and making room. He feels her wrap her arms around his waist. Tries not to let his discomfort show as she presses her face to his back. The scar burns as if the wound were still fresh. He has a sudden memory: teeth and gristle and digested bones. Feels his gorge rise, even as his bloodstream seems to fizz with a new, vital energy.

He'll tell her soon.

Tell her what he's remembered.

And tell her what he's done.

FIFTEEN

'What a to-do, eh, Sal? What a ruddy to-do!'

Sal gives a tight smile. She isn't sure whether 'to-do' is official police parlance. She presumes there's probably a form somewhere.

Detective Sergeant Elsie Crisp squats down and pokes the fire. Stands up, knees cracking like dry twigs. Slurps her tea.

'How are you holding up?' she asks, and it's hard to tell whether the concern is genuine. She's a good police officer, so her lies are hard to spot. 'Horrible time for you, isn't it? Losing Lewis, ending up back here – then this. I mean, you could go around wondering whether you were cursed! Next time somebody offers you some lucky heather, get your hand in your pocket. You poor thing.'

Sal's leaning against the sink. It's getting hot in the kitchen, and she's shed her outer layers. Her wet socks are drying on the stove. She finds her attention returning to her own naked toes. They're shrivelled and as pale as the inside of a seashell. They remind her of uncooked sausages.

'You would have made a wonderful Family Liaison Officer, Elsie,' says Sal, staring into her empty mug. 'Although the Samaritans would have been sorry to lose you.'

Elsie gives a big harrumph of laughter. She starts peering at the glass vials and bottles piled high in Wulfric's cramped little larder. 'New Moon Water,' she reads. 'God, there's enough herbs and dried flowers here, Sal? He's not on the wacky baccy, is he? And marjoram. That's a herb, yeah? No eye of newt, is there? Wing of frog, or whatever . . .'

'You've been a police officer for twenty-five years, Elsie. You still say wacky baccy?'

Sal looks back over her shoulder. Watches the snow fall, settle, lie. It's getting worse. The Mountain Rescue team has managed to get a forensics tent over the spot where Barry lies, beneath sodden cardboard and a foot of snow. They're doing their best in the circumstances. There's not a great deal anybody can do with half the roads impassable and the others too risky to trust. Schools are closed and there are whole swathes of the valley without electricity. The news on the radio just keeps getting bleaker. Families cut off; some shivering in the dark, unable to get out for supplies but somehow, miraculously, able to phone the Radio Cumbria call-in show. She'd hoped to listen to Dagmara's interview but she knows from long experience that trying to listen to anything while Elsie is intent on conversation is a true fool's errand. She's turned the radio off and given herself entirely to Elsie FM.

Elsie fans herself with her notebook. She's still wearing her pyjamas under her jeans and V-neck jumper. A red flush is creeping over her neck and cheeks. There are beads of sweat standing out on her broad brow: hair scraped back in the kind of ponytail that Sal instinctively thinks of as 'Consett Facelift': all loose skin pulled back across the cheekbones and secured with enough grips to build a cage. Sal is excruciatingly aware of Elsie's ongoing battle with her hyperactive thyroid, her suspected vitamin D12 deficiency and the loss of her libido since the onset of the perimenopause. Sal isn't sure she has ever asked Elsie any more searching question than 'How are things?'

'I mean, it has you wondering,' muses Elsie, peering into her empty mug and trying to read meaning in the squished teabag. 'If he's had an accident and gone through the wall, that's one thing. But the acid? I mean, it's a bit unlikely that some stranger will come along and find a dying man and then happen to have a corrosive substance to hand. You wouldn't give it credence. Or did he get the old acid in the face when he was still driving, and that's what caused the accident? I mean, maybe he even did it himself. People do worse, believe me.'

DS Elsie Crisp has never been one to keep her cards close to her chest. She thinks out loud. She has the general air of a neighbourhood gossip, speculating on births, deaths and marriages over the garden gate. She always puts Sal in mind of some saucy postcard caricature: a clucking housewife in wellies, raincoat, headscarf and rollers, rolled-down stockings

and plum-coloured slippers. She's squat and broad and has a
tinge of blue in her greying hair.

Elsie glances at the clock above the fireplace. Makes a face.
She's getting tired of waiting. They were supposed to leave
an hour ago, but there's an overturned people carrier on
the quiet road that leads to the dual carriageway, and until the
Mountain Rescue team can get there and get it shifted, they're
going nowhere. 'You know I've read it, yeah, Sal? Full disclosure, I mean. I've read the book. And heard bits of the podcast.
The Canadian one. I mean, it's my job, isn't it? It's intriguing
– not just because I know you and it's all so . . . well, it's a
weird set-up, isn't it? You here . . . with him. I mean, when
he asks whose turn it is to take the bins out, do you never
look at him and say, "Well, it's yours, 'cause you killed
my mam"?'

Sal snorts a laugh. She can't help it. She likes Elsie. She
rates her as a copper, too. For all of her wittering, she's a good
operator. People let their guard down around her. They under-
estimate her, right up to the moment they realize they've been
outplayed.

'I see he's burning the evidence, eh?' asks Elsie, nodding
at the great piles of paper mounded up in front of the fire.
Sal's trying not to look at them. Trying to pretend they don't
exist. 'Somebody somewhere will be feeling mightily relieved,
I shouldn't wonder.'

Sal starts leafing through the court documents, picking up
transcripts and photographs at random. She feels the familiar
sourness in her gut as she stares into the black-and-white
photograph of Wulfric's bloated, swollen neck, the weeping
sore where the cord cut into the flesh below his jawline.

'Check your phone, would you, please?' Sal tries to keep
the breathlessness out of her voice.

Elsie pulls her phone from her back pocket. 'Result! Outside
in ten. Socks on, I reckon.'

Sal licks her lips and tries to act as if she's in control of
her actions. In truth, she barely trusts herself to speak. She
can feel all the lies bubbling away inside her like acid reflux.
She can't quite make her mind up what it is she's most afraid
of. Scrutiny, she supposes. That's what she'd come up with

when the most recent psychiatrist asked her what she was most afraid of. Scrutiny was the best word she could find to describe the deep, creeping dread of being examined too closely, being inspected for flaws.

'He'll come to his senses, y'know,' says Elsie with a kind smile. 'Lewis. You're made for each other. Men can be funny onions; that's what it comes down to. He's lost friends over it – that much is true. When people heard where you were living – I mean, it's obscene. I bet your phone was pinging like a game of pinball.'

Sal nods. It's best to remain non-committal. She'd had a handful of texts and a couple of 'Hope you're OK' messages, but apart from the predictable flurry of 'I can help you get over him' texts from male colleagues, she hadn't noticed any outpouring of support.

'We're funny onions too, y'know,' says Elsie, tapping her nose. 'All of us. Twenty-five years in the job and that's the best I've got, really. I mean, look at your Wulfric. Whether he did it or not, he did rid you of a bona fide evil bitch, if you'll pardon my Albanian.'

'Albanian?'

'Oh, I let the *Daily Mail* dictate which country I should deride at any particular time. Keeps me current.'

Sal finds herself smiling. She's only a few years younger than Elsie, but spending time with her feels like being in the company of a slightly naughty auntie.

Elsie Crisp was still plain Liz Jessop when she first signed up to become a trainee police officer in 1992. She picked up the new surname when she married her cut-price Hell's Angel boyfriend Eddie Crisp in 1998. He told her it was a traditional Northumbrian name, with a proud heritage, of which their sons and daughters would be proud. He started calling her Elsie almost by accident, but the term of endearment fit her like a silk stocking. She's been Elsie Crisp ever since, though she did revert to her maiden name during a brief secondment to Fire Investigation.

From upstairs comes the sound of floorboards creaking. Something heavy is being moved. Dust slowly spins down from the cracks in the ceiling timbers.

'Not going to off himself, is he?' asks Elsie. 'I don't think I've got the right form in the car.'

Sal pushes her hair back from her face. Wonders what Hagman's doing up there. He's been hiding away since the Mountain Rescue vehicles arrived and disgorged a mess of crime scene investigators and a couple of extra uniforms.

'He's never been very good at offing himself,' says Sal with a tired smile. She shows Elsie the photograph from the court bundle. 'Rope broke. He was a bigger man then. He was lucky it snapped when it did.'

'Do you mean that?' asks Elsie, narrowing one eye. 'I mean, "lucky"? Really?'

'If he'd died, nobody would have believed that he didn't do it.'

'Nobody believes that now, Sal. He was in prison for more than twenty years.'

'Innocent people do go to jail sometimes, too, Elsie.'

'That's not something we tend to say out loud, Sal. Anyway, the way Lewis explained it to me, you were OK with him doing it. Killing her, I mean. Now you're saying he didn't? Come on, love – pick a lane.'

Sal sighs. It's all too complicated when she tries to turn her feelings into words.

'Do I believe he stabbed her in the neck with his glasses? No, I don't. Do I believe that somebody else did it and he tried to take the blame? No, I don't believe that either.'

'So what do you believe?' asks Elsie, as if she won't be happy until she gets a simple answer.

Sal pulls on her socks. Sucks her lip. She isn't sure she's ever been asked the question so directly. God, how she wishes Jarod were here. He's the only one who understands any of it, and yet she knows that even he has his secrets. They may share parts of their consciousness when the dreams and nightmares come, but in their wakeful moments, they live their lives in directly opposing ways. He has never believed that Hagman killed Trina. He even gave an interview to the Canadian podcast producers behind the ghoulish series *Murdering Mum*. Trina's death had been episode five. It still has a decent star rating on Spotify.

'I believe he came here to kill her, and he found her dead,' says Salome, and speaking the words out loud brings with it a feeling of release, as if all the stale air in her lungs has suddenly rushed out through her mouth. 'He knew he'd be blamed so he tried to end it. Rope snapped. All turned to shit.'

'So that means somebody else did it,' says Elsie, pulling a face that could serve as a dictionary definition of the word 'sceptical'. 'The list of suspects – none of it's ideal, is it? I mean, who else lived there? If it wasn't Hagman, then . . .'

Sal nods. Elsie's quickly thought her way into Sal's predicament. If Wulfric Hagman didn't kill Trina Delaney, it could really only have been one of the other occupants of the house. It could only have been one of her brothers or her sisters.

Elsie starts rummaging through the court transcripts again. 'So how long did you know Hagman? You know, back then. What was he like?'

'He was in and out of our life for a couple of years. More than that. He was the local bobby, you know? And I don't think he'd ever seen anything like us. We turned up in the middle of the night and took possession of a farm that nobody else gave a shit about. She was forever begging the council to look for something rural. She'd been brought up in the countryside and she always blamed living in urban environments for our lives going to pieces. She always said that if she could just get us out into the countryside, then everything would be better. She'd be able to breathe again. She'd stop hearing the voices. She'd stop hating.

'She heard about Pegswood from a bloke she invited back to our place. I'll have been seven, I think. Told her about all these old farms just sitting idle. Structurally sound. No running water but streams nearby. No heat or light but no shortage of oil lamps and gas bottles. She did her research and found Pegswood, between Alston and Garrigill. Loaded us into some friend's campervan and dropped us off in the middle of nowhere. The police didn't know we were there for weeks. And it was Wulfric who came to find out who we were and what we were doing.

'Mam was happy enough in those days. She was still high on it all. You have to remember, there was a time before all this – a time when she was still decent, y'know? Jarod and me, we do have good memories of her from when we were small. Life got away from her. It was temper. Rage. But when Wulf met her, she was still hanging in there. Bright eyes, pink cheeks. She was probably pregnant, though I can't get my timelines quite right. But she was this loud, curvy, batty woman in overalls and a bobble hat surrounded by all these urchins who thought life had just given them something wonderful.

'It was Wulf who had to tell us that we couldn't stay. We were trespassing. Squatting. He would be back with a notice of eviction if we didn't cooperate. He looked so ashamed of himself when he was saying it. Mam managed to talk him round. We needed time. We had nowhere to go. There was an abuser in her background and she couldn't go back to him. He was a police officer, wasn't he? Helping people and keeping them safe – that was what he signed up to do. He'd never met anybody like her before, and she just wrapped him around her finger. Leaving the house was never mentioned again. Wulf took care of it for us. Even when the social workers tracked us down, their documents all had mentions of the close relationship we enjoyed with the local community police officer.'

'He was shagging her?'

Sal lets her distaste show in her face. 'Don't, Elsie. I promise you, he wasn't after anything like that when it started. To be honest, he was kind of feckless. A bit wet. We knew he'd grown up on a farm nearby, but he wasn't any good at anything that made our lives easier. He could barely fit a hose to a gas canister. Mam did all that. But when he came to see us, he'd tell us stories and draw pictures, and we'd go out into the woods and learn about the names of the plants and the flowers and local history. If he was getting into bother for it at work, it didn't cross our radar. And he must have been getting an earful most days.

'We were a bad lot – there's no other way to say it. Jarod terrorized that poor woman at the post office in Nenthead. Cassandra did one day at school and got sent home for blocking up the toilets with the headteacher's anorak. I was a tearaway, same as the rest. We had fights with the kids in Allendale. Rock fights that left you bloody. I gave as good as I got. Wulf must have been tearing his hair out trying to keep it all from getting too official.

'I don't know when it happened, but the next thing, Wulf's living with us, too. He's in Mam's bed. And Mam seems happy for a bit. It was good for all of us. Mam being happy meant there wasn't as much shouting in the house, and that meant we didn't all spend our time outdoors. Inside, we couldn't get into bother. So they were peaceful times, y'know.' She shakes her head. 'Then Barry came along.'

'He was your brother's friend – is that right?'

'Mine, too. In a way. We met him at Weardy.'

'Weardy?'

'Youth initiative for kids in the valley. Dagmara ran it. Mam wasn't going to let us go, but Dagma came to the house and pretty much told her that she wasn't taking no for an answer. Mam was always OK with Dagmara. Respected her more than the others. When she battered any one of us harder than she meant to, it was Dagmara's disappointment she was most frightened of. Of course, Mam's disappointment usually came out in another battering, but she let me and Jarod go along. Dagmara even came to pick us up to make sure we didn't miss any.

'Barry used to be one of the kids there. Then he got too old, so Dagmara let him volunteer. He and Jarod got on OK. They liked the same bands, the same books. Barry wasn't anybody's idea of a bad lad. He was a bit silly sometimes and he'd egg you on to do things he wouldn't do himself, but he was OK, y'know.'

'And how old was he when your mam started to . . .'

Sal shakes her head. 'Twenty? Twenty-one?' She's aware of the silence in the room. The scraping sound from above has fallen silent. Whatever Wulf's doing, she fancies he's stopped to listen.

She starts struggling with her boots. She can feel tears running down her nose but isn't aware of starting to cry. She can hear Elsie leafing through the papers. She can feel the burn of Elsie's gaze upon the back of her neck. Can hear her absorbing every last spit, cough, punch and fuck of Sal's putrid childhood.

'Jesus,' whispers Elsie to herself. 'There wasn't much of this stuff in the papers. Maybe I just wasn't reading the right ones, eh? Jesus, Sal.' She furrows her brow. Chews on her lip as if something isn't right. 'What's Beecher even thinking having you along? I mean – is he being cruel or kind or what?'

Sal tugs at her wet laces. One of them snaps in her hand. She closes her eyes. She can still see the flames dancing on the inside of her eyelids.

'I'm proper sorry about all this, Sal,' says Elsie, and there's a sincerity in her voice, a softness. 'I'm sorry it's all come back like this. This Barry – he must have been a suspect, too, eh? I mean, you all must have been. I'm just so sorry this has all come back.'

Sal looks around. This is the house where Wulfric Hagman grew up. He inherited it when his dad died. Transferred it into Jarod's name halfway through his life sentence. He'd offered it to Sal first of all, but she'd turned it down instinctively. It had been Dagmara's idea. Sal hadn't put forth any opinions at the time. It would be better if one of the others had it. Jarod needed somewhere to put down roots having spent a decade floating from one life to another: new jobs, new relationships, new highs and lows. He was addicted to every vice, and there wasn't a drug that he hadn't sought out in an attempt to kill some of his memories and resuscitate others. Sal had been happy to let him take it. She'd been too busy thinking about her future to let herself be pulled back into the past. She was going to become a police officer. She was going to help people. She was going to make amends.

'Come back?' asks Sal quietly.

'What are the chances, eh? You being the one who finds the body? You being here – in this house. I mean, it has to be connected, doesn't it? Do you think he was coming here?'

Sal rubs her forehead, discreetly checking whether there's a spyhole in her brow. Is Elsie reading her thoughts?

'He'd have no reason to come here. We've had nothing to do with him since the trial . . .' Sal stops herself. She doesn't want to say anything to a fellow police officer that she may later have to contradict. 'I've not spoken to him since I was a teenager.'

'And Jarod? Hagman? All your brothers and sisters – I mean, where are they now?'

Sal shrugs, trying to act like she doesn't care. 'Scattered like poisoned grain,' she says with a half-smile. 'That's not my phrase – that's one of Mam's. She always said she'd kill us before she had us taken into care and "scattered like poisoned grain". She loved poetry, did Mam. She and Wulf used to talk about poetry. Barry did, too.'

'And you, Sal. You've got a degree, haven't you? A love of words – at least that's something she left you.'

Sal nods. Manages a smile. Rubs the misshaped hinge of her jaw. She lets her gaze drift upwards. She imagines Wulf lying on the floor, ear to the bare wood. Imagines her way into his head and heart and feels the pulsating waves of his fear and regret. Imagines him that night, waking on the floor of the kitchen in Pegswood Byre to discover himself responsible for murder. And knows, all the way to her bones, that his first thought would not be for himself. It would be for her. For Sal. For the child he made a promise to.

She thinks of what he'd said as he wiped the blood from her eyes and mouth and hair: his promise that this beating would be the last. He didn't care if Trina was in love with Barry. He didn't care that he'd been suspended and was under investigation for a campaign of sexual violence against Trina and her children.

She'll never hurt you again, Sal. She'll never hurt anybody.

He'd made that promise three nights before Trina died. He still hadn't gone back on the drink. It would be forty-eight hours later that he permitted himself to abandon sobriety, and to throw spirits down his neck like petroleum. He'd set out from home a little after eight p.m. Death followed him like a shadow.

'You up to this, Sal?' asks Elsie gently.

Sal manages a smile. 'Of course,' she says.

The lie tastes sour upon her tongue.

SIXTEEN

Meat glistens, pinkly, in the periphery of his vision. He screws up his eyes. Works his jaw in circles and hears something crunch and pop in the cartilage of his left ear. He lets his gaze drift back to the butchered corpse. Sees wet, succulent flesh, exposed muscle, bloodied bones. Sees a drift of grey fur, pulled inside out like a damp sock. Entrails, too: a silver dish of purple gristle and twisted sinew, all laid out on a rectangle of nearly see-through newsprint.

Rabbit, he tells himself, absurdly pleased that the word hasn't deserted him. For stew.

He tries to summon a memory of the flavour. Tastes the echo of red wine and rosemary and tough, chewy meat. Tastes the deep iron reek of stirred blood.

He pushes on, moving through his consciousness like a burglar, tiptoeing past sleeping beasts and locked doors.

Deeper, Wulf, lad. See. Remember!

He feels himself falter. For a moment, he loses the glittering thread connecting him back to the surface. For a moment, he's a daft old bugger, on his knees in the cramped little bedroom of a house he used to own. He's a daft sod in his old-codger clobber and shiny pink chin, big old headphones clamped to his ears: an audio loop set at 6Hz playing on a loop into his brain.

Earlier, Wulf, lad. Before then. Before you found her. What do you see?

Hagman forces himself back into his memory. He can never get past this point, no matter how hard Dagmara pushes him. He remembers waking up next to Trina's dead body – his glasses sticking out of her throat. Before that, it's just darkness. The last memory he can recall is from at least two hours earlier. She's laughing down the phone at him. Making him listen. She's telling him what the nonce-bashers are going to do to him in prison. She's making obscene noises.

Grunting. Moaning. Barry, too. Every time he hangs up, she calls back.

He stares into the memory. Sees himself, in the piss-stains and mould of the stinking bedsit he'd holed up in: a TV, a kettle, some pictures and papers, and his uniform, fresh and neat on a hanger behind the door. He's got a bottle in his hand. He keeps sitting down and standing up, rocking in his chair, rubbing his eyes with the heels of his hands. His beard tastes of gin.

Hagman reaches deeper, riding the vibration. Can feel the memory, trapped beneath sheet ice: fists banging as if on glass. Can feel him making up his mind, accepting his fate.

It has to end, he says, aloud. Death's the only way.

There's no future for any of them. He needs to cauterize the open wound. Needs to inject against the poison that will follow should they both live. He's pulling on his uniform over his pyjamas. He's picking up the little photograph of his kids and putting it in his jacket pocket. He's reaching from the hallway into the open kitchen, taking a small notepad and pen from its magnetized perch on the fridge. He's scribbling a note . . .

Hagman feels as if he's drowning. Feels the need to surface before he runs out of air. But he's never got this far before. Never seen the memory with such detail. Never felt so close to . . .

There's a sudden buzzing from nearby: a new vibration running across the naked floorboards and making his kneecaps feel numb. He snatches the headphones off. Pinches his nose. He realizes his chest is heaving and there are beads of sweat standing out on his brow like raindrops.

'Sort it, Wulf. Get it together,' he mutters to himself as he rummages in the folds of the rag rug for his phone. He stumbles slightly, light-headed, unsure of himself. Pleads with himself to focus, to try harder, be more.

The phone stops ringing just as he closes his hand around it. He puts out a hand to steady himself. His legs ache. There's a headache clustering around his crown and down into his face. He's not ready for what's to come. He's looked at his future and there's nothing in it that he wants. Now he needs to make his peace with his past. Has to know, for better or worse, whether he killed Trina Delaney. He doesn't care about clearing his name. It's just for him. For Jarod. Sal. Dagmara. He'd like to be able to look them in the eye and proclaim his innocence or guilt. He isn't sure he'll have time now. He fancies he'll be back in jail within the week: another notch against his scorecard. He'll be known as the cop who killed his ex, then waited a quarter of a century to finish off her lover. The tabloids will love it. There'll probably be podcasts. Documentaries. He doesn't think he can stand that. He just can't imagine any way to live through it.

The phone buzzes again in his hand. He anchors himself. Counts down from five, tapping the centre of his chest, until his heart rate slows. The call is from Polly – the tall, willowy Communications and Policy Lead at the Juris Project. His heart sinks. She believes him to be innocent and is committed to clearing his name. She's going to be so upset with him.

'Oh, what a relief! Wulfric! Goodness, it was so much easier to track you down when you were in prison!'

Hagman finds himself snickering, despite the jangling in his bones and the tightness across his brow. Polly Lockhart may spend her days fighting unlawful convictions, but she still approaches her working day like the campaigning journalist she used to be. She's impatient, hungry and resolute. Hagman admires her. Wishes he shared any of her virtues.

'Sorry,' he mumbles. 'It's been . . . it's been a difficult time.'

'I've seen the weather reports,' continues Polly with excitement in her voice. 'Did I hear a bus had overturned somewhere? Last I heard, grannies were chopping up the furniture to feed the fire and orphans were freezing to death on the roadside. Making quite a big deal out of it all, actually. The MSM, I mean.'

'MSM?' asks Hagman, struggling to keep up. 'The food additive?'

'Mainstream media,' explains Polly, enunciating each syllable. He hears her breathe out for longer than would seem necessary. Realizes she's vaping while she talks to him. They've met in person several times, and she always smells of a different flavour vape juice. The last time, it was Turkish delight. He imagines her at her desk, snug but stylish on the third floor of an old office building in Hoxton. A staff of twenty now, plus plenty of volunteers. Fifty thousand followers on Twitter, apparently, though Hagman can't be sure if that's good or bad.

'You OK up there, though?' she asks with what sounds like genuine concern. 'Must be horribly bleak. Can't be much good for the spirits. You're keeping your chin up, yes? So much to fight for, Wulfric. We need you to stay strong.'

Hagman chews on his lip: a child afraid to tell Mammy that he's got a detention. She's going to be furious with him. Furious and sad. He can't stand the thought of either.

'I've been thinking . . .' he begins, then stops himself. 'Barry Ford,' he says, and the name feels like razor blades in his mouth. 'Sal, erm . . . look . . .'

'You're sure you were a policeman, Wulfric?' laughs Polly, through another cloud of steam. 'Clear and concise, yes? I'll make a note to chase up on that media training, OK? It's in the budget, so don't worry. And once we get the real story out there, there's going to be a real clamour for a hearing and you need to be prepared.' She stops, and he imagines her running back through her shorthand notes. 'Barry Ford, yes. That's what I was ringing for. Have you got a date in the diary yet? I've tried him and there's no answer, and I really do need to be able to tell the documentary makers to be there so they can film the moment. I know it feels a bit intrusive, but it's going to be so instrumental to all that comes next.'

Hagman feels as if all the air in his body comes out in a rush. She doesn't know.

'I'm sorry, Polly,' he says quietly. 'I don't know what you mean. I've been trying to find a way to tell you. I don't want to proceed with this. I can't. I thought I could, but it's too much for me. It was too much before, and now, with what's happened . . .' He runs out of words. Feels cold air against his brow and totters his way to the window, leaning against the thick, butter-coloured walls and staring out into the endless vastness: snow devouring the view he's known most of his life. Pegswood Byre is three miles down the valley. He could walk it. Could press his face to the cold stone one last time.

He reckons the roof joists would probably take the weight, this time. Reckons they probably always could.

'That's not really my area,' says Polly, bulldozing through his complaints. 'We have a trained counsellor to support you through all areas of the process, so we'll make an appointment to get you some help, yes? It's bound to be daunting, but that's why we're here! So come on, tell me about Barry. Was it as awkward as he feared?'

Hagman feels like he's turned over two pages at once. He runs back through the last three minutes and realizes he's missed something crucial.

'Sorry, why are you talking about Barry? Have I missed something? I was about to tell you . . . Sal . . .'

Polly gives a little harrumph of annoyance. Hagman has never heard a harumph from anybody under the age of thirty before. She does it well. Probably tuts like a champion, too.

'I'm looking at my work log, Wulfric – I've got asterisks scored into the page next to your name – "follow up on contact with Barry". So I am.'

'I haven't heard from Barry Ford since the trial,' says Hagman slowly, his words cautious footsteps on shifting ice. 'Last I saw him, he was coming down from the witness box and he wouldn't look me in the eye. Not that I tried to, of course. Not that I'd have been able to meet his.'

'Sorry, Wulf, I'm confused – our investigator made contact with Barry a fortnight ago. They spent twenty minutes on the phone. He was thinking it over. Thinking of changing his statement – that's what's got us all excited. I left you a voicemail about it, on the house phone. Emailed Dagmara, too. Are you saying you don't know about this?'

Hagman steadies himself against the wall. He feels like he's still inside his memories, drifting on a frequency that muffles the impact of Polly's words. Barry was thinking of changing his statement? Jesus, that could change everything. According to Dagmara, he wanted to put that part of his life behind him – he was moving forward, making something of himself, living a half-decent life. He'd earned the right to put those dark events in his rear-view mirror. Hagman hadn't argued. He never argues.

'Barry's dead, Polly. Sal found his body beside a smashed-up car this morning. Less than two miles from our front door.'

Polly starts coughing, her words coming out in a wheeze. 'Dead?' she asks, and he hears a thump as she throws something at the wall of her office, followed by a frantic hammering on the window behind her desk. 'Violet. Natalie. Soph! I've got Hagman at last. He says Barry's dead.'

Hagman hears muffled shouts. He pictures the other members of the Juris Project tossing coffee cups and cigarette butts aside and rushing into Polly's office: pale faces and wide eyes around their designer spectacles and expensive hair.

'You're on speakerphone, Wulf,' explains Polly, and the other new listeners shout incongruous hellos. Sometimes, he misses prison.

'Sal found Barry's body this morning,' he explains again. 'Looked like a car crash at first, but there are postmortem injuries. He . . . well, Sal says there are signs of acid being involved.'

There is a chorus of 'Oh my God', and a moment later, he's off speakerphone and clamped to Violet's ear. Violet is older than the others. She's Chief Exec. She founded the Project. Believes in it. Believes in their clients.

'Wulfric, hi, it's Violet. I'm so sorry – this must be absolutely dreadful for you all. We had no idea! And Sal found him, you say? Oh, of course, she's a Collision Investigator now, isn't she – it's in her file. But, look, are you OK? I mean, given the proximity, and your history, what have the police said? The regular police, I mean – not Salome.'

Hagman's head is reeling. He can hear it in her voice as her mind sprints ahead of her words. Too many coincidences. Too close to home.

'They do think in straight lines, in my experience,' says Violet cautiously. 'The police, I mean. I presume Sal will tell CID who he is and what he did, and once they learn you were back in touch . . .'

'We weren't,' says Hagman breathlessly. 'I was explaining to Polly . . . I haven't seen him in years. Haven't heard from him . . .'

There's muffled conversation at the other end of the line as the assembled lawyers and campaigners argue over the conflicting accounts.

'Our investigator had a very encouraging sit-down with Barry Ford two weeks ago,' Violet says. 'We were giving him space to think it over. He said he needed to work out how best to proceed. He wanted to talk to you before anything else happened. Said he didn't think you'd want him to be anywhere near the campaign. You despised him, he said.'

'He didn't make contact,' explains Hagman. 'I swear, I didn't know any of this.'

There's more muffled chat. It's Polly who comes back on the line, her voice rising over the sound of angry exchanges and suddenly ringing phones.

'Wulf, look – we're going to regroup here and come back to you, yes? Sounds like you've got your hands full, what with the weather and, well . . . everything else.'

He can hear it in her voice. They're wondering whether they've got it wrong. Wondering whether they've just facilitated his vengeance. Whether they have well and truly backed the wrong horse.

'I've been burning the case documents,' says Hagman, rising on tiptoe to feel the breeze from the open window touch his face. 'I can't do this. I was going to tell you. I'll never remember. I just want it all to stop.'

'Sorry, Mr Hagman, what was that . . .?'

He doesn't notice when she says a hurried goodbye and ends the call. Just stays leaning against the wall, phone to his ear. He can feel them all scurrying away, just like before. Can feel the people who purport to care for him, to love him; can feel them abandoning him like rats slithering out of the port-holes of a sinking ship. He's alone again. Nobody gives a damn, not really. He was a cause for a while. Now he's a murderer again. He'll always be a murderer; he knows that. And he'll never be able to tell Sal and Jarod that he didn't kill their mam, simply because he'll never know for sure whether it's true.

Take a walk, Wulf, lad. You'll be inside again soon, lad. Take a last look. Go see her again.

Hagman listens to the only friendly voice he has left. It's avuncular. Chummy. It's rarely steered him wrong.

He feels insubstantial. Ghost-like. Barely here. Fancies he could drift through the open window and waft his way across the snow-filled moors and fields like smoke.

He takes his coat from the peg by the door. Kicks the floorboard back into place and stamps it down. A moment later, he wrenches it up again, as if a thought has struck him. He reaches inside and rummages around in the dark, cobwebbed space for the things he doesn't want Jarod to see. He pulls out a ball of green bailing twine. Stuffs it in his pocket. Eases his feet into his wellies. Pulls on his bobble hat. God, how he wishes he still had his uniform.

He's setting out for Pegswood Byre, just like he did nearly thirty years ago.

He's going to remember.

Even if it kills him.

PART TWO

SEVENTEEN

The air is so cold it's painful. Sal can feel a stinging, tingling sensation in her teeth, on her palms, behind her eyelids. Her breath, as it rises above the plastic lip of the cup, looks like a soul rising from a corpse.

'He's doing a good trade,' says Elsie, through a mouthful of sausage, bacon and mushroom sandwich, with extra brown sauce. She nods in the direction of the catering van that's set up in the car park of the shuttered pub, just off the main shopping street. There's a queue of rosy-cheeked, brightly attired locals standing in a vague approximation of a question mark. They have their backs to the wind and appear to be rather enjoying themselves – voices bright and loud, brocaded with bouts of laughter and good-natured shrieks. 'Good to see the British entrepreneurial spirit on full view, eh?'

Sal huddles into her coat. Sips her tea. 'Entrepreneurial is a French word, and the bloke who runs the burger van is Albanian, but yeah – a great day for Britain. Maybe I'd be more impressed if the good old Brits could deal with snow.'

Elsie rubs her hand across her nose, leaving a tiny smear of sauce on her top lip. 'Eeh, Lewis did warn me! Never discuss politics with Sal – you'll kill yourself before she runs out of steam. He said you were thinking of running for the Green Party but were worried you'd have to do the recycling properly and cut down on the chicken nuggets. He said you were a Communist when you were young. Bet you kept that quiet when you were applying, eh?'

The words are a slap upon scalded skin. She feels her throat close up, a cruel heat spreading across her throat and cheeks. Were her eyes not already weeping, she knows they would be prickling with fresh tears. She has no doubt Lewis said it. Has no doubt he said more.

They're standing outside a neat semi-detached, waiting for Leanne Whittle to get home. One of the neighbours saw her set off down to the village shop a few minutes before the all-terrain vehicle dropped them off. She didn't look so well, he'd said pointedly. Looked as though she'd been in the wars.

'Sorry, Sal – that came out proper snarky, didn't it? Butty hadn't hit my guts yet. I'll perk up when I'm fed.'

Sal leans against the front wall. She feels like a teenager staring up at a boy's bedroom, waiting for the all-clear. She saw a lot of boys in her teens. Dagmara didn't judge at first. She told Sal she knew she had to work through what she had endured. By the time she tried to rein her back in, she'd done herself nothing but harm.

'Still nothing from Lewis?' asks Elsie, swilling her mouth with a lukewarm latte and spitting it on to the snow. He'd called Elsie on the journey over, but whatever passed between them in their terse, two-minute chat, Elsie had chosen to keep to herself.

Sal checks her phone. Two voicemails are waiting, alongside a text from Beecher. She opens it first.

Sal. Hope you're keeping warm. Just want you to know, however this all pans out, I'm so proud of you. You're an asset to this investigation.

She feels her lip curl. Makes fists with her toes inside her boots. She knows what he's doing. He feels guilty. She can see it clear as day. Her mind starts to race, wondering what he's feeling bad about. Is it specific or general, an ongoing sense of shame over breaking her heart? Or has he done something new? She doubts it has anything to do with Barry Ford's death. He's going out on a limb for her. By rights, she should be well away from this investigation. At some point, he's going to have to account for his every decision. No, it must be something personal. She starts running through the possibilities. Not his ex-wife. No, and none of the neighbours have ever thrown him as much as a wave. Who had he spoken about? A colleague? Somebody from one of his overnight stays: a court case or a seminar or a debrief with Area Command. Who had he mentioned? There was that senior officer he'd spoken about, wasn't there? But that was a year ago, maybe more. Kept saying she looked like different actresses; every time anybody with dark hair and big tits had come on TV, he'd say they reminded him of that woman, that . . . Magda Quinn. That was it.

'Nothing,' says Sal, as Elsie waits for a reply. 'Hey, Elsie, do you know a Magda Quinn? She's a DS, I think. Northumbria.'

Elsie screws up her face. Nods, her lips tightly pressed together. 'Think so, aye.'

Sal stares at her. Elsie holds her gaze for a moment, then looks at the ground. Rubs her nose. Looks away.

Sal sees inside herself. Visualizes her own heart. Sees it collapse inwards in a great implosion of icy air. She snatches her hands across her eyelids. Glares down at her phone through misted eyes. There's a message from Nola.

Could really use a chat. Don't know if that's cool.
Really HATING it all right now.

There's a sad-face emoji at the end. Sal feels anger rising in her. Feels sick and light-headed with the sheer injustice of it all. She grinds her teeth as she keys out the message. Reads it back and decides that she's the worst person in the world. She begins to delete it, feeling all sorts of terrible. She's fought so hard to control her temper and she almost unleashed it on a girl she loves. She begins to delete it, rubbing the snow from the screen with her thumb.

'Sal, she's back.'

Sal looks up. A little way down the hill, a mother and three small children are making their way up through the snow. The biggest one is pulling the smallest one along on a red sledge. The middle child is carrying a shopping bag. Leanne has her hands in her pockets. She's fifty yards away when she notices the two strangers standing at her door. She comes to a dead stop, the largest child bumping into her shoulder. It takes a moment before she starts walking again.

'Reckon she knows?' asks Elsie.

Sal doesn't reply. She slips the phone into her pocket. Looks up and has to force herself not to physically react. Leanne is close enough for Sal to get a good look at her. Sees the fragile, slight creature huddled inside a too-big duffle coat. It's soaked through and seems to weigh almost as much as she does. It stoops her shoulders. She's wearing faded pyjama bottoms and sodden brown Ugg boots. In the space between her hood and her scarf, only half of Leanne's face is visible. The other is obscured with bandage and gauze: tramlines of clear tape sticking the dressings over her drawn, pinched face.

She starts speaking when she's still a few paces away. Her accent is soft, slightly high-pitched. It's a voice for bedtime stories. It sounds kind. 'Have you found the car? You're police, yeah? God, how did you even get here? He is all right, yeah?'

Sal lets Elsie lead. Wishes she'd told her about the sauce on her upper lip.

'Ms Whittle? Hello, I'm Elsie, from Cumbria Police. CID. Might we have a word in the warm?'

Sal stands silent until Leanne looks her way. Gives the kids a quick glance. They look well fed and cheerful, though, in Sal's experience, appearances are very often deceiving. She was a world-class actress as a child. She played whichever character Mam told her to – even taking phone calls in the guise of the various adults who were claiming benefits at their home address. Mam always found a way to make money out of her children's talents. They sought her approval as much as they feared her wrath. They fought to be the best. The favourite. The one who got to be her Special Soldier until she tired of them and chose another. They all feared becoming worthless.

Sal feels Leanne's gaze upon her. She gives her a little half-smile, softening her eyes. She's about to introduce herself when Leanne saves her the trouble.

'You're Salome,' she says, and an odd grin splits her features. She covers her mouth with her hand, but not before they glimpsed the missing teeth in her top row.

'Sal Delaney, yes,' says Sal, as warmly as she can. 'I'm a Family Liaison Officer. I'd be glad to make a brew while you two have a little chat. Maybe these little smashers and me could get the pens and papers out?'

Sal hears herself gabbling. Switches off from her own prattle.

She knows she comes across as warm and engaging. She wishes she felt it, too.

'You know our Sal, do you?' asks Elsie, following Leanne through the gates and into the driveway. 'Eeh, the North East – no forks in the family tree.'

Sal glances at Leanne as she helps the plump, dimple-faced Oompa-Loompa pull the sledge through the gates. She doesn't recognize the woman. Hadn't known the name before today.

'We have a friend in common,' says Leanne brightly. 'Dagmara. Told me all about you – big star next to your name on her Wall of Fame.'

Sal feels a familiar dread settle inside her. She wishes Dagmara would take the picture down. Jarod's, too. Doesn't deserve to be up there among all the success stories. She's a fuck-up. Jarod's damaged goods. They shouldn't be inspiring anybody.

'An impressive person, that Dagmara,' says Elsie as they step into a cluttered hallway: bags and bicycles, coats and a mound of mismatched shoes.

'Excuse the clutter – we've kind of been going through a time . . .'

Sal goes through the motions. Keeps her manner professional and courteous as she sets about introducing herself to the children, helping them out of their hats and coats and suggesting that they might like to show her their rooms. Elsie leads Leanne down the hallway. She takes the kids upstairs and makes the right noises as they show her their precious things. She pretends to be terrified when the littlest one holds up a stuffed crocodile, and the other kids find it funny, too. She spends fifteen minutes entertaining them with voices and impressions: physical tricks and ideas for games they might want to play with Mr Potato Head and Pingu. She could do this in her sleep, were it not peopled by monsters.

She listens out for tears. Hears none. Elsie's done this scores of times. Sal wonders whether she would really rather be in the room; would rather be asking questions, sifting the evidence, probing for inconsistencies. She can't say for certain that she would. She can't help thinking that she's doing more good here, pretending to be a cavewoman while three children make a memory that might be their best for a while.

'Sal? Any chance of a brew?'

Sal makes her apologies to the children. Pretends to catch a bullet in her teeth, fired from a gun made of finger and thumb. Wonders if perhaps she shouldn't drop that one from her repertoire, given the circumstances. She busies herself in the kitchen. Finds a tray, wedged between the fridge and the worktop. Flicks the kettle on. Plucks three mismatched cups from the mug tree. Puts her hand up to open the cupboard and stops short. There are holes either side of the handle; the wood splintered and scored. She glances at the other cupboards. Sees the same indentations. Feels her stomach clench.

She turns as Leanne appears at the kitchen door. She's taken her coat off and is wearing cold, wet pyjamas. Her hair hangs in tendrils across the whiteness of the bandage. Her other eye is weeping.

'Oh, God, I can't have you running around after me – we're so low on supplies at the moment, I'm amazed you'll . . .'

Sal watches as the pretence spills out of her. Watches as she screws up her face and glares down at the floor, wrapping her arms around herself.

Sal turns away. She wants to hug her. Would love to be a human being right now; instead, she has to be a police officer.

'I'm here to help you however I can,' says Sal, reading from the script in her head. 'Is there somebody I can call for you? A family member? I'd be happy to . . .'

Sal realizes she's talking too loudly. Stops short. Gets a hold of herself. She looks at the bandage. Sees the gap in her smile.

'Did he do that?' she asks, nodding at her face. She doesn't feel like a police officer. She feels like Mam. Feels like Trina Delaney when somebody other than her had given one of her kids a telling-off. 'Barry? He hurt you?'

'We're just chatting at present, Sal,' says Elsie from the doorway. She's making faces at Sal, telling her to stop asking. She's interfering. She's not doing what she's here for. 'If you could just rustle up those teas and then we can properly discuss . . .'

'Acid,' whispers Leanne, and the word comes out like a hiss. She says it again.

'Let's go back in the living room, eh, Leanne? We can have a proper natter about . . .'

Leanne shrugs her off. When she raises her head, she's curling her top lip back, showing the gap in her top row of teeth. Before Sal can react, Leanne raises her hand and grabs the edge of the bandage. She rips the tape free, as tears fall from her good eye and snot bubbles against her lip.

Sal doesn't speak. Just stares at the puckered mess of gleaming pink flesh: some shimmering lotion daubed into the whorls and twists where the acid devoured her face.

'Is it him?' she asks, glaring at Sal. 'You promise me? You promise me it's him?'

'As I explained, Leanne, we've found the vehicle you reported missing and need your help in identifying a gentleman found dead at the scene, but we haven't got a—'

'Sal?' she asks, as if they're old friends. 'Sal, is it him?'

Sal can't help it. She nods. Watches as the tears fall, Elsie's angry glare burning her cheek.

'He did that?' she asks again.

Leanne slides to the floor, hugging her knees, tears spilling as if she were rising from the sea.

Sal bends down. Finds her gaze. Holds it. When she tells the lie, she needs it to look sincere. 'He can't hurt you any more, Leanne. You're safe now.'

For an instant, Sal thinks she's attacking her. She lunges forward as if going for her throat. And then she is hugging her, arms about her neck as if they were old friends reunited after years apart. Sal can feel her sobbing. Can feel her tears and snot and her words dribbling against her shoulder.

'Thank you,' she whispers again and again. 'Thank you . . .'

EIGHTEEN

They take their time with her. Handle her as if picking up a cobweb. She's got her legs drawn up on the grimy velvet sofa before she speaks again, mug in hand and with a half-dry towel around her shoulders. She refuses to change her clothes. Her movements are minuscule, fragile. Sal thinks of her second youngest sister. Remembers how she looked the first time Mam lost her temper with her.

'Leanne here was just telling me about the last few days,' says Elsie, trying to keep the anger from her voice. She's staring at the side of Sal's face. Sal can't bring herself to meet her eye. 'The vehicle in question belongs to Leanne's nan, Ann Kelly – is that right? There was an argument . . .'

'Tell me about your injury,' says Sal, ignoring Elsie. She's sitting on the sofa beside Leanne, trying to take in the details of the room while giving Leanne her full attention. The room looks half burgled: toys spilling out from trunks and boxes; carrier bags disgorging handfuls of laundry, uniform, clothes. There are no pictures on the walls; dirty mugs and full ashtrays are mounded up on the mantelpiece. There's another broken lock on the cupboard under the stairs, a patch of carpet torn up to reveal sodden underlay and rotten floorboards beneath. 'It was Barry?'

She gives the slightest of nods. 'Sounds weird, hearing you say his name. He's always been Yeti to me. Even to the kids.'

Sal isn't familiar with the nickname. He was Baz when she knew him, though she called him other names behind his back. He was the fucking devil, for a time. 'He did this on Friday?' she asks. She has to force herself to stay present, stay focused. Her head's reeling, stomach clenched.

A shake of the head, this time. 'Valentine's Day,' she says, and her voice cracks as she looks at the memory. 'I don't think he meant it. Not really . . . he wanted to scare me. It was meant to be a threat. He was as scared as I was.'

Sal bites back the words that threaten to burst free from her mouth. Manages to keep her expression neutral, her gestures soft.

'He wasn't always like this,' she says, pulling the towel around herself. 'I swear. He was faultless right up until he wasn't.'

'Faultless?' asks Sal, surprised by the word choice. 'Faultless as what?'

'As a partner. As a stepdad. He ticked every box, I promise you. Paid the bills, didn't raise his voice, made time for the children. Honestly, it was like he'd read a manual on how to do the job. He was so good to us it was almost boring.' She laughs, but there's no humour in it. 'Jesus, I used to say that to him. Used to tease him and poke at him and try to wind him up, just to get a reaction.'

She looks down at her tea. Sees her reflection in the shimmering surface. Looks away. 'I'd only been with bastards before. Men who hurt me. Narcissists. Bullies. I've only ever picked selfish, violent men. Or maybe that's just what I turn them into. Yeti was the opposite. Flowers. Chocolates. Classy lingerie. Theatre tickets. He'd even bring me stuff for the kids. Bought me a puppy on our third date. I'm there with a newborn baby and two bairns, and he's treating me like I'm a Kardashian. I thought it was all a trick – even thought he might be a pervert trying to get near the kids. Took me a long time to trust him, but by the time he moved in, I swear, I'd half convinced myself I loved him.'

'You didn't love him?' asks Elsie, shifting some board games and plonking herself down on a maternity chair. 'Did you ever tell him that?'

'I called him everything you could think of to hurt a person,' sniffs Leanne. 'He always kept his voice calm. Took what I dished out. Never blamed me for anything and solved every problem I had. I mean, he was a closed book – didn't talk much about himself, didn't mention his family or any friends or anything. But he was teaching football to kids on his weekends, y'know? Doing charity fun runs and amateur boxing competitions. He had direct debits going to pretty much every decent cause you can think of. I mean, on paper he was about as safe a bet as you could ask for.'

'And then?' asks Sal, raising her voice over the storm in her head. From upstairs, she hears a peal of laughter, followed by a chorus of thumps. The kids are still playing.

'And then I got pregnant,' says Leanne softly. 'Pregnant with his baby. I thought he might actually be pleased. He was good with kids. Good with mine, anyway. When I told him, you'd think I was a doctor giving him bad news. That was the first time he put his hands on me.'

Sal can't help herself. She puts her hand on Leanne's forearm. Moves closer.

'You're not pregnant any more,' says Sal, glancing at Leanne's slight frame and doing the arithmetic in her head. Mathematically, the youngest child couldn't be Barry's, and he'd referred to his brood of stepchildren in his social media posts. 'I'm sorry.'

'He went crazy,' continues Leanne, pressing her elbows into her sides as if bracing for a blow. 'Throwing things. Smashing things. He was so angry with me. Not just angry, no . . . no, he was proper scared. I'd never even seen him lose his temper. I used to joke that he had all the depth of a puddle, that there was nothing beneath the surface. He was the original grey man, y'know. Then this monster just came out of him.'

'When was this?' asks Elsie, making notes on her phone.

'Last summer,' says Leanne. 'July. The kids were with my nan and grandad so we could have some time together on his week off from work. He works for the council. Northumbria. Potholes, general maintenance work. Has some businesses on the side: cars and boy stuff. I told him the first night we were alone.' She shakes her head. 'He smashed the place up. Threw me against the wall and slammed my head off the door. Stormed out and didn't come back for three days. When he came back, every bit of the man I knew had vanished. He was somebody else entirely. Walked in like nothing had happened, even as I'm crying and shouting and trying to slap him and hold him all at once. He hit me in the stomach. Didn't even bat an eyelid, just punched me right in the gut.' She shrinks in on herself. 'I wet myself. Lay there on the floor for what felt like hours. I could barely feel my legs. There was blood in my pee when I finally got to the toilet. I started bleeding that night. The baby was gone by the morning. Not even eleven weeks.'

Sal squeezes Leanne's clasped hands. 'You're doing so well, Leanne. You're being so brave.'

'I know you're going to ask why I took him back,' she sniffs. 'Why I didn't call the police or the social. Don't you think I wish I had? But we've been through all that before – me and the kids. People poking around in our lives and our business. And I thought that if I didn't upset him again, he'd go back to how he was. It never happened. He was still nice as pie to the kids when they came back, but even as he'd be playing with them on the floor, he'd be looking over the heads at me and giving me this nasty little smirk. He'd say things in their games, little comments about the big toys being able to gobble up the little toys – hurt them, kill them. The kids thought it was all so funny, but I knew it was a threat. He was telling me what he could do to them if I dared tell anybody about what happened. It got worse and worse. He put locks on all the cupboards. Set tracking apps on my phone. He wouldn't let me leave the house unless he was with me. He would make me put my make-up on and take happy pictures with the kids so I could upload them to my social media accounts. He'd tell me what to write, all about feeling hashtag "fucking blessed" and having the perfect family. He was playing make-believe. And whenever I found the strength to say no or answer back, he'd find a new way to hurt me. He was so much bigger than me. He'd do this thing . . . the typewriter, he called it.'

Sal sits back as if stung. She remembers. For an instant, she's on her back on her mam's bedroom floor. Barry's kneeling on her arms, sitting on her stomach. She's bleeding from the nose, squirming beneath him, arms pinioned beneath his weight. He's jabbing at her chest with his fingers as if she's an old Imperial typewriter. He's dictating a letter, slapping her across the side of the head every time he reaches the end of a line. She can hear Trina laughing from the bed.

'It was all about keeping up appearances,' says Leanne. 'He wanted the world to see this perfect happy family, but, for whatever reason, the idea of having a baby of his own just

did something to him. Whatever he'd been hiding, it came out.
And I was too terrified to do anything about it. He had me
take the older kids out of school and move them to the
little village one that's miles out of my way. Played the part
of the perfect stepdad. The kids didn't want to move. They
were starting to see through him anyway. So I tried harder to
keep the peace, and I ended up shouting at them, screaming
at them, taking it out on them. That was when he said he was
going to call social services. They'd be better off without me,
he said. Kept telling me I was insane – that nobody would
believe me over him . . .'

'Bastard,' mutters Elsie without apology. 'Fucking bastard.'

'Christmas was the worst of my life. I had to pretend. Had
to make a big show of everything being lovely, even while I
was dying inside. He made me keep my family away, you see.
Wouldn't let anybody come to the house. Wouldn't let me
speak to them on the phone. He'd dictate my text messages
to my nan. Would stand there, arms folded, just out of shot,
while I forced the kids to play nicely on their Zoom calls and
act like perfect little lords and ladies. But not seeing her at
Christmas – that was what got her really worried. And then
Valentine's Day . . .'

'That was when he attacked you with the acid?'

She nods. 'He'd been getting worse. He was on his phone
all the time. He was missing days at work. There were letters
coming to the house with "Urgent" on the front. He was
starting to miss payments on the utilities, on the rent. That
was when the school got in touch. The kids had said some
weird stuff about their stepdad; about locks on the cupboard
doors and Mummy being sad and having bruises. They wanted
to send somebody to do a welfare check. There wasn't going
to be any hiding it. I felt like there might be some hope, some
light to look forward to. I got giddy on it. Got drunk. Told
him what had happened: proper laughing at him, proper
triumphant . . .

'He kicked my legs out from under me. Kicked my knees
so hard I hit the deck like I'd been thrown. He knelt on my
arms like he'd done so many times before. Then he reached
into his jacket. Told me he had a little surprise for me – that

if I didn't do what he said, he was going to make the kids
watch while he burned my face off. I was screaming. Squirming.
The kids came running in, and I think he got distracted or lost
his balance, but the stuff in the bottle sloshed in his hand. It
splashed my face. Splashed my shoulder.' She raises her head
and angles her neck so that Sal can stare at the ruination of
her cheek. 'I've never known pain like it. If I'd had a gun, I'd
have shot myself right there in front of my kids, just to stop
the agony.'

'Did he help you? Take you to the hospital?' asks Elsie,
back teeth gritted.

'He brought somebody over. Some nurse he knew. She
seemed more afraid of him than I am. She did what she could
for me. She thought that if they got me to a doctor, they might
be able to save the eye. By the time I finally got there, it was
too late. They patched me up. I'm on a waiting list for an
operation.'

'Friday,' says Sal gently. 'Tell me about Friday.'

'He was barely here after that. He would call me hundreds
of times a day, checking up on me, making sure I was still in
the house. He'd sometimes put money in my account if I
begged. He got rid of my old phone and got me a new one
in his name so he could see everything I was looking up online
and everybody I was messaging. He was still making me keep
up the happy-families routine, but I couldn't be in the pictures
because of what he'd made me do to him. Nan saw through
it. On Friday, she turned up unannounced. The kids were at
school, and I was in here, staring at the wall, smoking again,
sobbing, drinking. When the doorbell went, I threw myself
behind the sofa like a scared little girl. I heard her shouting.
She was yelling that she just wanted to see me, just needed
to know I was OK. I phoned Yeti. I swear, by then, there was
nothing left of me. Christ, he even sold Rosco – grabbed him
out of my arms and sold him to some woman he knew. He'd
have sold the kids' toys if they'd been worth anything . . .'

'And he came over?' prompts Sal.

'She was shouting through the letterbox. Making a scene.
He was there inside half an hour. Turned on the charm. Told
her I was having a spa day and that I'd been working on

getting myself a new beach body and hadn't wanted anybody to see until it was time for the big reveal. He manipulated her the way he did everybody else. Even charmed her. Told her there was something wrong with her car and that he'd sort it out for her. Told her to leave it with him and he'd have it back by the next day. Drove her home in his work van. Then he came back. I thought he was going to kill me. I was ready for it, I swear. He didn't say anything. Just looked at me, hiding behind the sofa. Looked at me like he'd never seen me before. Then he said he was going. Said he wouldn't be back.'

'He said he wouldn't be back?' parrots Elsie.

'I didn't believe him,' says Leanne quietly. She looks towards the patio doors, at the slushy white snow in the little patch of back garden. Her gaze falls on the empty kennel. Her face twists. 'He'd said it before,' she continues. 'I think he just did it to be cruel – to dangle the light in front of me, then pull me back into the dark. But maybe, this time . . . I don't know. Maybe he meant it. The last thing he did was take a crowbar from his toolbox and drop it at my feet. I thought he was going to use it on me. When I flinched, he laughed. Then he walked out. Took her car. Nan's. She texted me the next day, wanting to know whether it was fixed. She didn't fall for any of my lies. Lost her temper with me. Said that if it wasn't back on her driveway by Saturday night, she was reporting it stolen. What could I do? And he wasn't replying to my messages. Wasn't calling. Day before yesterday, just as the snow was really coming in – that was when I dared to believe he might be gone. That was when I took the locks off the cupboards. Thought about showing my face outside again. Started going through his things, what little there were . . .'

Sal can't help but interrupt. She needs to know something. Needs to know now. 'Dagmara,' she says, as gently as she can. 'How do you know her?'

'I went to Weardy,' she says with a gentle smile of remembrance. 'And Dagmara helped my mam when she had her own problems. She's known me since I was a bairn. I started taking my eldest there a few years back. When I was with my ex. Dagmara was good to me like she's good to everyone. Got me away from him. I can't bear the thought of her finding out

I was lying to her about being safe and happy. I know I should have done everything differently. God, she even used to tell us all about her police officer friend – the one who did what had to be done when nobody else was willing to do it. She sang your praises like you were her own bairn.'

Sal realizes she's jiggling her legs up and down. Isn't sure where her memories end and her imaginings begin. Her police officer friend? That could cover a multitude of sinners.

Elsie speaks first, using her slightly more formal detective voice. 'Leanne, can I ask you something? Are you familiar with Barry's involvement in a court case in 1996? He'll have been a teenager at the time. He gave evidence in a murder trial.'

Leanne looks to Sal for confirmation. If Leanne knows, she's hiding it well. 'He never talked much about his past. Said he was a tearaway, though it was hard to imagine it. That didn't really fit the image he liked to show. But I didn't like to push him. I wasn't brought up in the safest house, y'know? You don't poke unless you're willing to take the consequences. What murder? What trial?'

Sal sits back in her chair. Her mind's racing. There's sweat across the back of her neck. She tries to make sense of what she's learned. Sees Barry taking advantage of an opportunity – helping himself to a vehicle he's not likely to be traced to. Sees him making his way into the valley beneath the bulging, damp-fleece skies. She can't help but feel he was heading to the place she calls home. Heading to see Hagman, or Jarod – a bottle of acid in his pocket.

'Did he ever mention a Wulfric Hagman,' says Elsie, her voice sounding strained. She's reading a message on her phone while she speaks.

'That's a funny name,' says Leanne dreamily. She looks exhausted, suddenly. Looks like she could evaporate into nothingness. 'Hagman. No. No, never said.'

'Katrina Delaney,' says Elsie, looking past Sal.

'I know the name *Delaney*,' she says, lifting her head and giving a weak smile. 'You're Sal Delaney. You've got lots of brothers and sisters. You used to go to Weardy, too – like me; you've got a degree from Oxford and you've got a lovely family with a nice police officer. You're one of Dagmara's success stories – I told you she said that, right?'

Sal swallows down the acid that rises in her throat. She glances again at Elsie and realizes that her phone is active – somebody is listening in to the interview and sending her prompts on the screen.

'The necklace Barry wore,' says Sal, taking over. 'Did he ever tell you where he got it?'

'The Arab-looking thing?' asks Leanne, settling against the arm of the chair. 'He never used to wear it. Kept it in a drawer. He was fastening it around his neck the night he left. I didn't ask. I'd stopped asking.'

'Did he tell you where he got it?' presses Sal.

'Said it was a gift from his one true love,' says Leanne, and her eyelid flickers. She's beginning to fall asleep. Sal wonders what she's taken. What she's been dosing herself up with to get through the pain and the misery.

'Can we look around please, Leanne?' asks Elsie, rising from her chair. 'Can you show us where he kept his things?'

'Help yourself,' mutters Leanne, eye closed. 'Do what you like.'

Sal doesn't move. Just sits there, staring at a woman whose spirit has been broken by a man who managed to hide what he was for the best part of thirty years. He'd mistreated her as if making up for lost time.

And in her head, those three hateful words, again and again, like fingers pummelling her chest.

One
True
Love.

NINETEEN

Beecher ends the call. He's heard enough.

'You beauty,' says Quinn, giving herself a high five. She's dressed now. Looks to die for in her black dress and white jacket, hair flowing over her lapels like spilled ink.

'What are we celebrating?' asks Beecher, turning away from the monitor. 'I just heard that we're looking for the killer of a Grade-A fucking c—'

'Don't be crude, Lewis,' says Quinn, adopting an air of schoolmistress sternness. 'I can't abide foul language unless somebody's taking the trouble to pull my hair while they whisper it in my ear.'

Beecher's not in the mood for it. Leanne's words have left a sickness in the pit of his stomach. He feels ill. Can't seem to stop twitching his hands. God, Sal had done well. Earned her trust and got her talking within minutes of entering the gaff. Got more out of her than Elsie or any of his detectives could have achieved in a month of interviews.

'Sorry,' he says with a poorly disguised sigh. He scratches at his head and sees a tiny blizzard of dandruff flake down on to his tie. Hopes she didn't notice. Wonders if he would be out of order asking Sal where to get the shampoo she used to buy for him, which kept his skull from looking like a mermaid's arse. 'Seriously. It's good intel, but in terms of Hagman, I don't . . .'

Quinn makes her way into the office. She's got her tablet under her arm, her phone in her hand. She makes Beecher think of Viking shield-maidens: weapons clasped to their chest, ready to die for their cause. Beecher wonders if she's put a spell on him – slipped something in his drink. He doesn't remember thinking such things before.

'Lewis,' she says. 'I do worry about you, I really do. It fits the narrative perfectly, doesn't it? Barry Ford sees Hagman

killing Trina Delaney, right? Maybe he's even the one who
cut him down?'

'The alibi,' protests Beecher. 'He was with Dagmara
Scrowther. It's watertight.'

'We'll get to that,' says Quinn impatiently. 'Look, what I'm
saying is, for some reason, Hagman lets him live. Decides not
to bump him off the way he did Trina. But he tells him he'll
be back for him someday – scares him into believing he's the
bogeyman. Scares him into living this perfect existence of
good deeds and jolly selfies. Then Hagman gets out, right?
And there's all this talk of him challenging the conviction.
Ford realizes it's all going to be dredged up again. Maybe he's
terrified of Leanne learning the truth. Most narcissists are like
that – they fear the annihilation of their image.'

'I know, Magda. I was on the same course.'

'So . . . Barry cracks under the strain of it. Starts abusing
Leanne, taking his frustrations out on her. Wasn't that around
the same time he was arrested for the assault? Remind me to
check that name, yes? Anyway, he builds himself up into a
frenzy, right – there's the incident with the acid . . .'

'Incident? That's what you're calling it?'

'And he really fears it all coming down around him. Fears
Hagman above all else. So he decides to kill his bogeyman.
He takes the first chance he can to use a car he's not connected
to and then heads off into the valley.'

Beecher plays with the tail of his tie. For a moment, he
feels like Stan Laurel, about to be smacked for his stupidity.
He's about to try to fudge an answer when his phone buzzes
on his desk. It's Nola again. He lets her go to voicemail. He
can't face being cheerful Daddy right now.

'He heads to the farm, right? Jarod and Hagman's place,
yes? He's dead set on slaying his demon. But Hagman's too
clever for him. Kills him there at the house and sets about
trying to make it look like an accident, yeah? The same as
with the others. But the snow's coming in and the roads are
starting to be impassable and the sky's turning black – he has
to do what he can before the farmers come flying past on their
quads to bring the sheep down from the hills . . . can't deposit
him wherever he had planned. Has to do it close to home. So

the best he can do is to try and buy himself some time, right? Disguise him until he can think of a way to account for himself. So he takes the acid that Barry planned to use on him. Gives him a facial. Gets himself back home before the snow closes the valley off. Pure bad luck that Sal was called to the scene. He must have shit his pants when she told him about the necklace.'

Beecher can't find the words. He wishes none of this were real. He doesn't even know whether he believes that Hagman is a serial killer. Doesn't know whether he should put him in handcuffs or give him a medal. He knows what he would do to anybody who put their hands on Nola or Lottie. He'd slice him up so small that they'd never find the bastard.

'You're going to press ahead with it, then,' says Beecher, trying to find the strength to get out of his chair. He picks up his vape and breathes in a lungful of menthol. It makes him feel cold inside. 'You're going to start the arrest plan.'

'It's the perfect time,' says Quinn, stretching her back, then typing out a note on her phone. 'Bring him in for this, then hit him with the other stuff. We'll be friendly. He won't see it coming and he'll be all of a jangle after what he's just done.'

Beecher shakes his head. 'The picture you painted of him – he's not that man. He's fragile. Old. He's a sad case, really . . .'

'Oh, for fuck's sake, Lewis,' says Quinn, lashing him with angry eyes. 'You're still not on board? You're as bad as the rest of them sometimes. This is what it's been for . . . this is a career maker!'

Beecher feels himself folding inwards, his insides crumpling like paper cubes. He feels as though he's somehow sold a piece of himself – made a deal without knowing the stakes. He suddenly knows that Quinn doesn't give a damn whether Hagman killed anybody. It's about the headline-grabbing result. He hadn't seen it at first. Had believed her when she'd laughed off her brief spell in the public eye – the high-flying detective who bungled an investigation and blotted her perfect record.

'Is this about Doctor Holloway again?' he asks, without taking the time to soften his tone. 'For the last time, Magda, it wasn't your fault and nobody thinks it is! Christ, it's almost

like you've made up this whole "narrative" as you call it . . . like
you've just come up with this whole thing to prove that you
were right and everybody else was wrong. I mean, even the
whole cellmate confession – Christ . . . I feel like I'm coming
out of a bloody trance, love.'

Quinn glares through him. Licks her lips. Beecher suddenly
wonders whether she's about to unleash a forked tail, her
perfect back splitting open to reveal demonic wings. He's
starting to worry about himself. Feels like his thoughts are
somebody else's. Thinks of Sal, and her weird frequency with
Jarod: the way she talks of seeing his nightmares, feeling his
pain. That was how she knew he was still alive for all those
years when he was out of touch. She feels his heart against
her own. She claims to remember the womb, though Beecher
has never given the idea much credence. She's got a taste for
the esoteric, has Sal. Used to drive him up the wall with it.

'Don't take your guilt out on me, Detective Inspector,' says
Quinn coldly. 'You are my deputy SIO on this investigation
and if you don't want to be a part of this – of the culmination
of so much hard work – well, now's the time to step out. But
I warn you, you've got your ex-girlfriend sitting there sharing
war stories with the partner of Hagman's last victim. You've
already helped her cover up a procedural fuck-up. I'd say that
the way things go from here depends very much on choosing
your next few words carefully. After all, the police do love a
good cohesive and coherent narrative. Keep things simple,
yes? Not only have we saved the service's blushes by blocking
Hagman's attempt to clear his name, but we've even managed
to build a case against him for half a dozen others. We're
bringing in justice for all of them. For Trina Delaney. Jack
Stempel. Terry Carruthers. Tifo Trabelsi. William Fox-Barnard.
Jessica Platten.' She reels off the names like a religious incan-
tation. Takes a breath before saying the last. 'Doctor Perry
Holloway.' She sniffs as she says it: that wound's still raw.
'How about Tyson DeFreitas, eh? Mason Coolidge. Geoffrey
Lerner. Theresa Booth . . .'

'I know the names, Magda. I know the case inside out and
back to fucking front, love.' He drums his fingers on his forehead, as if typing. 'The thing is, right . . . I don't even know

if we should be trying to stop him! Those names you read off – they're a who's who of evil – you get that? There's not a man or woman among them who deserves to draw another day's breath. You've half got me convinced somebody's killing them off – but that sad little man that lives with Jarod? Jesus, he hasn't got it in him.'

Quinn looks as if she wants to punch him right in the face. She looks at him as though she's just wiped him off her blood-red heels.

'So you're quitting, yeah? You don't want to be a part of this? That's what I'm hearing, yes?'

Beecher arches his back. He already knows the right thing to do. Knows, as well, that he isn't going to do it.

'I'm in,' he says, forcing himself to meet her eye. 'But I tell Sal. And I tell her when I think it's right.'

Quinn smiles. It's not as seductive any more. He feels as though she's simply showing him her teeth.

'I'm happy to make sacrifices on the altar of your romantic entanglements, Detective Inspector Beecher. But do promise me you're going to look a little less glum when we're charging him, yes? They'll play that bit at the end of the documentary, I shouldn't wonder. That'll be the moment, yes. Make sure you look like it matters to you.'

Becher hauls himself up. For an instant, he imagines grabbing her by the throat and squeezing until her eyes pop and her lying tongue falls slackly down her open throat. He shakes it away. Knows where such thoughts can lead.

'Come on,' she urges, as if he's a shy toddler. 'Let's go and ask the lovely people to sign off on the arrest, and then we can work out how the fuck we're going to get out to the farm to arrest him. Maybe we should hold off until the cameras can make it over. I've spoken to the producer again. Snow's messing things up for them as well as us.'

Beecher isn't listening any more. He doesn't care. He wonders, as he so often does, what it would be like to be dead. He thinks about nothingness. Oblivion. It's only the spectre of hell that stops him. He can't be sure it isn't real. He knows he won't see heaven, not after what he's done, but hell sounds like somewhere he'd rather not see until he has absolutely no alternative. And there are his girls. Sal, too. A couple of mates. Dad. He talks his neck out of the noose half a dozen times a day. Has done since he started reading about Sal's past and allowing his infatuation with Quinn to blind his thinking. He wonders whether there's any way to make amends for what he's done. Whether there's any way to right the scale.

He picks up his phone and thinks, for a moment, about calling Nola.

Puts it away.

TWENTY

Nola's cleaning. Scrubbing. Putting some bloody elbow grease into it. She's humming: a high, bright madness in her throat. She always cleans when she's trying not to be a big girl's blouse – trying not to whinge and moan and go on like the world's about to fall off its bloody axis. Mam doesn't need that, thank you very much. Not today.

She's giving it her best. She likes to scrub the stains out of things: to really chisel away at the dried candle wax on her chest of drawers, then take her thumbnail to the bits of blu-tack on the walls and the pasta splashed on her shiny white desk. She uses all the nozzles of the vacuum cleaner to suck up the hairballs and false nails from the nooks and crannies of her little square bedroom. She's been working hard. The room is spotless but she's still wiping down, high on lemon-scented wet wipes and pine air freshener, furniture polish and room deodorizer. She feels light-headed. She'd like to open the window but doesn't know if she's allowed. They're not made of money, after all. They can't have hot air blowing straight out into a force-nine bloody gale. Mam's said as much. Says she'll send the bill to her bloody dad. He's got the money, after bloody all.

She's got her headphones on. She's listening to Agnes Obel. It's winsome and ethereal and makes her feel like she's dancing in the rain, pirouetting barefoot through dark, gaslit streets. She's wearing her little vest top and some jogging trousers. Her hair's sticking to her sweaty face. She can smell herself. She'll have a bath when she's done. Maybe chop the split ends out of her hair.

She's OK, she thinks. Doing fine. She's tiring herself out. She'll go check on Lottie in a moment. Maybe grab some water. Cheese and crackers. Just the bedspread to do. Bedspread? Ha! They'd laughed at school when she'd called it that. It was one of Dagmara's words: an old-lady word.

Quilt cover, that was it. Just the quilt cover to put on. She's not great at this bit. Has never managed to do it without grabbing hold of the quilt by its edges and crawling inside the cover until she reaches the seams. She likes it inside the cover, with its scents of fabric softener and detergent. She's putting on the nice white cover with the strawberries. She doesn't know if it's too young for her or too old for her, but she likes it, and Sal always said that she wouldn't want to know somebody who worried about what somebody else might think of their bedspread, and . . .

She thinks of Sal for a moment. Remembers sending the message. God, she's so cringe! She grinds her teeth, sucking on self-loathing, squeezing her thumbs in the palms of her sweaty hands. She hasn't checked her phone since she started tidying up. Plucks it from its place on the tall pine bookshelf, leaning up against a copy of *Lorna Doone*. She hasn't read it yet. Sal's told her not to feel bad about this. Said nobody has ever actually reached the end of a novel by Hardy or Eliot – they just say they have to show off to their friends. And *she* went to university on a special scholarship and used to work in a bookshop, so . . .

She reads the message.

Reads it again.

There's a strange feeling inside her: a low crackling, like the static on the telly or the fizz in the moments after a lightbulb has burned out. She feels sick, suddenly. Feels the urge to throw her guts up all over the nice clean floor. God, what was she thinking? She makes herself feel sick with her neediness, her weakness – all the things that Hank likes to tease her about. He's only being funny, according to Mam. He's nice really if you listen to Lottie.

She starts to read the message again and can't make it to the third word before her eyes blur with tears. She puts the phone down. Tries to tune back into the music. Picks up the duvet cover and the quilt and tries to control her breathing. They did yoga for a while at school. Some friend of Dagmara's had come in and taught them how to breathe. Nola had made half the class laugh when she'd joked that she didn't need any help with that – she could even do it in her sleep. The other half of the class didn't get it. One girl said she told proper dad jokes and was 'so cringe it makes my insides hurt'. Nola hasn't told any jokes since.

There's a roaring inside Jarod's skull: a sound like grit being passed through a grinder. It isn't the quad bike. He can feel its reassuring rumble against his thighs. The sound inside his brain is something else: something old, something new . . .

'Borrowed,' he mumbles to himself. 'Blue.' Realizes he's speaking, not thinking. Tells himself to stop. *They'll think you're mad if you talk to yourself.* That's what he'd been taught, before his mother's death, and after. He'd given the same advice to his brothers and sisters as Dagmara had given him. Keep it locked away, Jarod. Don't ever let it out.

He slows the quad, coming to a halt outside a sagging five-bar gate. Crows are taking off from the white-capped stones, feathers fluttering down among the billions of billions of billowing fractals. Jarod switches off the engine. Allows himself to stand in hushed amazement for a moment – to let the wind buffet him, cool him, spin him. He remembers the mole-catcher: dozens of sleek bodies pinned to the barbed wire, metal skewers through their noses, corpses shrivelling inwards as the seasons changed. He'd been one of Mam's Wednesday-night callers. Liked to watch. Killed himself with strychnine a couple of years back, according to the papers at the time. Used the same poison on himself that he used to kill the moles.

He peers at the only marker on the vanishing horizon: a line of frost-laden trees, ghost-white and stark. Remembers his way inside. Remembers Barry, giving him cigarettes, giving him sweets, telling him he'd be his mate if he'd let him come back to the Byre with him – to meet Trina, wind up that boring bastard Hagman. To get up to mischief. To have some fun. Jarod had done what he'd been taught to do. He'd been kind. Generous. He'd shown hospitality and welcome, just like the picture on Dagmara's wall had told him to. He was repaid for his kindness in blood.

'You hear that, Tips?' he asks, turning in the seat to give the soggy dog a rub behind the ears. He'd like to take his

gloves off to do it properly, but unsettling images keep flashing
in his vision: surreal projections, fractured imaginings. He sees
himself taking off his glove and pictures the flesh and fat and
meat of his hand sliding out – the crimson-smeared whiteness
of his skeletal hand sticking out of the sleeve of his coat like
gory twigs.

He glares across the whiteness, looking for something
familiar. He's five miles from home. Three miles from the
crime scene. If he takes some of the old roads and cuts across
the untended fields, he can be at Weardy before the broiling
black clouds disgorge their next cargo. He'll find some comfort
in work, he tells himself. He can keep busy. Do stuff. *Build*
stuff. Make Dagmara happy.

He feels a low trilling in his trouser pocket. He'd like to
answer the call but knows he can't do it with his gloves
on. He doubts it's important. Nothing's very important any
more.

Up ahead, a battered blue Toyota HiLux is making its way
down the curve of the road, two wheels seeking the extra grip
of the grass verge beneath the snow. Jarod recognizes the
driver – a tall, youngish man who farms out towards Sinderhope.
He spots Jarod. Gives a grin and a thumbs up – leaning across
to shout through the passenger window.

'We've had worse!'

Jarod knows he's supposed to smile back. He's spent years
training himself how to react correctly. He just can't seem to
make himself perform the command.

'That is you, Jarod lad? Heard there's some bother near
Bewley's place? Dead bloke – that right? God, Bewley'll be
shitting himself that he's liable for something. I was going to
have a nosey once I'd dropped some feed off for our Yvonne.'

Jarod feels as if he's moving underwater. Hears in slow
motion. Behind him, he feels Tips shivering against his sodden
coat. It doesn't feel real. Everything seems to be coming from
far away.

The driver starts to look a little put-out. He wrinkles his
forehead, blue woollen hat rising on bushy brows. 'You OK,
lad?'

Jarod screws up his eyes. Summons up a smile. 'Sorry, Dan,

I just choked on a bit of dirty snow – throat's throbbing like a bastard.'

Dan laughs, relieved. 'Been there, mate. I think I've still got a Lilt or two in that family pack on the back seat if you want a drink, like. By the bairn's seat. Don't look too closely at the fabric – think some of that stuff's evolving. I swear to God, I left the doors open once and came back to find a retching in the footwell. Makes you take a look at yourself, a moment like that.'

Jarod feels the buzzing in his skull begin to recede. Feels himself soften for a moment. Climbs off the quad as steadily as he can and plods his way across the narrow road to where the truck is idling. He places his face in the warm air spilling out of the open window. Looks inside at a chaos of papers, cartons, pizza boxes and fur. There's mud and snow and hay on every surface. Radio Cumbria is dribbling out of the speaker.

'Coming in bad,' says Dan companionably. He reaches across and pulls a can of Fanta from a half-finished pack. Hands it to Jarod, who takes it with thanks. He takes a sip and feels the sugar hit his bloodstream. He hadn't realized how thirsty he was. How hungry. How desperately he'd needed to replenish himself. He glugs it down in one. He's panting when he's done.

'Thirsty, lad?' asks Dan, impressed. 'God, that stuff's gassier than Foster's!'

'Thanks,' says Jarod again. He feels a trembling in his arms: needles stabbing at his skin from the inside. 'All go at Bewley's, aye. Car's gone through that wee wall at the bottom of the road – the one over the falls. Driver's gone through the window, best they can tell.'

Dan pulls a face: a toddler sucking on a lemon. 'Under the snow, was it? Christ, it's lucky they spotted him at all. There's some plods there now, are there? You're as well off out of it, I reckon. Keep your head down.'

'Doesn't make any difference to a dead man when they find him,' says Jarod, surprising himself. The words come from nowhere: a searing flash of certainty, as if they've been carved into the meat of his brain by an intruder. Temper flashes through him. He doesn't deserve to be feeling like this. Not

again. Not after he worked so hard to put himself right – to
make sense of it all; to pull on a mask he could wear for the
rest of his life. The thoughts that broil and pop and sizzle
inside his head are not his own. He can't untangle his memories from his imaginings. He wishes Sal were closer.
Sometimes, all he wants to do is press his head against his
sister's, to let their consciousnesses fuse – to walk around
inside one another's minds like honoured guests.

'I've seen a fair few four-by-fours heading up that way,'
confides Dan. 'Was thinking I should mention the silly sod
on the lane t'other night, as it goes.'

Jarod stares at him, hoovering him up like smoke. He's
wearing a Barbour jacket over padded shirt and vest, his
moleskin trousers wet to the knees. There's a smell of wet
hair and cowshit rising from the upholstery, tiny fragments of
snow dancing in the air from the blowers. 'Lot of fuss for a
car crash, if you ask me. But aye, some little thing, going like
the clappers over the lane from the falls. Almost had me off
the quad. Told meself, they're going to do somebody a mischief.
You don't think it was owt to do with it, do you? I mean, I
didn't get much of a look. Shouldn't have been out in the
weather that was coming in. Clouds could have swallowed it
up like a mint.'

Something tickles across the back of Jarod's neck. He has
to fight from squirming inside his skin, turning around within
the too-tight wetsuit of flesh. He doesn't want to talk to Dan
any more. He doesn't know whether Dan is trying to worm
some information out of him, and he doesn't like not knowing.
He doesn't like it when people say and do different things.
How is he supposed to choose the right mask if people keep
lying about what they want him to be? Memories assail him:
moving photographs thrown like playing cards. He almost
recoils under the onslaught.

He reels as he peers at the flickering collage of memories:
a flickering zoetrope of shadows and patterns. He finds himself
close to sagging under the weight of staring both within himself
and out at the gnarled whiteness beyond the HiLux, at Dan's
still-moving mouth.

His chest constricts. He feels the bubbles from the

guzzled-down soft drink log-jamming at his oesophagus. Feels hot sick climbing up his gullet. There's a familiarity in the feeling: a memory, pecking at his insides.

'You doing all right, Jarod? Missus said you weren't doing your spell bottles any more. Shame, that – though I reckon she knows how to get what she wants without using spells and potions, eh? Men aren't hard to control.'

Jarod isn't listening. He's remembering. He sees himself in the kitchen of Pegswood Byre. Sees a length of green twine around his bloodied hands. He's hauling on a rope, trying to shift fifteen stone of dead weight. He's sobbing quietly. He can taste sugary sweetness on his tongue, salty snot on his top lip. There's a pain across his forehead: twin spots of red, abraded flesh. He remembers what she did. Remembers what he did in return.

'I reckon you could use a lie down, lad,' says Dan, pulling a face. 'I'll leave you to it, mate. See you when I'm looking at you.'

Jarod stumbles back from the window as Dan slowly nudges the car forward. He almost falls. Keeps his feet, clawing wildly at the air.

He knows he should call Dagmara. She's always been able to calm him. He spent years in the wilderness trying to find ways to dull the parts of his memory that pained him and to find space for the return of those recollections too painful to witness again. He took part in rituals, ceremonies; drank ayahuasca until the hallucinations became more vivid than his reality. Only Dagmara has ever been able to help him disentangle what he remembers from what he fears.

He stares back inside himself. Looks again at the figure at the end of the twine: the blue bulk of his shoulders, the slack jaw and bulging eyes of his bloodied face. Fire belches up into his throat. He sags. There's a feeling inside his brain: a bottled spider – something menacing and purposeful – pincered feet skewering the grey matter of his prefrontal cortex.

Tips barks. Whines. Calls to his master.

Jarod stares again. Inside himself. Sees again the edge of the memory. Sees her. Sees her step forward and clasp her hands around his. They are the same hands. Same fingers. And together, they haul him to the ceiling – fastening the cord to the brutal-looking hook above the fireplace. He dangles above the body of Trina Delaney: a dragonfly bound in spider silk, spinning slowly in the half-dark air.

Sal,' he whispers.

Sees it.

Sees them.

Sees what they did.

TWENTY-ONE

A69, somewhere near Gilsland

B eecher's in the back of the big four-by-four. Magda's in the passenger seat. There's a uniformed sergeant driving. He's not speaking: two hard eyes peeking out from between the brim of his cap and the fringe of his coarse, dark beard. He's just following orders, and following them with the considered silence of a man who knows that he won't be the one who gets in trouble if things go wrong. He's driving into air that looks like it's being viewed through a cigarette paper: just gauze and fog and whirling snow, all warring beneath the darkening, purplish sky.

Beecher snatches a glance at the road ahead. Watches as the driver nudges the big warm vehicle right, slotting the front wheels into the two parallel black ruts in the snow. They haven't passed many vehicles. The motorway is still officially open, but only the occasional HGV and slow-moving all-terrain vehicle have passed them. They're all going in the opposite direction.

He has his phone pressed to his ear, straining with the effort of trying to follow the conversation over the ceaseless drone of the wheels on the snow.

'. . . very much a movable feast, Boss. Lots of moving parts.'

In his ear, Detective Superintendent Emma James is sounding distinctly harassed. She made it through the snow, got herself to the office. Did it on foot. Went above and beyond.

'I haven't even got the energy to school you on your mixed metaphors, Lewis,' snaps James. She's Head of Major Crimes: Beecher's boss. She hadn't been in favour of his secondment to the special operation being run out of Northumbria Police. But she'd acquiesced because he'd promised it would get a couple of unsolved murders off their own Cold Case list. He's managed his own caseload alongside his work with Quinn. He hasn't shirked a single responsibility. She's still annoyed with him. He fancies she's going to use the words 'into the loop' before very long.

'Sounds rather flaky in places, from what I'm reading here,' says James, and he can picture her in her office, all fleece and Gore-Tex and sensible hiking shoes: neat bowl cut and that same gloop of clarted-up mascara in the corner of her left eye. Can see her reading the cobbled-together briefing. Can feel her sticking her nails into the holes. Can feel her tearing.

'It's being out of the loop that feels so disrespectful, Lewis,' she says despairingly. 'I mean, I understand that you're not calling the shots here – it's Northumbria's operation – but . . . in these conditions, at this stage – and the original witness statements I've been re-reading . . . I can't believe it even got as far as it did back in 1995. They may be trying to cover their backsides against an unlawful conviction suit, but I don't think their problems will go away if you go and round him up and try to stick another half-dozen cases on him.'

Beecher has spent a lot of his life disappointing women. He's learned to be quiet until they've burned themselves out. He rates DS James. Knows how he'd feel in her position and doesn't blame her for being pissed off with her errant DCI. He prays she hasn't heard the rumours. Knows that people are already whispering in the canteen about the reasons for his split with Sal: his recent closeness with a DCI from Northumbria being a particularly juicy theory.

'We've got excellent intel from the ex,' says Beecher, parroting Quinn's words. She turns around from the front of the car and pokes her tongue out at him. There's a gleam in her eyes, a shortness to her breath. She's excited, limbering up: a trackside sprinter performing star jumps and stretches. 'Elsie's taking a statement now. Family Liaison are present.'

'Well, that's one comfort,' says James. 'You have formal ID?'

'On Ford? Not official, no. SOCO have recovered his wallet. Taken fingerprints. Body's in transit right now – they'll have more when they get him back to the chop shop, though they may have to take a blowtorch to him first.'

'Wrong tone, Beecher,' says James warningly. 'I'll have you on another course.'

'You heard what he did, yeah?' asks Beecher, sounding petulant. 'What he did to her . . . what he put her through.'

'I appreciate you're not going to be his biggest fan,' says James. 'The history. With Sal . . . How is she doing? It must have been awful up there. God, there are conflicts of interest everywhere I look . . .'

'She's OK,' says Beecher automatically. 'Doing her job.' He knows he should tell her that Sal is the FLO whose presence at the family home had afforded James a moment's comfort. At least something was being done properly. He doesn't think he can face it. Nudges the conversation on.

'No mobile phone recovered yet,' he continues. 'He used pay-as-you-go, so we can't trace who he's been talking to as yet. Finding that phone has to be a priority. Wallet's still there. Ninety pounds in cash. Driving licence. Few receipts and betting slips, a condom and a couple of loyalty cards. I've got officers going to his place of work.'

'This working theory,' probes James, sounding unimpressed. 'It's compelling, but I can't see any golden bullets, Lewis. There's nothing that isn't circumstance and conjecture. Unless you get a confession, there's nothing . . .'

Beecher closes his eyes. Swallows down the urge to concur with every bloody word she's said. 'I think that's very much the optimum outcome,' he says, choosing his words carefully. 'There's confidence that he'll be on edge. He'll be twitching. We can get him to spill.'

There's a little laugh down the line. It makes his stomach hurt. 'And if his solicitor asks why you've been letting your ex-partner live with this monster for the past few weeks . . .'

'Moving parts, like I said,' he replies. 'She couldn't be alerted to the investigation, could she?'

'You're saying she'd have warned him? Her mother's alleged killer?'

Beecher thinks for a moment about opening the car door and throwing himself out into the snow. He feels so fucking trapped. Feels squeezed between all these damn women, dictating what he can and can't do, what he can and can't say,

what he's allowed to do and not do. He tells himself he'd feel
the same way if they were men. Knows that he's lying.

'The acid?' asks James. 'Any news on the source?'

'We don't know where it came from. Not recovered yet, but
we can't perform a fingertip search under two feet of snow.'

'Jesus, so why the rush?'

Beecher is trying to think of a reply when Quinn reaches
into the back of the vehicle and plucks the phone from his
hand.

'Brrrrrsssssh,' she whispers, into the phone. She makes a
crackling, clicking noise. 'Going . . . tunnel . . . losing.'

She ends the call. Tosses it back to him. 'Mammy cross?'
she asks, affecting a teenage pout. 'She'll forgive you. You're
bringing back a gift-wrapped career case, Lewis. God, everybody is so bloody ungrateful!'

Beecher puts the phone away. Grinds his teeth. He feels
sick. Hungry. Wired. Feels like the worst bastard in the
universe. Needs to salve himself. Needs to bathe his wounds.

Does what he promised he wouldn't do.

Texts Sal.

**We're arresting Hagman on suspicion of murder. Stay
where you are.**

He puts a kiss. Deletes it.

Sends the message.

He can't bring himself to look at the reply.

Sal's returning to herself: re-inhabiting her mind, her bones;
forcing herself back into limbs and organs, synapses and
nerves. She feels jangly. Numb. She feels like she's been away.
Can feel the echo of distant cold air against her cheek. Can
taste sugar. Acid. Doesn't remember taking up this position,
on sentry duty, by the grimy sink in the poky kitchen,
scrubbing her hands raw in the scalding water, screeching a
damp rag into the insides of a dirty cereal bowl.

'Dozing away,' says Elsie, making Sal jump. 'I couldn't get
her to tell me what she's on. I'm thinking diazepam but
could be owt, really. If he can get acid, he can get whatever

knock-out drops you care to name. Done neighbours on both sides. They had their concerns. Did nowt about them. Bloke next door's got one of them clever doorbells that videos owt that passes by, so he's going back through to Friday night – see what we can see. I've phoned Mrs Kelly. Given her an update. She's on her way over with supplies, so you'll have company. I see you've got the little ones settled. We'll have that chat with them soon, eh? Let's see if we can wake her sooner rather than later – we need a couple of photos of him. Something with a DNA sample. Ask her about that hole in the floor, too. That came up in a temper, I reckon. Seems a place you'd hide something you didn't want the kids to stumble on. Bottle of acid, you think? Lads and lasses up the valley can't see owt but snow, but you never know, maybe they'll get lucky – find his phone . . . we'll have that number, too. The one he was using when he last rang. They can still trace the movements from the towers if they know the number, so we might get a better picture of where he went . . .'

Sal lets the words tumble into her like coins cascading into a well. She tries to steady herself, the way Dagmara had shown her – how she'd shown them all. She visualizes the candle flame: the soft white heat encased in the billowing robes of reds and crimsons and golds. She listens to Dagmara's voice. Feels her take her by the hand, sliding into the twists and thorns of the labyrinth in her mind, sliding under doors like steam. Feels gentle hands caressing the matter of her mind: kneading, caressing, remoulding. Feels the soft numbness spread out within her, languid and warm and delicious. She makes sense of herself. Tries to focus.

'Magda Quinn,' she says without turning around. 'Is Lewis sleeping with her?'

Elsie sighs. There's a scrape as she pulls up a chair and sits down heavily. When she speaks, she sounds older. Tired. 'All I know is what the gossips say, and they're wrong more than they're right.'

Sal nods. Picks up a beaker from inside the mound of suds and starts trying to get the dried chocolate off the handle.

'This investigation he's been working on,' begins Sal.

'I can't, love. You know I can't.' Elsie sounds genuinely

pained. 'I don't have owt to bloody tell. He's been working with this special operation – joint investigation with Northumbria. She's in charge. If you're asking me what they're doing, I couldn't tell you, love. I do know that HRH Detective Superintended Emma James was getting her knickers in a twist about the amount of time he was spending over in Newcastle when he should have been dealing with live cases. There was a bit of laughter from the lads, y'know – a few lewd comments about what he and the Succubus might get up to.'

'The Succubus?'

'Quite high-brow for a copper's nickname, isn't it? It followed her from Notts Police. So did the stench, like.'

Sal finally turns away from the sink. Surveys the sad, cluttered little kitchen. Raises her eyes to the holes where the locks had been fastened. An unkind thought flutters up: a leaf caught by the breeze. Dagmara! God, she was bloody everywhere. She must have known Barry was Leanne's partner. She knew everything about everybody. She knew enough to be bragging about his achievements that day at Weardy. No, she must have known more. And yet she hadn't said more than a few gabbled platitudes when Sal had broken the news about who she'd found. She hadn't acted right. Had Hagman? Was she missing some unspoken conversation, some shared secret, as the old friends stared at each other down the lens? She could have coughed up some information right then. Could have been helpful. Told her where he was living, about his stepkids and his blessed living arrangements. She could have dropped her a message as she was tramping around the crime scene dragging police tape behind her like an arthritic spider building a lacklustre web.

She stops herself. Tries to focus. She hates being angry with Dagmara. Feels guilty at once. She's alive because of her. Free. Everything she has is because Dagmara believed her all those years ago. Believed what her mother was, and promised to do all she could to help. Whatever it took.

'You're buzzing,' says Elsie, grateful for the distraction.

Sal feels tempted to let it ring. She dries her hands on her trousers and fishes the phone from her pocket. There's a text from Beecher. Another from Hagman.

'I was just thinking about you,' mutters Sal, trying to get the pitch of her voice right. She always likes to show Dagmara her best self. Everybody does.

'I thought my buttocks were burning,' says Dagmara brightly. 'You do know that's what happens, yeah? Somebody's talking about you, it's your ears. Thinking about you – backside every time.'

Sal feels her mouth twitch into a smile. Feels herself sag a little. She's heard Dagmara say such things too many times to count – invariably greeted by peals of laughter and a cacophony of silly noises. Kids love how she talks. She's not a proper grown-up. She's one of them, really. She gets cross and she gets silly, and she absolutely will not stop stamping her foot until she gets what she wants.

'I'm with Leanne,' says Sal, wanting to get it out of the way early. 'You didn't say you knew her, Dagmara.'

There's a moment's silence. She hears Dagmara suck in a breath through her back teeth: a mechanic looking under the hood of a broken car. 'Bad Dagmara,' she says and provides a sound effect of a slapped wrist. She softens her tone. Becomes the gentle storyteller who tucked her in and told her stories and made the memories go away. 'Sorry, Salome – you dashed off in such a rush. I've been worrying about you. About her. Does she need anything? It's been a long time since I saw her, but I could get there . . . I've finished my interview.'

Sal glances over at Elsie who's reading something on her phone. From the set of her jaw, she's not enjoying the contents.

'The appeal,' says Sal, screwing up her face with concentration. It feels like there's wire wool in her brain. 'They'll have contacted Barry, won't they? If they're really going to go ahead with it, they'll have been tracking down all the witnesses, surely. And you were proud enough of what he'd done with his life . . .'

'I didn't mean for you to hear that,' says Dagmara, with real sorrow in her voice. 'It was thoughtless of me. Stupid, really. I was all fluttery – you know how I can get. Just babbling really – trying to impress. That's the job, isn't it? And yes, Salome, I was proud of what he'd done. The changes he made.

The person he was – the person who watched your mother do those terrible things . . .'

'He did them, too, Dagmara. I told them, and I told you.'

Dagmara makes a soft cooing sound, a gentle *there-there*. 'That time is all of a jumble, you know that. She had you all twisted inside and out with lies and stories. You can't untangle what you remember and what Jarod's told you. God knows I've done my best to help you all decipher it.'

Sal leans back against the sink. She feels bone-tired. Wishes she were still in her stinking bed in the creaking caravan: just she, her brother and her mother's convicted killer, snuggled up tight three miles from where it happened. Those were the good times.

'Sorry, sorry,' she mutters, feeling wretched. 'And yes, maybe it would be good for Leanne to see a friendly face. I'll be here if you can get through the snow.'

'They really seemed to love each other,' says Dagmara sadly. 'A beautiful family.'

'All a front,' she says. 'Put her through every kind of hell over the past few months. Making up for lost time; that's how Leanne's described it. Made her take the pictures to show the right face to the outside world and all the while he was doing the self-same thing to her as he used to do to me.'

Elsie jerks her head up. Sal turns her back. A fat, iridescent tear wells on her eyelid, but she refuses to let it fall.

'That's not right,' says Dagmara. 'No, he got himself right. He was working. Trying. Helping people. He did what he promised after the trial.'

'I've still got the scars he put on me, Dagmara. Scars inside. Out.' She slaps the side of her head with a flat palm. Feels the sting of it. Thinks of Mam's big meaty palm smacking off the side of her head. Remembers the simple thrill of taking it: riding the wave of jingling bells and buzzing static, taking it and grinning up at her, big eyes and Shirley Temple curls. *Is that it, Mam? Is that the best you've got?* Remembers the night she pushed too far.

'Sal, I swear, I didn't know any of that,' says Dagmara, flustered. 'Oh, God – oh, that poor girl. The children? Did he hurt the children?'

Sal hears the panic in her voice. Can't help but feel the tug of compassion – the desire to make her feel better, the way Dagmara has always done for her.

'They saw some bad things but no physical injuries,' she says. 'Leanne not so lucky.'

She senses Elsie staring at her. Feels uncomfortable. Feels like she's given too much of herself away.

'There were letters,' says Dagmara. 'Over the years. When the appeal first started to become a possibility – when Wulf started waking up from it all and daring to believe he might not be to blame . . . I had to track him down. See if there was anything new he wanted to say about what happened that night. He always gave the same reply. He was putting the past behind him. He was living right. He was making amends, and he didn't want anything to do with any appeal to clear his name. He was clear about that. Said he was a new man now. That he just wanted to forget it ever happened. I mean, the solicitors, the appeal team – they couldn't just take my word for it. I've had the very devil of a time trying to stop them stirring his life upside down . . .'

'You protected him while he was pouring acid on his girl-friend's face, Dagmara. When he was punching their unborn baby out of her belly . . .'

'Jesus, Sal, that'll do!'

Sal snatches a look Elsie's way. She's standing up, face carved in stone. She's gone too far. Told too much.

She fumbles with the phone, all jittery, all fingers and thumbs. Jabs at the screen. The message from Beecher flashes up. She reads it twice. When she speaks again, she doesn't know if she's telling Dagmara or Elsie, or just repeating it for confirmation.

'They're arresting Wulf,' she says without emotion. 'Lewis.'

'Wulf,' says Dagmara, her voice tinny as it bleeds from the phone. 'That would be bloody suicide. That would be bloody stupid, Sal. Check again, please. Tell them I'll be straight there. We can sort this . . .'

'I have to go,' says Sal, and she ends the call before she can cause herself any more harm. Gives Elsie her attention.

'This is what Lewis has been doing, isn't it? Investigating

Wulfric Hagman? Looking into the one decent man in my life?'

'Decent man? He killed your fucking mother!'

'Good!' screams Sal, mouth so wide that she hears a pop in her jaw. 'Do you know what she was, Elsie? Do you know what she did? What she made us do? To each other? To ourselves? To her boyfriend. There was only ever Wulf and Dagmara – the people who were there to make sure that she never went further than we could come back from. Wulf was obsessed with Mam, yeah, but he stayed for us. Left his wife to keep us safe from her. I think he even made her happy for a while. Started getting us right, even when everybody in the valley was laughing in his face for shacking up with Mad Trina and her feral bastards. And she destroyed him, Elsie. Broke him down and tore him into little pieces. Pissed on what was left.'

Elsie pushes herself back from her chair. She looks like somebody has reached into her throat and begun to squeeze her thorax. Her eyes are glassy. She can't find her breath. 'Sal, I didn't . . . I didn't know any of that. How much of this does Lewis know?' she asks quietly.

'All that he needs to,' she says, and from upstairs comes the thump of the children finishing their movie and jumping down from the bed in search of fresh mayhem. Sal wipes her eyes. Manages a little smile of apology. She hadn't meant to get so cross.

'He knows what Wulf did for us,' she says at last. 'Knows what he means to me. To Jarod. And he's on his way to arrest him. He'll make it stick, too. Sounds good, doesn't it? Vigilante killer cop slays love rival . . .'

She walks past Elsie. Runs briskly up the stairs and puts on her best face for the children.

In her head, the same refrain: *What if he didn't do it?*

And its echo: *What if he did?*

TWENTY-TWO

*B*loody deathtrap, thinks Hagman as the old farm building materializes out of the snowy air like a coal-rimed iceberg. He's sweating, despite the sparkling, frigid air. The walk's taken it out of him. The walk and the thoughts and the memories.

There's not much left of Pegswood Byre. It's a slumped black hump on the landscape now. Fallen slates and rotten timber. Crooked carcasses of crenellated outbuildings – half-rotted bodies rising from the soil and the snow.

The arsonists came after the trial. The journalists, too: their lies endlessly more flammable than the lighter fluid and petrol of the local yobs. Nobody's even bothered to condemn the place. Once in a while, it will pop up on a YouTube video: the house where a copper killed the woman who spurned him. He's always named. Perhaps the appeal will put a stop to that, clear his name.

Clear your name? Fat chance of that, Wulf, lad. You're fucked, mate.

Hagman chides his inner voice for the foul language. He's always tried to set a good example. Always tried to do the right thing.

Did you, lad? Did you really? Shagging Trina? That was out of the goodness of your heart, was it? Ditching your wife? Paying off your girlfriend's bills with the family savings? Arrested on suspicion of taking indecent images of a child? Suspended?

Hagman trudges on, his feet crunch-crunch-crunching over the settled snow. He wants to stop for a breath. Wants to turn back. But the old building pulls him on as if he were being reeled in on an invisible line.

He pushes past a snarl of dead brambles. Feels his boot scrape across an uneven patch of rock, concealed beneath the snow. A memory falls. He sees Trina. She's on her knees by the new flowerbed that she's dug with the twins. She's got little hand-stitched pillows tied around her swollen knees: mad floral patterns stitched with different coloured threads. There's sweat on the back of her neck. Sweat on her shoulders, where her roundness escapes from a too-tight vest. She's grunting as she plants seedlings, poking at the brown earth with a tablespoon. Sal's helping. She's eight or nine: dark eyes and curly hair, smudges on her cheeks and dirt under her nails.

It's Jarod who sees him first. Jarod, sitting in a rickety chair round the back of the sagging building, overlooking the yard. Hagman's in the patrol car. He's heard there's a family moved into one of the abandoned farms up above Alston. He's here to move them on, the same way he's done with the half-dozen other families who've had the same idea. He hates this part of the job. Hates enforcing laws that do more harm than good. He can't understand the problem. The house is empty. She needs a place for her and the kids. They don't give a damn about the complex land management agreements or the ongoing dispute about whether leasehold fees are due to the landowner. It's been empty for nigh-on twenty years. He admires any mum who'll take a risk for a better life. He sometimes wonders whether his wife is preparing to do the same: to take a great leap into the unknown. She doesn't look at him the same way she used to. Perhaps she never did.

He's a joke, really. He might be OK to look at and harmless enough as a copper, but he can't think of a single person who genuinely admires or respects him. He knows he'll fuck this up, too: knows he'll be too bloody soft to say no to this big, round, hard-faced woman; all stumpy arms and breasts that seem to take up all the space between her waist and neck.

He shakes the thought away. It's too clear. Too bright. He knows which memories he can trust. It's the deeper ones he needs to access – the ones that Dagmara has been trying to tease out for too many years. He feels himself getting closer to it the nearer he gets to the Byre. Can feel the echo of that night. But he can't seem to focus on the picture . . . keeps seeing little scraps of memory. Sees himself bringing Jarod back after he was caught robbing the post office in Nenthead.

Brought him back after he got into the old mine workings, too. Jarod wasn't like the other tearaways he'd had to deal with in his role as community cop. They were cheeky little sods: yobbos and bored farm lads, looking for a few extra quid or a way to have a good time in a valley known as the North's last wilderness. Jarod and Sal weren't like any of them. They weren't like anybody he'd met before. Neither was Trina. Christ, how she'd played him! How she'd wrapped him around her finger with her soft eyes and trembling lip, and her story of unnamed loan sharks in Newcastle hounding her for money, for blood. She'd pleaded with him to let them stay – just until she could sort something out. She'd introduced him to Sal. She'd smiled politely, as she'd been taught. Even reached up to shake his hand. He knows now what it took for Trina to pretend to be meek and motherly. But she fooled him, that first time. They all did. Played their roles. Even agreed to have an off-the-books meeting with his old friend: a social worker he'd known since he was a kid.

Dagmara, when she found time to visit the property, hadn't been fooled by the performance. She saw children at risk of harm. Saw a mother putting on a show, making all the right noises, parroting phrases and serving up mugs of nettle tea on a tray; her darling children playing at her feet like a low-budget version of *The Sound of Music*. She'd made a referral. Got things moving. Started a care plan that got the kids into school. Picked them up in her own little car to make sure they went to the youth initiative she'd started for troubled teens.

Trina played along with it. She knew she was shielded from the worst of it. She had a copper on her side. A copper who couldn't seem to get her out of his head, a copper who started spending more time at the Byre than he did with his own wife. The first time they slept together, he told her he loved her. Said he wanted to be there for her, forever. Said he'd leave his wife, if she'd have him. Let her have the damn house. Let her have the kids. This was what he wanted – this passion, this madness, these children. She never said a kind word to him again from that day forward. She had him under her spell.

And that's when she started to show him what the children endured when he wasn't there. People started to comment on the scars, on the weight loss. He was starting to look at the whisky bottles again, the way he did when he first left the valley to go and try to become something other than his father's son.

He stands in front of the open door. The rotten wood hangs on one rusted hinge. He wonders how many times he's stood here. Whether he stood here that night.

He forces himself to look inside. Summons up the image of the single flame: Dagmara's voice.

He sees himself. Sees his cold hands knocking on the wood. She's home; he's sure of it. Can see her sitting up on the big squishy four-poster bed. She's naked, in his head. Not alone, either. He knows Barry isn't around. His foster mother has been complaining: getting in Dagmara's ear about the amount of time he's spending at the Byre when he should be home preparing for his GCSEs. Too late to do anything about it now. Not here, at the last. Not swaying, drunkenly, on the doorstep, in the uniform he's not allowed to wear any more. Trina did what she said she would. Told his superiors she'd found him taking photos of her naked, sleeping child, the accusation enough to get him suspended.

Did he really come here to kill her? He asks himself again as he pushes forward into the boot room. It smells of damp and sheepshit, wet fabric and mildewed walls. He steels himself. Tries to remember what it felt like to be a police officer – to be something approximating a person.

The vision in his mind fades like a negative held up to sunlight. He can't get any closer to the image. Just the doorway, and his own pitiful voice, begging her to open up, to tell them it's not true, to clear his name, to take him back. He remembers the sensation of the bailing twine against his fingers. Remembers the certainty coming over him – the indelible stain of murderous intent. He wants to hurt her. Wants to hurt himself.

Then there's just the rabbit, and the pain in his throat, and Trina's dead body on the flagstone floor. He has no memory of either act. Has no reason to think himself not guilty. Better people than him have committed murder. He knows what drunk, angry, jilted men are capable of.

The kitchen is a foot deep in mud and hay and animal droppings. The sink's been ripped out. Cupboards, too. The metal hooks still hang from the rafters, but the roof sags in the middle, offering a jagged porthole to the upper floor. To Trina's bedroom – to the place where he thought himself briefly, deliriously, alive.

Hagman shivers. Stands in the middle of the room and slowly turns a lazy pirouette. He knows there's something trapped inside his head: some memory that refuses to grant him peace. He tells himself he can deal with the truth, whatever the truth might be. Has lived a great chunk of his adult life as a convicted killer. He isn't sure he has the fight for what's to come. Hates his feebleness, his weakness. Hagman had never witnessed her beating the kids. Didn't see what she did to them all when he wasn't around. Just saw the cuts and bruises and made his excuses for her. Rough-and-tumble, he said. Kids being kids . . .

There's a dead bird on the rotten timbers by the window-sill: ragged feathers and tiny, fragile bones. Can't help but think back to those brief, happy days – him and Sal at the table, pasting wildflowers and bird feathers on to a circle of bright cardboard. They were making a garland for Mam. They used her favourite flowers and favourite birds. Sal wrote her a card from all of them. Told her she was a brilliant mammy and that they all loved her so very much. Hagman learned from Dagmara that she'd made Sal burn it in the fireplace as soon as Hagman had gone. She didn't want to read lies, she said. Sal despised her, she said. They all did. They were going to tell. But if they thought there was any escaping from her, if they thought anybody was coming to help . . . she promised them they'd be dead long before the blue lights started to flash.

Hagman pushes on into the living room. Sees Trina sitting on the sunken sofa, wildflowers sprouting from the soggy fabric at the arms. She's drying dandelions with a hairdryer, plugged into the generator on an extension lead. She's drinking some sticky liqueur from the bottle. Jarod's at her side, listening as she tells him how to do it. Tells him about the new moon. Sometimes, he saw glimpses of the person she was when the

twins were young. Sometimes, she could be funny.
Knowledgeable. Kind. The darkness inside her devoured the
light as if it were made of acid.

He glances to the far corner of the room. A space has been
cleared amid the debris and filth. A military-style camp-bed
is tucked out of view of the open, glassless windows: metal
tubes and green canvas. There's a blanket and a scrunched-up
coat, sweet wrappers and tobacco pouches.

Hagman feels the cold breeze chill the sweat on his neck.
Moves towards the bed as if being powered by a remote control.

He squats down, a pain in his knees. Picks up the coat.
Holds it to his nose. Rummages in the pockets. Pulls out a
crumpled sheaf of grimy paper: envelope torn open with a
finger, names printed in black on the white space. The letters
are addressed to Barry Ford. They've been sent to his work
address; the Works Department at Northumbria County
Council. Feeling unsteady, he sinks on to the bed. Selects the
top letter and starts to read, squinting in the dying light, occasional snowflakes dancing around him like moons orbiting a
pale, fragile planet.

Dear Mr Ford

As we previously discussed, the Juris Project is committed to quashing unlawful convictions and overturning
erroneous guilty verdicts. To that end, we are representing
Mr Wulfric Hagman, who was found guilty of the murder
of Trina Delaney in 1996. As part of that process, our
team is seeking to revisit the testimony of everybody who
gave evidence during the investigation. I would urge you
to call our investigator on the above number so we can
arrange an interview to discuss some of the more complex
aspects of the case. I enclose your original statement, for
reference. I'm led to believe that you have previously
been unwilling to engage with the possibility of a retrial
or appeal. While I appreciate that these memories may
be painful, Mr Hagman spent more than twenty years in
prison for a crime that he maintains he did not commit.
I urge you to make contact at your first opportunity.

Hagman squeezes his eyes shut. Wishes he could still weep. His eyes are sore, his throat tight. For a moment, all he can see is Barry as a dead-eyed, blond-haired young man who used to grin, all silly and self-conscious, as Trina did the things to him that she enjoyed. As she filmed them. As she made Hagman watch. And then he pictures him as he was a few nights ago. Sees him as he was, crawling through the gathering snow: glass in his hair, blood on his face, on his hands. Sees him, lying there, gulping, gasping, waving for nobody, staring up at nothing as if talking to God.

When the phone rings, he doesn't answer. He already knows they're coming for him. If he was a copper, he'd be gunning for Hagman, too. It's open and shut. The appeal will be dead in the water before the end of the day. He'll be in a cell before nightfall. He wonders how long he'll last among the general population; whether they'll put him back with the paedophiles and the rapists, the way they do with all convicted coppers and prison wardens. Wonders who his new padmates will be, who he'll have to do little favours for; who'll protect him and who won't. Whether he'll need to start taking tablets again: the special pills that kill his dreams and let him sleep without nightmares. The only time he tried coming off them, he let himself down. Spilled his guts to the rapist he shared the wing with. Made a mess of things. Left himself open.

He can't face going back to that. Can't face any of it. He'd rather die than do any of that again.

He lifts the blanket on the bed. There's a length of green bailing twine underneath.

The world goes quiet. Shrinks down. Everything else falls away. It was always going to come to this, he tells himself. Was always going to happen here.

Don't, Wulf, lad. They'll think the worst. They'll burn your body and scatter it in the silage tank. You'll be a bogeyman; a monster. They'll tell stories about you to scare the children . . .

He's stopped listening. Slowly, deliberately, he begins to unwind the twine. He won't write a note this time. He'll let them think he did it. He'll take the blame for Barry, like he's taken the blame for Trina. He made a promise, years ago. Vowed to keep them all safe. Failed in every conceivable way.

He rubs at his throat. Looks up for something firm, something unyielding – a place to fasten the noose.

Memory hits him like a train.

He sees himself dangling there, turning crimson, eyes bulging like a dying cod. Sees the cord biting into his neck. Sees himself swinging; legs kicking, scrabbling. Feels the darkness, the nearness of oblivion.

Stares into the vision. Examines it from every angle, like a photograph on a computer screen.

'She wasn't there,' he croaks, pulling the cord tight in his palms, a thrum of tension emanating from the tough twine.

He manages to still his fumbling fingers long enough to unearth the phone in his trouser pocket. He needs to call Dagmara. She'll be so pleased with him. He's seen it. Seen what he did do, and what he didn't. Sees himself, swinging above empty air. There's no dead body. No Trina. Just a reeking rabbit laid out on newspaper, and dirty dishes in the sink.

He doesn't get a chance to call. His eyes are drawn straight to the messages. Dagmara. Sal. Both warning him that the Major Incident Team are coming for his head.

He feels himself grow small. Grow still. Grow calm. None of it matters any more. He didn't kill Trina Delaney. He hanged himself out of sheer frustration and shame. Chose to end it in the kitchen of her stolen home because he knew nobody would ever believe him.

Deep inside his mind, he hears the creak and twang and slap of the cord snapping clean in two. Remembers the impact. The pain.

Remembers the nearness of another shape. Remembers the shadows creeping in from the walls. Sees bare feet, in the corner of his vision. Dirty. Big wide feet, like their mum.

Loses consciousness before he can count how many people are watching him gasp for breath. Sees children. So many children, silent and grey in the dark of the room. They assemble like wraiths. They see his sins rise like steam.

Hagman puts his arms around his head. Lowers himself on

to the bed. Puts Barry Ford's blanket over his head and breathes him in.

When he's sure he can trust himself not to drop the phone, he types out a text message. Sends it to a number he's memorized.

Detective Superintendent Quinn. I'm at the place where it began. Come alone. Tell Whitehead I said hello. x

Puts a kiss, just for fun.

Presses send and settles back: an arsonist watching a petrol bomb arc through the purpling sky.

TWENTY-THREE

Nola's packing. She hates them. Hates them all. Hates herself most of all.

She's throwing things in a rucksack. Biting her tongue. Picking the lesions around her nails. She can taste blood. Can taste hot tears.

She's fiddling with a stuck zip now. Tugging at it. Teasing at it. Her hair's in her eyes. She's sweating on her top lip. *And the stupid fuckety bastard zip won't fucking give . . .*

She throws herself down on the bed. Screams into the pillow. Breathes. Pictures the flame and the soft words and the gentle hand in hers. Knows what to do.

She'll go to Dagmara, like they all do when things get bad at home. Just because she's one of the good girls, it doesn't mean she hasn't got problems. Dagmara will see that. She'll walk if she has to. She can listen to her radio interview on the way. They can pot some plants, maybe, like she did with the damaged children who came to her for help in putting themselves back together after seeing horrible things. She gave off good energy. People felt safe around her. She was what people needed when they needed it most. She'll only take a change of clothes and a book or two. She doesn't want to be away long. She'll tell Dag everything, and she'll make it stop. She should have done that a long time ago. She grabs for her glasses case, her phone. It'll be better soon. She'll tell. She'll do what they say you should do. She'll tell a grown-up . . .

'What are you doing, Nola?'

Lottie's standing in the doorway, all muzzy-edged and lovely. She's wearing her pyjamas and bedsocks pulled up to the knees. She looks a little dozy, the way she gets when she's been staring at her tablet for too long, emerging from the trance looking boss-eyed and vacant and generally disappointed that reality doesn't contain Peppa Pig.

Nola curses. If she had a whip, she'd lash herself. Stupid!

She should have put something against the door. She doesn't want to be slapped in the face with yet more reasons to feel shitty about herself. She can't leave her here. What was she thinking? How could she be so cold-hearted? Selfish? So cruel? They were right what they said about her, Mam and Hank, when they thought she wasn't listening. *A cold fish, that one. No joy in her. No laughter. Lewis and me, we might have had a chance if she hadn't turned up nine months after the bloody wedding. And no, she weren't conceived that night – he'd had eight pints of Stella and three Jagerbombs . . .*

'They're arguing again,' says Lottie, trundling sleepily into the room. She's holding her misshapen yellow friend by the tail. He's called Happy Tiger. She takes him everywhere. Hasn't let him out of her sight since she saw him in the window of the charity shop and started making lovely little chirping noises and pointing at the glass. Nola had bought her it, out of her own pocket money. 'Arguing about you, I think. I dunno.'

Nola sits down on the bed. Tries to wipe her eyes, sniffs back snot.

'Don't,' gasps Lottie, panic gripping her little round face. 'He hates that. Hates noises like that. Be sweet. He likes sweet.'

Nola puts her arm around her little sister. Pulls her in.

'Happy feels weird,' says Lottie, holding up her companion and inspecting his lopsided face and button eyes. 'He looks sort of cross. I mean, he's always grumpy, but it's like he's giving me the Death Stare – you know how Dad gets when waiters ask him if he's happy with his meal while he's still chewing his food . . .'

Nola zones out. She doesn't know what to say if he asks. He's going to feel so guilty that he didn't answer her calls. She feels her heart aching with regret, hating herself for making her dad feel anything but good. She sits forward as if bracing for an impact on a crashing place.

'. . . look, Nola. See, doesn't Happy look weird?'

Nola's patience snaps. She snatches Happy Tiger out of her sister's hands and holds it up, staring at its lopsided eyes. 'No, Lottie, your teddy doesn't look weird, and its expression hasn't actually . . .'

She stops. Presses her fingers around the bear's glassy eye.
There's something under there. Small and hard, like a pebble
in a shoe. She pushes it with her nail. Finds a tiny, barely-there
seam, stitched under the fur.

'Grab me those tweezers, please, Lottie.'

Lottie looks aghast. 'Does he need an operation? Is it
cataracts, like Nana?'

'Please, Lottie. Be a good girl.'

Lottie does as she's asked. Hands the tweezers over like a
nurse assisting in a surgery. Nola unpicks the stitches. Peels
back the thin white material. She finds the tiny object tucked
into a little fold of stuffing behind Happy's eye. She pulls it
free with her fingers. Holds it up.

'Did somebody shoot Happy?' asks Lottie, mystified.

Nola peers at the little capsule. It's black, with two concentric semi-circles of perforations punched into the hard plastic.
There's a little hatch at the back. Underneath, there's a slot
for a SIM card, and a tiny, red light.

Nola feels her heart quicken. Tries to tell herself to be calm,
to not jump to conclusions: to take a moment before doing
anything rash.

'What is it?' asks Lottie, again. 'Is Happy OK?'

From downstairs comes a sudden surge of angry shouting.
Mam first: screeching, cursing banshee-like, great guttural
squawks that never quite become words – just undiluted
ululations of sheer, raw pain. Him next. Shouting, at last.
Raising his voice. Telling her she's mad. She's a fucking
psycho. She's just like his ex. He doesn't need this any more
– not her, nor her awful, bratty little daughters . . .

Lottie snuggles up to her sister. Nola covers her ears and
presses her head against her cheek, trying to transfer some
sense of safety, of calm: to be what Dagmara is for everybody
else.

When Nola raises her head, there's no sound. Whatever was
happening downstairs, they've shouted themselves out. They
do this all the time, she reminds herself. They'll be out in the
garden shed now, doing what they do to make up.

Then she hears the creak on the stairs.

Nola raises her head, pulling Lottie in as tight as she can.

She wants it to be Dad. Wants it to be Sal. Wants it all to be better again. To all be like before.

A shadow falls in the doorway.

A figure steps forward, hands and face dripping with spilled and spattered blood.

'I'm sorry,' whispers Mam. 'I'm so, so sorry . . .'

She jerks backwards as if pulled on an invisible lead. There's a fist in her hair. And then her head's smashing off the doorframe, her nose crunching against wood, and he's hurling her backwards down the stairs: all thumps and crunches and breaking bones.

He steps into the room. There's blood on his shirt. He's been stabbed under the arm. If it pains him, he doesn't show it.

TWENTY-FOUR

Quinn can feel her pulse thumping, redly, against the cuff of her expensive duck-down puffer coat. Can feel her heart thudding against her ribcage like the pedal of a bass drum.

'Elsie's spoken to the neighbours,' shouts Beecher from the back seat. He's reading a report on his phone. He looks grey. Drawn. She can see him losing faith before her eyes, an apostle poking a lifeless Jesus. He's doing his best to go through the motions, but she can just about hear him writing up his excuses in his head for when everything turns to shit. Were she less wired, she'd give him a little tenderness. Hold his plump hands and assure him that she's got this; she's got the angles covered. God, how she wishes she could tell him the truth. It's not that she dislikes lying to him – she just wants somebody to pat her on the back and tell her she's played an absolute blinder. She won't be getting words of gratitude from Callum Whitehead any time soon, even though she's done all he wanted of her and more besides. There won't be any appeal; she can guarantee that. He'll cough to the other murders. She knows that. They have an understanding.

'Albanian guy with the food van outside the home address . . . he's told Elsie he saw Ford driving away in Kelly's car. Said it wasn't long after six p.m. Ford had a rucksack with him. He was looking at his phone. Smoking a tab. He remarked on it because he'd never seen him smoke before. He'd always been a bit holier-than-thou about how to behave in front of the kids, according to what he's saying here . . .'

Quinn gives him a grateful nod. Faces forward again, trying not to grip the leathery edges of the upholstery. She feels as though somebody's carbonated her blood, and wonders if her pulse is visible in her neck: a blue bird snatching flies.

Her phone is buzzing inside her jacket pocket, but it takes her a moment to notice it above the thrum of the tyres and the rushing of blood in her head. She's ascribed each of her important contacts their own ringtone and, more crucially, their own distinct vibration. She hates being taken unawares. Likes knowing who she's about to manipulate the moment her phone starts to buzz. She sucks in a big gulp of air, an excited white smile splitting her red lips.

She turns her shoulder to the back of the car before she reads the message, blocking Beecher's view of the screen. She reads Hagman's missive. Reads it again, just to be thorough.

'Change of destination, Tommy,' she says to her driver. 'Pegswood Byre. I'll put the postcode in for you – you keep those big brown eyes on the road, yes?'

It's going to work, she tells herself. She's going to put the cuffs on a serial killer. Sod the documentary – there could be a bloody movie in this.

'What was that, Magda?' shouts Beecher from the back. 'Who was that?'

Quinn finds herself suddenly rather tired of her junior officer's company. 'We've got eyes on him,' she lies, as she feeds the new address into the satnav. 'Heading for the old place.'

'It's just a ruin,' yells Beecher, bewildered and terse. 'Wasn't easy to get to even when the roads weren't covered in snow. This is madness, Magda. We need Operational Support. How many bodies do we have on the ground?'

She waves a hand: a taffeta-clad duchess dismissing a nuisance waiter. 'Just follow my lead,' she says. 'I'll go in alone.'

Quinn feels a sudden flash of irritation with herself. God, if not for the weather, she could have called the director of the documentary and arranged an exclusive ride-along. They could have used drone footage: bleakly beautiful tracking shots of the gathering tundra and the lowering sky. She rummages in the glove box and finds her lapel camera. She likes to record her interactions when there's a chance people will go back on their word.

'Oh, this is interesting . . . listen, it's just coming through . . . our mate Barry, well, the bloke he walloped – the arrest that blotted his record – the dates match up. He beat the living shit out of him the same week he took his fists to Leanne.

Bloke was a temp from an agency, casual staff along on Ford's
work crew. Made some off-colour remark and Ford went for
him. Took the rest of the lads to get him off him. Reckoned
he was trying to bite his eyes out. None of them had seen owt
like it. Sacked on the spot, like. Hassan's got the financial
records through, and Ford was on his uppers. Beating the shit
out of her must have been easier than telling her he'd lost his
job, eh? Hang on, going through the direct debits now. More
going out than coming in. Transfers . . . regular payments over
the past year . . .'

Quinn isn't listening any more.

The driver slows as he nears the exit: a single-track road
leading through a line of black, snow-mantled trees, branches
virtually touching fingertips overhead. It takes a moment for
the vehicle to find the ruts in the snow. The sergeant flicks the
headlights on to full beam as they crunch over the unblemished
snowfall: huge cones of fluorescent white lighting up the
sparkling air and creating eerie shadows as they scythe across
the tangled branches. Quinn thinks of lifeboats. Icebergs.

Her phone buzzes against her palm: two little zaps followed
by a longer burst. It's Whitehead again. Getting twitchy now.
She ignores him. Lets him stew.

'. . . you listening, Magda? . . . oh, fuck off . . .'

Quinn snatches a glance.

'Ex-wife,' he grumbles. 'Third bloody time.' He answers
the call and barks, 'Not bloody now' into the handset. Ends
it with a jab of his index finger. Rubs at his forehead as if
massaging a heart.

Quinn turns her back on him. Gives the driver a nudge.
'Looks better up ahead. Put your foot down a little, eh?'

Fifteen minutes, according to the satnav. Then he'll give
her what she wants, and she'll do the decent thing in return.

She stares through the glass. Watches the fat flakes tumble
in their millions. She feels oddly awestruck. Feels unpleasantly
insignificant.

She shakes away her intrusive thoughts. Focuses on the here.
The now. What had he been prattling on about? The ex-wife?
He couldn't be referring to Sal. Wouldn't speak to her that
way, either. No, must have been the girls' mum. Three calls?

She finds herself feeling uneasy. Feels like she did when she was a graduate detective, bright-eyed and fearless, learning to listen to her instincts, her gut – the little voice in her head that likes to stir the ashes of her paranoia. She shifts in her seat. Changes her angle again. She knows she's going to have to reassure herself. Knows she's going to look. To snoop. It makes her feel sick to know she's going to use the tools of a killer to save a life. Calls up the app on her phone. On the screen is a black-and-white image of Nola's bedroom. It's a static image: the foot of the bed, the edge of the doorframe. She zooms in, widening the image with finger and thumb.

Rewinds the footage. Sees Hank in the doorway. Sees the stains on his shirt. Sees him take Nola by the hair and throw her out of shot.

Acid rises in her gullet. *Not now*, she pleads. Not this moment. Not when Hagman's waiting.

She has to tell him. Has to. They need to scramble everything they have available: there's an immediate risk to life. But he'll lose his mind; she knows that. He'll fight for the wheel if she knows him the way she thinks she does. He'll punch and kick and bite and claw, and he sure as hell won't do what she needs him to do, which is to stay quiet and let her finish the operation. She'll tell him everything when it's done. She'll explain, and he'll understand, or he won't. She doesn't care much either way.

But she can't not care about the girls. She's no stranger to moral compromises. She's done things that would sicken her if she allowed herself to dwell. She doesn't know whether she's a terrible human being or just ambitious and goal-oriented. She fancies the outcome is much the same either way.

She texts Whitehead. She fancies he's good for one last little flex of his influence. Types out a message: a precis of events. She'll have Hagman imminently. And she needs somebody to ring in a 999 call on an untraceable line. Screams heard at Nola and Lottie's home address. She puts two exclamation marks. It's non-negotiable.

She sends it. Receives a thumbs-up acknowledgement a moment later.

Looks at the clock.

Five minutes. Jesus, it was remote. You could forget that other people existed out here. Wouldn't be surprised to glimpse a pride of woolly mammoths lumbering across the gathering tundra.

'Magda, are you listening . . . and, mate, I know you're trying to impress the boss, but you need to slow down like – there's a bend coming up . . . mate, mate . . .'

The tyres lose their grip. There's a screech and a sudden metallic clanking, and then Magda's head hits the glass: cobweb cracks spreading away from the impact point, and for a moment her ears are ringing and there's blood in her nostrils, and then she's airborne, and upside down, and something breaks inside her, and they're tumbling, crashing, dangling in their seats. The vehicle then flips itself right, again, again: crunching metal, compacting: Magda's vision is an explosion of dust and glass and snow.

The car comes to rest on its back at the end of a great furlough of churned earth and compacted snow. The lights are smashed, front and back. The engine's dead. The wheels continue to turn for a while, before slowing to a dead halt.

Then there's just the silence.

And the settling snow.

TWENTY-FIVE

Hagman hurries his way back through his own footprints. He's moving faster than he was when he arrived. He can hear his blood in his ears. Can hear his heart. There had been no mistaking the sound. He'd reacting instinctively – hurrying towards the sounds of violence as if he might actually do some good when he arrives.

For a few fleeting moments, he feels like a copper. This is the way he imagined feeling every day of his working life: a guardian, a protector – somebody to call. He signed up so he could become the thing that his own life had been missing. Became a protector, because nobody had ever taken it upon themselves to be that for him.

Shut up, Wulf, lad. Stop malingering. Shift it . . .

He hurries on, trying to differentiate between the voices and the thoughts and the memories that spin around his head like bluebirds in a cartoon. He's out of breath, and as he coughs to clear his throat, he can taste the blood in his lungs. It was Trina who got him smoking, too. Told him she couldn't fancy a bloke who didn't have the taste of harsh Camel cigarettes on his tongue. He'd taken it as instruction, of course. Moulded himself into whatever it was she claimed to want. Never got it right. By the time she was making him watch other men try to give her what she wanted, he barely knew who he was any more. He just knows he wasn't Barry Ford.

An image flashes in his mind. Barry. Leather jacket with tassels and glasses down his nose; floppy hair and cigarette burns on his knuckles and up his arms. Cock-sure, rodent-faced, fang-toothed little rat. Hagman had arrested him twice before he turned up at Pegswood Byre with Jarod and started making moony eyes at Trina. He'd heard she was fun to play with. Trina ate him up. Let him in. Found a playmate.

He sees himself in the passenger seat of Dagmara's car. She's mid-thirties. Stocky, flame-haired, formidable. She'd

been working with Trina more days than she got paid for. She
was making inroads with the twins. They were helping her set
up the new youth club. Sal was devouring books from the
local library and catching up on the other pupils. Jarod was
turning his hand to mechanical engineering: helping out any
number of locals who owed Dagmara a favour and were willing
to let him tinker under the bonnets of their cars, lawnmowers,
quads and combine harvesters.

It'd half killed Dagmara when he broke the news: Trina
was using again. Drinking again. She was hurting Jarod more
than Sal this time. Barry was bringing out the worst in her.
They egged each other on. Pushed one another into new
cruelties and perversions. He didn't know how to stop it. Didn't
know what to do.

Match made in hell, said Dagmara, sipping herbal tea from
a thermos and squeezing his arm. God knows she's been
through a hell of her own, but whatever it was that let her
have her kind moments when the bairns were young, there's
nothing there now. In any sane world, we'd have the bairns
out of there, but unless the twins will give a statement and
stick to it, we'll be back where we were before. Where we
are now. Best thing that could happen for those children is
Trina going to sleep one night and never waking up.

Hagman had barely acknowledged it at the time. He was
drunk on his own misery. The wife had never looked at him
with anything other than contempt, but since word had got
around that he was sharing a bed with Mad Trina, she'd closed
the door to him. Closed the door of his own house – the house
he was born in, that his dad died in – and told him she was
going to go through with the divorce this time. He hadn't
cared. All he'd wanted was for Trina to make sense to him
– to explain what he'd done wrong, and why she'd been so
nice and wacky and sexy when they first met and now seemed
hyper-fixated on the destruction of his soul.

He would have to find somewhere else. Needed to start
getting serious about what mattered. Needed to fix things for
everybody. Fix things for Sal and Jarod and Dagmara and
himself. Fix things for Barry, too, even if the smarmy little
shite deserved to be bleeding out at the bottom of a mineshaft.

He could do it, too. Could make it happen. One little push, perhaps. A loose screw, a frayed wire, a patch of black ice and a sharp stone. He thought about it endlessly: ways to kill, people to kill, ways to do some good with one act of harm. Then Trina called his boss with her claims about the photos of Sal . . .

He's so deep in thought that it takes him a moment to spot the crumpled wreck of the four-by-four. It's come to a halt on its back, half a mile from Pegswood, partially concealed by the bank of snow. He snatches a glance at the stone wall by the bend in the road. It's been annihilated: great grey chunks scattered among the smashed glass and twisted metal.

Hagman stands perfectly still, watching his breath drift into the shimmering air. He blinks repeatedly. Feels like he's in one of Dagmara's 'safe spaces', trying to make sense of what's real and what's imagined by flicking his eyes to the left instead of the right, or perhaps the right instead of the left, trying to see outlines instead of vague shapes, to know what happened rather than what he fears.

He hurries forward. He wants to help. On some level, it's all he's ever wanted.

He wonders if it was like this for Barry. Ice, a squeal of brakes, the chaos of crunching metal and exploding glass. Wishes he'd seen. He's fantasized about Barry's death many times and would like to know if he had been accurate in his imaginings.

Hagman crops, crab-like, into the random wedges of shallower snow. Stumbles on a discarded metal bracket. Sees the smashed plastic casing of the brake lights: a bead of disappearing red.

He bends down. Remembers the words as if the last thirty years were a mere aberration. Remembers how to be a police officer – somebody who's here to make things better, to save those who need help. Christ, had he ever been that naive?

The words die in his throat as he peers in through the broken glass. Dangling upside down in the back seat is Sal's ex-partner. Lewis Beecher. Nola and Lottie's dad. There's blood dripping from his nose and his ear. His left arm is horribly twisted at the elbow. He reaches in to unclip his seatbelt. Stops.

Slowly, he repositions himself. Looks at the people in the front seats. The driver's dead: his body compacted into an unnatural shape between the crumpled front end and the seat.

There's a noise from the passenger seat. He sees dark hair, hanging like vines. Sees the dark, almond-shaped eye. There's a smear of crimson at her mouth, a trickle of viscous blood running down to drip-drip-drip on to the inverted roof.

Hagman sits back on his haunches. Lets himself breathe. Glances back to the road. It's a bad bend. He covered half a dozen bad crashes here when he was a plod. Two were fatal. Had he done this? Were they names to be written in his ledger? Has he killed Sal's ex? Has he killed the police officer who promised to listen should his memories ever delineate into real shapes?

He screws up his eyes. It's all such a blur. He can see himself banging again at the door, his blue uniform dripping with fine, blustery rain. He's drunk. He needs Trina to know that he didn't do what she's accused him of. Needs to know that he forgives her, no matter what she's done. All she has to do is look upon him kindly again and he'll never mention the past few weeks and months. She can cast Barry aside as easily as she did him. They can be a family. He can keep the children safe. She can admit that she framed him. They can move away, perhaps. Or into his own farm, now the wife has packed her things. It can be perfect. It can be beautiful.

And then he's waking on the floor. He's resting his cheek on her fleshy, bloody calf.

He can't hold the edge of the memory. It's as if some sinister force has reached into the matter of his brain and excised the bits that he needs. Two decades of Dagmara whispering in his ear and it's still not much more than a blur.

He reaches into the mangled car. Unclips the seat belt and tries to brace her fall. Puts his hands under her arms. Heaves. In painful inches and increments, he drags her through the broken window. Puts his fingers to her neck. She's breathing, but her breath is fluttering; the pulse is barely there at all.

He's breathing heavily by the time he gets her clear of the car. Does the same for Beecher, too. There's an awful lump behind Beecher's ear. He's breathing, but there's nothing in his eyes. Hagman takes off his coat. Lays it on the snow and heaves Beecher on top of it.

He's shaking when he finally stands up, the effort of the exertion greasing his body with sweat. He needs help. Needs people.

Hagman searches in his trouser pocket for his phone. There's a new message from Dagmara. One from Sal, too. He ignores both. Keys in the first two digits for the emergency service. Stops before hitting the third nine.

Quinn's bag is open in the battered footwell, spilling papers, files. Her mobile is tucked away under the seat, the screen smashed but legible. It's open on her messenger service. He sees his own words. His own invitation . . .

He wishes Jarod were here. Dagmara. Not Sal. She'd know what to do, of course. She's the best of them. But he needs to keep her way from all this. That's never been open for negotiation. It's all for Sal, deep down. All to make sure she never has to tell the truth about that night, when . . .

He fumbles at the phone with his trembling hands. One of the little icons on the screen flashes open. He's watching a live feed – a bed, a doorframe; a smudge of red paint. He closes it down in case he sees something he's not supposed to. Looks for something to wipe the blood from her head. Rummages through her bag. He can't help his eyes falling on the briefing document. Sees his own face staring back at him – a younger man, battered, bruised: the imprint of Callum Whitehead's boot ground on his temple and cheek.

He pulls it from the bag. Shakes free the fragments of glass. Sits back in the snow, six feet from the vehicle. Reads. Reads every word.

When he reaches the end, he lets it fall from his hand. Stares at the falling snow through bleary, tear-glazed eyes.

He knows the names of the dead. Knows how they died: the wheres and whens of their demise. Knows why, too. Abusers. Pimps. Paedophiles. Violent men, perverted men, dangerous men. Women, too. Women like Trina . . .

He centres himself. Thinks of the flame.

Shuts down the voice that whispers, softly, in the centre of his head.

Remembers.

Sees.

TWENTY-SIX

J arod parks the quad in the little car park at the rear of the building. There are no tracks in the snow; it's a perfect white canvas, waiting to be defaced. He feels a perverse ripple of deep-down pleasure as he churns through the virgin whiteness with the big, meaty tyres. He's always liked making his mark. Couldn't see a bare wall without tagging it. He rubs at the scar tissue on the back of his hand. Remembers to breathe. Draws a box in his head and writes the number *100* on it. Wipes it away and draws *99*. He'll keep doing it until he hits zero.

'Focus, lad. Build a snowman. Think of Sal. Breathe.'

He'd like to throw himself down in the snow and make angel shapes with his arms and legs. But he doesn't think he'd get back up again. He feels like there's somebody else moving around inside him. There's an echo to his heartbeat, as if it is splitting slowly in two. He thinks of cells. Twins. *You ate your triplet inside me*, said Mam. *Devoured him. Ate him up. You were twice the size of your sister. Monster. Devil! I'll tear him out of you, my good boy, my baby boy, the one you sucked the life from . . .*

'Tips,' he says quietly, as the dog jumps down from the rear of the quad and disappears into the deepest patch of snow, biting at the falling drifts that hang like frozen lace in the nearly black air. 'Tips, come on, lass.'

He feels like a penitent approaching a church and begging for sanctuary. He doesn't know what he's done wrong, but he knows it was bad. He's hurt somebody. Told lies. He feels as though he's fallen into one of his own nightmares – swapping places with his other consciousness. He needs Sal. Needs Dagmara. Needs to ask them to make it stop.

He finds the key on its chain around his neck. Slips it into the wooden door and pushes into the cool air of the brightly painted boot room. There are pictures of colourful flowers and trees painted on each wall. The word 'Welcome' is written in a score of languages, all etched on multicoloured leaves hanging from the chocolate-coloured branches of the central oak. He takes a deep breath. Tastes the poster paints and the sweat and the sweeties, outdoor clothes and floor polish.

'Dag,' he says. 'Dagmara.'

The words bounce off the floor and the ceiling as he pulls off his boots and slops soggily into the main room. The walls shimmer with photographs of all the kids who've passed through Weardy's doors. Bunting and streamers hang in loops; escaped helium balloons are slowly losing their grip on the ceiling. There are huge murals on the wall. A pool table neatly tidied away. Boxes of board games. Great chests of toys. There's a full catering kitchen behind a partition wall: pots and pans and plates and cups. Dagmara teaches the kids how to cook, sometimes. She used to teach them to iron and vacuum and hang out the washing, too. Taught them how to be just that little bit nicer to one another. Showed them how to meditate. A little self-defence. The council put a stop to that. He wonders how she still manages to keep fighting. All the people she's helped, all the scraps she's endured – he knows she'll keep going until she drops.

He remembers that he's here to fix the little wall in the peace garden. Dagmara's left him one of her special tea infusions: a decoction in one of those glass bottles. He takes a sniff. It smells like warm seaweed. He takes a sip – it's disgusting. It's always disgusting. He tips it into the sink. Feels the shiver of guilt.

'Job to do, lad. Get on wi' it.'

Can't quite seem to make himself leave the safe, dry space. Can't help but let the memories and the imaginings bubble up and breed.

He sees them on the floor together. Him and Sal and Barry Ford. Barry's got blood coming from his nose. Sal's hand is wrapped in bandages and a clear polythene bag. Jarod's got burns on his knuckles: black scabs obscuring the tattoos on the back of his hand. It was Barry who first inked him, when he was just a kid. First put his mark on him. First showed him who was boss.

'Stop it,' he says aloud. 'It's not real. It's a bad dream.'

He sinks to his knees, hands loose, eyes closed, mirroring the movements he sees in his memory. The three of them: points of a triangle, eyes closed, barely breathing, sitting up like petrified monks in a golden temple. None of them are moving. There's a single flickering flame on a saucer in the middle of the triangle. There's jam and white powder at the corner of Jarod's mouth. Can taste it in his hindbrain. Can taste it now.

He feels Tips lapping his tongue at his cheek. Reaches up instinctively and holds her closely, wet cold fur against his grimy cheek.

Remembers.

From somewhere nearby, the low, trilling vibration. He feels it in his bare feet. Looks at the grimy wet prints he's left on the floor. Lets himself drift inside it; a feeling of weightlessness, of blessed oblivion. He thinks of New Mexico: the red dirt and the vast sky and the ditch-water foulness of the ayahuasca on his tongue. Feels his mind become smoke, greasy whorls of ineffable sadness.

'You didn't mean it, Jarod. She pushed and she pushed. It's no sin to slay a beast. You did good, lad. We can make this go away. Say nowt. Let me hang . . .'

He feels his memories changing shape. They drift in and out of one another. For an instant, he is Sal, hauling the blue-clad colossus aloft on a length of cord. He feels the sting of it in his teeth – the incongruity, the impossibility. He's been seeing this picture for nigh-on thirty years. Here, now, it feels like a dream.

He needs Sal. She always puts him right. He'll explain about the medication. She'll hold his hand and soothe him, and she'll tell him to talk to Dagmara and . . .

There's a sudden movement behind him. He's half drugged, half broken, disassembling, evaporating, turning to nothingness. But he turns his head just in time.

Something hits him right in the centre of his skull. He feels himself tumbling backwards as if he's been shot through the eyes.

He hits the ground so hard that his teeth mash together. He tries to move. Can't. Feels gentle hands moving him backwards:

something at his throat, a loop around his neck, biting into
the soft flesh beneath his jaw.

A face, staring into his own. A face from the dank, fetid
well of his nightmares.

He swallows. Tastes chemicals. Tastes ash.

'It's OK,' he whispers, letting them work. He feels the knot
tighten. It'll be over soon. Over, and he can rest.

A flash of black and white, a sudden blur of wet fur . . .

Shouts and yells and gathering darkness.

Then the sticky touch of blood.

Her name, a dying prayer:

Dagmara.

He's growling. He's got his teeth locked together like a pit
bull's clamped around a stick. But he's still talking, deranged
in his rage. Spit spumes on to his chin. His eyes are bulging,
sweat on his forehead, blood on his cheek.

'Bitches! . . . Fucking bitches! She did this. She did! And
you. You evil little bastards.'

He's got Nola by the hair. He's dragging her towards the
stairs. There's a knife in his hand, dripping with red. He seems
to forget it's there. He's feeling victimized. Persecuted. Picked
on. Even smacking her head off the wall had left him
disappointed. It hadn't made the noise he had hoped.

'Stop it!' screams Lottie, trying to hold her sister's clothes.
She's sobbing. Her face is the ash and snow of the view beyond
the glass. 'Please, don't hurt her.'

'I could have kept going!' he hisses, shoving Lottie away
with his arm. 'Could have been good for you. I fucking tried,
didn't I? Tried with all of you. And it wasn't enough, was it?
Never enough. And that silly bitch – copper's wife? You know
how many families there were before you little bastards? How
many times I tried.'

Lottie pulls herself off the floor. Nola twists in his grasp.
Feels a burning pain at her crown.

'You're coming with me,' he says. 'I'll be dead or inside
by this evening, but I'm damn well going out happy. I hope
he feels like shite until his last breath. Hope he sees this every
time he closes his eyes . . .'

Nola lashes out with her right hand. He's not prepared for it. He's struggling with the door, trying to push Lottie back into the room; his hands are slippy with their mother's blood.

She finds her voice. Calls out for help. Shouts for her father. For Dagmara. For Sal.

He laughs when he hears her name. 'Nobody cares, love. I saw the message she sent you. Doesn't give a shit. Nobody does. You'd be better off with me. I'd be nice to you. Nice to Lottie, too. I just need some of this, for me. Helps me be better – keeps me decent . . .'

A rage unlike any she has ever known floods her system. She thinks of Sal. Of the few stories she shared – about the life she endured. She thinks of her father's stories. Of the kids at Weardy. Of Dagmara, telling them, over and over, to live well. To be the best version of themselves. She thinks of Mam. *God, please . . . Mam, I'm so sorry, so sorry, please . . .*

He loosens his grip on her hair as he yanks her down the hallway. Jerks his head up as a thunderous knocking comes from the doorway.

'Bastards!' he yells.

He's at the top of the stairs now. He's got the knife in his bloodied hand. Lottie is tugging at his arm, screeching, sobbing.

She looks down. Mam is on the top step. There's blood on her face and on her hands, but she's clawed her way up from the bottom step to the top. She reaches up. Her eyes meet Nola's. Something passes between them.

He screeches in agony as Mam hauls herself up and sinks her teeth into his Achilles tendon, biting down through gristle and bone. Nola brings her head up like a battering ram. Sal taught her this. Showed her what to do when you're fighting somebody bigger than you. Smashes her skull right into the centre of his face in a gory crunch of blood and cartilage.

It's Lottie who trips him. They'll never say. Eventually, they'll forget the truth, the sequence of events. His arms pinwheel madly. And then he falls, toppling past Mam, clattering and crunching down the stairs: bones breaking like burning twigs.

The door bursts open in a shower of splinters. Two police officers rush into the hallway, slipping in blood.

Nola gathers Lottie into her arms. Holds her close. They sink to the floor, reaching down, trying to haul Mam on to the landing. There are stab wounds to her chest. Her back.

'I killed him,' whispers Lottie. 'I killed him.'

Nola pulls her close as the police officers shout their names, call for back-up, thunder up the stairs and demand immediate medical attention.

Nola looks down. Happy Tiger's lying on his side. She crawls forward. Picks him up. Passes him to her sister and watches her snuggle him in.

And then there are arms around her, and people are saying her name and she suddenly knows it's OK, it's over, he's dead. She looks past the bulk of the police officer. Stares down into his lifeless eyes. If this is a sin, she's willing to burn for it.

There are no tears. There won't ever be tears again.

Through the fog, she hears the officer shouting into his radio. 'It's Beecher's kids . . . his ex . . . we need help . . .'

No, we don't, thinks Nola, closing her eyes. *We did. We don't any more.*

TWENTY-SEVEN

Sal's stroking the littlest of the children. She's called Lacey but she'd like to be called Violet. Her favourite stuffed toy is a lamb in a fluffy waistcoat. She's called Baarbara. She was still talking about their adventures when she fell asleep, her head in Sal's lap. The two older ones have retrieved an old games console from the graveyard of toys and are trying to wire it into the clunky, boxy TV. It's still got a VCR and DVD player.

Sal tries to slow her heart. She feels as if she's running from something – as if she's always been trying to stay one step ahead of the thing that's screaming for her attention. She feels as if it's wrapping long seaweed fingers around her throat, into her mouth, her nostrils, pulling her down, tugging her back . . .

She feels Jarod suddenly. Feels the strange moment of refraction when her cognizance slips and she senses the eerie nearness of her twin. He's in pain. He's afraid. He needs her.

She jumps at the sudden *drrriiing* of the doorbell. Eases Lacey on to the sofa and tells the boys to keep it down. Leanne's asleep upstairs now. She dropped off once she'd finished gathering up photographs of Barry and letting Elsie rummage through the pockets of his clothes, hung haphazardly in the cheap white wardrobe.

It rings again as she approaches the door. Through the frosted glass, she can see a small figure, blue and pink and red. She pulls it open, shivering in a sudden swirl of icy air.

'Oh, sorry, I was expecting Elsie,' says the short man on the doorstep. He has a moustache. A sensible coat. An air of good, solid dependability. Looks like the sort of chap you'd trust to run the lottery syndicate. 'I'm her neighbour. She wanted me to look at my CCTV footage for her?'

'DS Crisp?' asks Sal, for form's sake. She mimes shivering, steps back into the hallway, expecting him to follow. He stays

where he is. Holds up a tablet, flakes of snow melting on the
screen.

'Took me an age to go through it, but the old doorbell cam
came up trumps,' he says animatedly. His breath hangs in
curtains around his face. There's a BMW logo on his bobble
hat. There's a frozen dewdrop in his left nostril.

From behind, Sal hears the kids shouting. Feels like she's
back in her old life. In her stomach, fire and ice.

'You'll see, here's the gentleman of the house . . . making
his way out at seven fourteen p.m., yes. He has a holdall and
what looks like a toolkit. And here . . . You can see a car
following him, shortly after.'

Sal feels like there's chaos in her head: all static and explo-
sions in the centre of her skull. Suddenly, she feels sick. There's
a constriction at her throat.

'I've seen it around before, I think,' says the neighbour
jovially. 'It's not Leanne or Barry's. Perhaps one of their
friends'? Might be irrelevant but Elsie – lovely woman, by
the way – said this was the sort of thing that might help plot
out the old timeline. As you can see from the snow on the
bonnet, it had clearly been sitting idle. And look, the lights
don't come on until it's almost out of shot. I'm such an
enthusiast for your craft; it's rather thrilling to be able to assist.
Can't be easy, in this weather. I've been out doing my civic
duty, helping pull the strugglers out of the snow. BMW X6.
Winter tyres. I don't think I've ever been happier.'

Sal isn't sure she can tell what's outside and what's in.
There's a ringing in her ears. She's having trouble focusing.

She glances up, searching for her reflection in the hall
mirror. She looks ashen. Ghostly.

'Little things are good on the snow, aren't they?'

For an instant, she's staring into the flame. Dagmara's talking
to her. Telling her she's a good person, a good soul – that
everything will be OK. She'll make it so she can't remember.
She'll never know what she did. They were helping her at
Weardy, that's all. She had friends. Influential friends. She
could make it all better, but they'd have to trust her. They'd
have to make sure they never let themselves dwell upon the
events at Pegswood Byre. They were to repeat the lies until

they became the truth. She'd keep it from them, even if it killed her.

Sal looks at the screen. At the little car. The bald head in the driver's seat.

Not many people know Dagmara wears a wig.

From somewhere beyond the end of the street, she hears sirens. Lots of them.

'Are you feeling quite well?' asks the man, looking concerned. 'If you're diabetic, I think I may have a Murray Mint . . .'

Sal looks past him. The world tilts again. Light floods her. She smells floor polish. Clay.

Sal rummages in her pocket. Calls Jarod. It rings for an age. Finally, the *click* of an answer. She hears breathing. Hears retching, hacking coughs, great spasms of choking breath.

'Jarod . . . Jarod, where are you? I felt . . . I don't know, I . . . I'm remembering stuff. Seeing things. I need to see you . . .' She stops, out of breath, out of words.

Slowly, like breath on a window pane, a sense of dread steals over her. She knows, now. Knows what Dagmara did for them. What she'll keep doing for them.

For them? She asks herself. No. Just for her. Just the chosen one. Just Mam's special princess, with her big brown eyes and lovely curls and brain bigger than Durham Cathedral. She'd do anything for Sal. Jarod could go hang.

'Dagmara . . .' she whispers, glancing back at the little car on the little man's screen. He looks positively mortified, unsure how to hold himself or his face.

'Pegswood,' says Dagmara, all of the sing-song playfulness gone from her voice. 'I'll tell you all of it.'

'What have you done?' whispers Sal. She hears the coughing subside. Feels heat in her brain, a sudden flush of cold air in her lungs. Feels her brother fighting for his life.

'What I had to,' says Dagmara, and she ends the call.

Sal stares at the phone. At the neighbour. At the car on the screen. Elsie's upstairs, finishing the search. The kids are OK. Whatever happens now, she doesn't see how she can be a police officer come tomorrow. Not after what she did.

She manages to summon up a professional face, an official-sounding voice. 'Sir, I appreciate this is a bit irregular, but might you be willing to assist the police in their enquiries? To the tune of a four-by-four . . .'

TWENTY-EIGHT

Hagman drags Quinn's body into the barn. Pulls her through the mud and the snow and the sheepshit. Dumps her, breathlessly, on to the fold-out bed. He's dripping with sweat, an icy rind of chill perspiration clinging to his skin. There's blood on his hands.

She makes a strange gurgling noise, and he realizes her tongue is lolling back into her throat. He remembers his training. Eases her on to her side, forefingers in her wet gullet, pulling the long, pink tongue out of her airway. She starts coughing. Begins to jerk. There's blood in her hair. On her cheek. Her eyes flutter open, wide and fearful, half clouded in one misshapen iris.

'Can you hear me?' he asks, looking into her eyes. 'You've been in an accident. People are coming.'

She pushes back against the bed. He can see the wildness in her eyes as she jerks her eyes around the room, looking for a gap in the darkness. Finds none. She tries to speak. Can't find the words.

'Sssh,' says Hagman gently. 'Don't get yourself in a lather. You're going to be OK. I'm not going to hurt you.'

She blinks desperately. Swallows down a mouthful of dirt and blood and snow. 'Not you . . .' she whispers. 'Never you . . .'

'No,' says Hagman. 'No, it never was.'

He grips the notebook in his left hand, waving it in front of her. 'I think I know what you want,' he says quietly. 'The deal, such as it is. Am I right?'

'You drop the appeal . . .' whispers Quinn weakly. 'And we . . .'

Hagman smiles. 'Yes, try and finish that sentence. You can't do it. You're a police officer. No matter the victims, people can't go around ending lives – even if it's for the common good. I still believe that.'

'What she did . . .' begins Quinn.

He rubs at his throat. 'Gift-wrapped, I suppose. I'd made the connections, I think. Before it all went to hell, I saw the same name on the same reports. Saw the victims and their connections to her cases, the kids under her care. God, when I pulled that noose over my head . . .'

'She did it,' gasps Quinn. 'She tried to kill you, too.'

Hagman shakes his head. 'No. No, she saw an opportunity.'

He remembers pulling the noose around his neck. Fastening it beneath his jaw. Remembers his fingers fumbling with the knot as he tied a loop around the meat hook. Remembers stepping out into the empty air in the dark of Trina's kitchen. She wasn't there. She'd never been there.

'It snapped,' he says. 'By the time I was on the deck, there was a body under me. Trina's body. And I'd been so starved of oxygen, well . . .'

'She's manipulated you all these years. Fumbled around in all of your heads. The names in that book, the people she's killed – they were evil. They were hurting people. She removed them. Made lives better. Made the world better. I don't care what Whitehead's offering – I can't let her . . .'

In the doorway, a sudden movement. A silhouette, an outline against the white snow and black, black air.

Hagman shields his eyes. Squints. Watches as she steps forward into the shaft of light that punches down through the open timbers.

She has the grace to do it theatrically. To remove her wig like a player on her stage.

Dagmara lets the moonbeams illuminate her scarred, hairless skull. There are ridges and bumps and still-weeping sores.

'You can,' says Dagmara, standing up straighter. She arches her back. Stands taller. She's shed some of her layers. There's no fat under her grimy jumpers – just hardened, work-toned muscles. 'Wulf,' she says softly. 'You poor sap.'

She unclips the top of her walking stick. Reveals the short blade inside.

'She'll be here soon,' says Dagmara, eyes soft and dream-like. 'Cate. No . . . no!' A harsh laugh, bright and mad. 'No, not Cate. Cate died. Cate died, didn't she? Because we believed him when he said he would change. Believed that he was going to stick to the action plan and stop drinking and stop beating his kids until they passed out. So he killed her. Killed her in front of me. Snatched her away . . .'

'Dag, come on, there's time to stop all this. This isn't you . . .'

'It is, Wulf,' she says apologetically. 'This is me at my most honest. This is my most authentic self. Here, in the dark, about to end somebody who's thrown away their right to be alive.'

'But you helped me,' says Hagman, eyes filling up. 'You were the one who wanted me to appeal. You were the one who kept me pushing. You gave me a home. Visited me all those times. Helped me with my monsters . . .'

'You're not a bad man,' she says pityingly. 'You shouldn't have shacked up with that demon, though, Wulf. Shouldn't have turned a blind eye to what was going on. Shouldn't have played along and hidden what she was doing. I knew. Whitehead knew. But no, you believed you could turn things around, love her into being anything other than the vile abuser she truly was . . .'

'I'm sorry,' sobs Hagman, folding in on himself. 'I thought I was doing what was right . . .'

'No, you didn't,' she snaps. 'I do what's right. I remove the obstacles. I give them a warning, and if they don't change their ways, then I come calling. They see me, at the end. See me like Barry did.'

Hagman falls silent, choking on his tears. On the bed, Quinn rises. 'You're bleeding,' she says, gesturing at Dagmara's right arm.

'Some of it's mine,' she says, as if noticing for the first time. 'The rest's a bit of a broth, if I'm honest. A real treat for the lab. Three different blood groups and one canine. They won't believe it!'

'How many?' begs Quinn. She looks like she's fading. Her eyes are cloudy, her voice weak. But she needs to know if she was right.

'A bloody who's who, love,' says Dagmara brightly. 'Pimps and paedos and perverts. Some monster mums, too. God, Trina got away easy. It was a Godsend. One of those mad moments.

Me and her, alone, and her ex-lover dangling by a cord. Poor bairns – to see that, and them too little to reach him. I think the light went out of their eyes that night. I mean, who else were they going to call? Sometimes the universe just makes things come together perfectly, don't you think? Took a lot of love to make them forget. Love, and a few little helpers in a pill pot. It was a kindness. Same as their mam got. One stab, that was enough. First one I'd done with a blade. It was just there, see. She'd been making a nice tea for her and Barry. He was losing interest. Getting frightened of the things she was making him do. He enjoyed it, but he thought they were going to get caught. So she turned on him. Hurt him like she did the bairns. He went running and found he had nowhere to run but to me.

'I took him home. I swear, I must have passed Wulf here on the drive. Trina's out on the moors yelling for that sorry sack of shit, and the man who really loves her is in the kitchen begging for another chance. It was a bloody farce. I told Barry that I would get his things. It would be over. He could come back with me. There was a badness in him, but he was young enough for hope, y'know? And she's coming running down towards the house. There's rabbit blood on her hands and she's sobbing for her boyfriend – a man barely out of his teens. All the while, he's inside, begging, sobbing, tying himself up. And she's giving it to me on the front doorstep – both barrels of her venom right in the face. I tell her I've come for his things, that Sal and Jarod won't be coming back, that she's lost everything and I'm glad. By the time we see him swinging, well . . .'

'She cut him down,' says Quinn. 'At the very least, she tried to save him.'

'*She* did?' spits Dagmara. 'She was laughing her head off. Looked like she'd never seen anything more beautiful. And there was the knife. One stab, right to the neck. I'd never seen so much blood. Never done one right up close like that before. I watched her die. Saw the imps come and start dragging her down into the fire.'

'And then the rope snapped?'

'Aye, the fucking rope snapped. Scared the life out of the

bairns – silly sods running back when I'd already told them to stay put. He was dead, love. Dead when I left him. There's nobody who will convince me otherwise. Dead, and there was no way to hurt him any more. He could take the blame, she was gone, and a whole lot of kids could get on with their futures. He had to go and wake up, didn't he? Like some fucking Poundland Jesus. Messed everything up.'

Wulf raises his head. 'The appeal.'

'Barry,' she shrugs. 'Almost had me fooled. He gave the statement I told him to give. Changed it when I heard you'd woken up from the kicking Whitehead put on you. You didn't remember anything. As long as the kids didn't either, I could sustain things. I gave you the appeal to focus on – to give you something to fight for. I like you, Wulf. You're harmless.'

'You killed Ford,' says Quinn, trying to sit up.

'He had it in his head that you were going to end him,' says Dagmara with a smile. 'I gave him a warning, a while back; he thought it was you. I used acid, like Dad used to do for me when I was wee. Focuses the mind, doesn't it? I told him how to live a good life. Told him to be the best version of himself. If he slipped up, I'd be there. Five generations of degeneracy spawned that little shit, and he wasn't anywhere near the worst of them. He did OK, too. Thought he had me fooled.

'I made my own enquiries, though. Saw what he was becoming. What he was doing to her. Fear of you had driven him back inside his own head, you see? He was collapsing. All his walls, coming down. All the violence and the hate and the perversions that he pushed down inside himself – it all started coming out when the appeal started making headlines. You were free, Wulf. And as far as he knew, one slip up and you'd come for him. He came for you on Friday. Wanted to make a deal. Thought he could somehow play it to his advantage, and if he didn't, well, that's why he'd nabbed the acid off the poor bastard at work. It was more than good fortune that I saw what he was doing to their mam.'

'The bugs . . . Beecher's girls . . .' begins Quinn.

'Bit of therapy and they'll bounce back. Not sure who'll look after them, though. Passed their dad in the snow back there looking none too chipper. And Mam's dead at the bottom of the stairs. You reckon Sal will step up?'

'You drove Ford off the road?'

'In my little tin can? Ha! Not as such. Just got ahead of him down one of the old permissive paths. Parked on the road and turned my lights off. Hit full beam as he came around the bend. He went through the wall like it was made of shoe boxes. He was nearly dead when I found him.'

'Not dead enough.'

'No. I had to be a woman of my word. I let him see. Made sure it was the last thing he saw. Then I made him drink what he'd brought along for you, Wulf. You ever seen a thorax smoke? When you know they're evil, you can let yourself enjoy it . . .'

Quinn falls back on the bed. Hagman realizes he's holding her hand.

'The kids,' he says. 'You brainwashed them. Climbed inside their skulls. You left them not knowing what they did and what you whispered in their ear. Same with me. They don't know if they killed her! If they strung me up! You've no right, Dagmara – no fucking right!'

She moves. Jerks forward. She lunges with the stick, lancing the blade towards Quinn's throat. Hagman raises his hands, desperately. There's a searing pain as the blade skewers his palm. Instinctively, he lashes out with his boot. Kicks her in the kneecap. She stumbles. Lifts herself up, murder in her eyes.

'It's not for me,' she whispers. 'It's for the children . . .'

Sal rises up behind her from the darkness. She's gripping a damp rock in her shaking, ice-white hand. She smashes the skull of the woman she loves most in the world. Watches her fall to the floor of Pegswood Byre: an echo through the decades, a body in another man's grave.

Then there are just the tears.

And the falling snow.

TWENTY-NINE

S al isn't sure which hospital bed she's supposed to linger at. Beecher and Quinn are both in Intensive Care. They'll live. His ex-wife, too. She'd lost half the blood in her body, but she still hauled herself up the stairs to save her girls. Sal can't imagine she'll be particularly welcome – can't see herself holding her hand and telling her she hopes she pulls through.

Nola and Lottie are with Elsie. They were patched up for cuts and bruises. Sal tried to call when she heard what had happened. Nola didn't answer. It was only then that she saw the message she'd accidentally sent. She isn't sure she'll ever be able to make amends.

Dagmara's been airlifted to the RVI in Newcastle, her skull fractured.

Sal leans against the cold bare wall. Reads the signs pointing the way to Oncology, Haematology, Radiology. She doesn't know where to go. Where to turn. Who to be.

'Hero of the hour, eh?'

Uncle Wulf is standing a few paces away. He's holding two hot drinks on a tray. His other hand is stitched, bandaged, wrapped in plastic. It will heal. So will the rest of him.

'I don't think I'm even going to be a police officer by morning,' says Sal, and she doesn't know how she feels about it. 'So many lies. Everybody playing everybody else. I don't know if I'm fit to run a bloody snack van, let alone try and make the world a better place.'

Hagman takes up sentry at her side. He's wearing borrowed clothes: jogging trousers and a thick shirt. He looks haggard. Drawn. But there's a lustre in his eyes that makes him seem, for a moment, like the young man who entered her life on a white charger, then failed to slay the dragon. She doesn't know how she feels about him yet. She knows he didn't kill Mam. But he didn't make it stop, either. He tried to protect Trina from the consequences of her actions and, in so doing, left Sal and Jarod at her mercy. He only tried to kill himself when he realized she wouldn't ever have him back. But twenty years inside? Not knowing whether you're guilty or not? Your only ally climbing around inside your head and smudging your memories? She feels he's paid the price. She puts her head on his shoulder.

'Jarod,' says Hagman quietly. 'He's OK?'

Sal isn't sure how to answer. She doesn't know where he is. She can feel him. Knows he's out there somewhere, trying to put himself together. She's called him a dozen times without reply. In the end, she left a voicemail, trying her best to explain. It had sounded absurd.

'No,' says Sal softly. 'No, he's not OK. And he won't be. But he'll keep going. We've promised each other. We have to become old together. That's the rule.'

Hagman smiles. Sips his tea.

'Do you think she'll survive?' asks Sal. 'I have so many things I need to ask her. All that she did. For so many years . . .'

Hagman nods. 'She'll survive. She'll probably find people to help on the inside.'

Sal squeezes her hands together. Feels a tear leak from her eye. She sips her hot chocolate. Inside her head, the shapes are moving and rearranging like tectonic plates. She still doesn't know what she remembers. Still doesn't know what she wants the truth to be.

'She was coming to make a deal,' says Hagman quietly. 'Magda Quinn. She was willing to turn a blind eye to Dagmara if I dropped the appeal, make the potential embarrassment for the police go away. She found the connection to Dagmara as soon as she started looking properly. Pieced it all together and found she'd got something a damn sight more exciting than me. Callum Whitehead – ex-bigwig, pride of the Masons – he got her the resources to look into me. She told Lewis and her officers that I was the target. All the while, she had her eye on Dagmara and a chance to restore her reputation in the force, whatever it took. Even if it meant turning a blind eye to murder.'

'She couldn't have turned a blind eye,' says Sal. 'Not to that.'

'Dagmara slew monsters,' says Hagman. He changes his position. Looks at her tenderly, eyes wet. 'I don't have it in me to slay anybody, Sal. But I'll spend the rest of my life wishing I had done the right thing by you and Jarod. I'm weak. I'm an absolute coward. More trouble than I'm bloody worth.'

Sal feels a great warm surge of compassion flood her. Wishes she felt able to hug him. Felt able to hug anybody. She thinks of Beecher – all those years breaking down her defences, convincing her to let herself be vulnerable, to let in the light. And Dagmara, always there, always probing, always checking: manipulation disguised as meditation. She wonders how many minds she turned inside out. Whether it was wrong to do so. She helps people forget. Hides their worst memories from themselves.

'There was a bug in one of Lottie's toys,' says Hagman, quietly. 'A bleeding spy camera! According to Elsie, Dagmara's prints are on it. They're taking her place apart now. Found empty boxes for another half-dozen of them. She's been watching. Families she doesn't trust. Domestic arrangements with people she thinks might be doing harm. Quinn went through the financial records and tracked down the exact devices she was using. Used the serial numbers to piggy-back the live feed. She saw what Dagmara saw. She sent the help for Nola and Lottie.'

Sal lets it all sink inside her. Shakes her head. 'I don't know whether I despise her or think she's amazing,' says Sal, taking off her glasses and cleaning them on her sleeve. 'Think I know what she did . . .'

'Don't think about it,' says Hagman. 'Not now. Not yet.'

'Do you think she's insane?' asks Sal, wishing it were that easy.

'No,' says Hagman, at last. 'I think the rest of us are.'

They're silent for a while. Eventually, Sal says, 'What do you think will happen?'

Hagman gives a snort of laughter. 'She'll want her say. When she wakes up, she'll want to explain herself. She's been waiting for this all her life.'

Sal drains her hot chocolate. Thinks, *You're very well
informed for a pariah.*

'Whitehead,' says Hagman, reading her thoughts. 'There's
talk of a settlement.'

'You mean a pay-off? A bribe?'

'It was always his style,' says Hagman. 'That, and putting
the boot in. But he really believed I'd done it – taken dirty
photos of you, and then killed your mother to shut her up.'

'Did *you* believe you'd killed her?'

Hagman closes his eyes. 'No,' he says. 'But I knew I hadn't
protected you. I'd not kept Trina at arm's length. I deserved
the hell I'd landed in.'

Sal feels her pocket vibrate. It's Nola. It's a link to a funny
video: a woman pole-dancing in her living room and knocking
her toddler off their tricycle mid-pirouette. Sal finds herself
smiling. It's a start.

For a time, they stand in silence. Neither knows what
tomorrow will hold. Neither knows what they want. But here,
now, in the quiet of the corridor, they can take a breath. They
can centre themselves. They can stare into the flame and let
go of the pain.

She takes Hagman's hand in hers. Squeezes gently.

She stares down the long corridor to the double doors. They
bang open as a paramedic wheels in a stretcher: an elderly
lady holding her injured arm, face tight with pain. An elderly
man huffs along at her side, fussing, worrying, touching her
as if seeking reassurance that she's still alive. She sees
the love radiating between them: the symbiotic tug of their
aching love for one another. Wonders what they wouldn't do
to save one another.

Thinks, *Dagmara . . . show me how. Teach me. I can
slay the beasts.*

And behind her eyes, Jarod begins to weep.